Then and Now

William Somerset Maugham was born in 1874 and lived in Paris until he was ten. He was educated at King's School, Canterbury, and at Heidelberg University. He spent some time at St. Thomas's Hospital with the idea of practising medicine, but the success of his first novel, *Liza of Lambeth*, published in 1897, won him over to letters. *Of Human Bondage*, the first of his masterpieces, came out in 1915, and with the publication in 1919 of *The Moon and Sixpence* his reputation as a novelist was established. His position as a successful playwright was being consolidated at the same time. His first play, *A Man of Honour*, was followed by a series of successes just before and after World War I, and his career in the theatre did not end until 1933 with *Sheppey*.

His fame as a short-story writer began with *The Trembling of a Leaf*, sub-titled *Little Stories of the South Sea Islands*, in 1921, after which he published more than ten collections. His other works include travel books such as *On a Chinese Screen* and *Don Fernando*, essays, criticism, and the autobiographical *The Summing Up* and *A Writer's Notebook*.

In 1927 Somerset Maugham settled in the South of France and lived there until his death in 1965.

W. Somerset Maugham
Then and Now

Mandarin

A Mandarin Paperback
THEN AND NOW

First published in Great Britain 1946
by William Heinemann Ltd
This edition published 1997
by Mandarin Paperbacks
an imprint of Reed International Books Ltd
Michelin House, 81 Fulham Road, London SW3 6RB
and Auckland, Melbourne, Singapore and Toronto

Copyright © by The Royal Literary Fund

A CIP catalogue record for this title
is available from the British Library
ISBN 0 7493 0436 7

Printed and bound in Great Britain
by Cox & Wyman Ltd, Reading, Berkshire

No one could write a book of this kind out of his head, and I have taken what I wanted where I could find it. My chief source of information has naturally been the works of Machiavelli. I have found much that was to my purpose in Tommasini's biography and something in Villari's, and I have made some use of Woodward's solid *Cesar Borgia*. I wish to acknowledge the great debt I owe to Count Carlo Beuf for his lively and accurate life of Cæsar, for his kindness in lending me books which otherwise I should never have known about, and for his patience in answering the many questions I put to him.

1

Plus ca change, plus c'est la même chose.

2

Biagio Buonaccorsi had had a busy day. He was tired, but being a man of methodical habit before going to bed made a note in his diary. It was brief: 'The City sent a man to Imola to the Duke.' Perhaps because he thought it of no importance he did not mention the man's name: it was Machiavelli. The Duke was Cæsar Borgia.

It had been not only a busy day, but a long one, for Biagio had set forth from his house at dawn. With him on a stout pony went his nephew, Piero Giacomini, whom Machiavelli had consented to take with him. It happened to be Piero's eighteenth birthday, October 6th, 1502, and so was a fitting day for him to go out into the world for the first time. He was a well set-up youth, tall for his age and of an agreeable aspect. Under his uncle's guidance, for his mother was a widow, he had received a good education; he could write a good hand and turn a comely phrase, not only in Italian, but in Latin. On the advice of Machiavelli, who passionately admired the ancient Romans, he had acquired more than a cursory knowledge of their history. Machiavelli cherished the conviction that men are always the same and have the same passions, so that when circumstances are similar the same causes must lead to the same effects; and thus, by bearing in mind how the Romans coped with a given situation, men of a later day might conduct themselves with prudence and efficiency. It was the wish both of

Biagio and his sister that Piero should enter the government service, in which Biagio held a modest post under his friend Machiavelli. The mission on which Machiavelli was now going seemed a good opportunity for the boy to learn something of affairs, and Biagio knew that he could not have a better mentor. The matter had been settled on the spur of the moment, for it was only the day before that Machiavelli had been given his letter of credence to the Duke and his safe conduct. Machiavelli was of an amiable disposition, a friend to his friends, and when Biagio asked him to take Piero with him immediately agreed. But the lad's mother, though she saw that it was a chance that could not be missed, was uneasy. He had never been parted from her before and he was young to go out into a hostile world; he was besides a good boy and she was afraid that Machiavelli would corrupt him, for it was notorious that Machiavelli was a gay fellow and a dissolute. He was, moreover, not in the least ashamed of it, and would tell improper stories about his adventures with women of the town and with maid-servants at wayside inns which must bring a blush to a virtuous woman's cheek. And what made it worse was that he told them so amusingly that though outraged you could not keep a straight face. Biagio reasoned with her.

'Dear Francesca, now that Niccolo is married he will abandon his loose habits. Marietta, his wife, is a good woman and she loves him. Why should you think him so foolish as to spend money outside for what he can get at home for nothing?'

'A man who likes women as much as Niccolo will never be content with one,' said she, 'and if she is his wife less than ever.'

Biagio thought there was something in what she said, but he was not prepared to admit it. He shrugged his shoulders.

'Piero is eighteen. If he has not lost his innocence

already it is quite time he did. Are you a virgin, nephew?'

'Yes,' answered Piero, with so much candour that anyone might have been forgiven for believing him.

'There is nothing that I do not know about my son. He is incapable of doing anything of which I should disapprove.'

'In that case,' said Biagio, 'there is no reason why you should hesitate to entrust him to a man who can be useful in his career and from whom, if he has sense, he can learn much that will be valuable to him all his life.'

Monna Francesca gave her brother a sour look.

'You are infatuated with the man. You're like putty in his hands. And how does he treat you? He makes use of you, he makes fun of you. Why should he be your superior in the Chancery? Why are you satisfied to be his subordinate?'

Biagio was of about the same age as Machiavelli, who was thirty-three, but because he had married the daughter of Marsilio Ficino, a celebrated scholar patronized by the Medici who then ruled the city, he had entered the government before him. For in those days influence got a man a job as often as merit. Biagio was of the middle size, plump, with a round face, a high colour and an expression of great good nature. He was honest and hard-working, a man without envy who knew his own limitations and was satisfied with his modest position. He liked good living and good company, and since he asked for no more than he could have, might be counted a happy man. He was not brilliant, but neither was he stupid. Had he been so Machiavelli would not have endured his companionship.

'Niccolo has the most brilliant mind of anyone at present in the service of the Signory,' he said now.

'Nonsense,' snapped Monna Francesca.

(The Signory was the City Council of Florence and

since the expulsion of the Medici eight years before the chief executive body of the State.)

'He has a knowledge of men and of affairs that men twice his age might envy. Take my word for it, sister, he will go far, and take my word for this too: he is not one to abandon his friends.'

'I wouldn't trust him an inch. He'll cast you aside like an old shoe when he has no further use for you.'

Biagio laughed.

'Are you so bitter because he never made advances to you, sister? Even with a son of eighteen you must be still attractive to men.'

'He knows better than to try his tricks with a decent woman. I know his habits. It's a disgrace that the Signory allows harlots to flaunt themselves in the city to the scandal of respectable people. You like him because ha makes you laugh and tells you dirty stories. You're as bad as he is.'

'You must remember that no one tells a dirty story better.'

'And is it that that makes you think him so wonderfully intelligent?'

Biagio laughed again.

'No, not only. He made a great success of his mission to France and his dispatches were masterly, even the members of the Signory who don't like him personally were obliged to admit it.'

Madonna Francesca shrugged her shoulders crossly.

Meanwhile Piero, like the prudent young man he was, held his peace. He looked forward without enthusiasm to the job in the Chancery to which his uncle and his mother had destined him, and the idea of going on a journey was very much to his liking. As he had foreseen, his uncle's worldly wisdom triumphed over his mother's anxious scruples, and so it came to pass that on the following morning Biagio called for him and, Biagio on

foot, Piero on his pony, they went the short distance to Machiavelli's house.

3

The horses were already at the door, one for Machiavelli and two for the servants he was taking with him. Piero, giving his pony to one of the servants to hold, followed his uncle into the house. Machiavelli was waiting for them with impatience. He greeted them curtly.

'Now let us start,' he said.

Marietta was in tears. She was a young woman of no great beauty, but it was not for her beauty that Machiavelli had married her; he had married her, that very year, because it was proper that he should marry, and she was of a reputable family and brought him as good a dowry as a man of his means and position could expect.

'Don't weep, dearest,' he said, 'you know I shall be gone only a little while.'

'But you ought not to go,' she sobbed, and then, turning to Biagio: 'He's not fit to ride so far. He's not well.'

'What is the matter with you, Niccolo?' asked Biagio.

'The old trouble. My stomach is out of order once more. It can't be helped.'

He took Marietta in his arms.

'Good-bye, my sweet.'

'You will write to me often.'

'Often,' he smiled.

When he smiled his face lost the sardonic look it generally wore, and there was something engaging in him so that you could understand that Marietta loved him. He kissed her and patted her cheek.

'Don't fret, my dear. Biagio will look after you.'

Piero, on entering the room, had stood just within the door. No one paid him attention. Though his uncle was Machiavelli's most intimate friend, he had seen little of him and had not exchanged more than a few words with him in all his life. Piero took the opportunity to have a good look at the man who would be thenceforth his master. Machiavelli was of the middle height, but because he was so thin looked somewhat taller than he was. He had a small head, with very black hair cut short which fitted his skull like a velvet cap. His dark eyes were small and restless, and his nose long: his lips were thin, and when he was not speaking so tightly closed that his mouth was little more than a sarcastic line. In repose his sallow face wore an expression that was wary, thoughtful, severe and cold. This was evidently not a man you could play pranks with.

Perhaps Machiavelli felt Piero's uneasy stare, for he gave him a quick, questioning glance.

'This is Piero?' he asked Biagio.

'His mother hopes you will look after him and see that he doesn't get into mischief.'

Machiavelli gave a thin smile.

'By observing the unfortunate consequences of my errors he will doubtless learn that virtue and industry are the highways to success in this world and happiness in the next.'

They set forth. They walked the horses over the cobblestones till they came to the city gate, and when they got on to the open road broke into a jog-trot. They had a long way to go and it was prudent to spare the horses. Machiavelli and Piero rode together and the two servants behind. All four were armed, for though Florence was at peace with her neighbours, the country was unsettled and you could never be sure that you might not run across marauding soldiers. The safe conduct the travellers carried would have been of small help to them then. Machiavelli did not speak and Piero, though not by nature shy, was somewhat intimidated by that sharp, set face, a slight frown between the brows, and thought it wise to wait till he was spoken to. The morning, notwithstanding an autumnal chill, was fine, and Piero's spirits were high. It was grand to be setting out on such an adventure and it was hard to keep silent when he was bubbling over with excitement. There were a hundred questions he wanted to ask. But they rode on and on. Soon the sun was bright in the heavens and the warmth of it was pleasant. Machiavelli never said a word. Now and then he raised one hand to indicate that they should walk the horses.

4

Machiavelli was busy with his thoughts. It was much against his will that he went on this mission and he had done his best to get someone else sent in his place. For one thing he was far from well and even now as he rode he had an ache in his stomach; and then, having recently married, he did not wish to pain his wife by leaving her. He had promised her that his absence would be short, but in his heart he knew that the days might run into weeks and the weeks into months before he got permission to return. His mission to France had taught him how protracted diplomatic negotiations might be.

But these were the least of his troubles. The state of Italy was desperate. Louis XII, King of France, was the paramount power. He held a large part of the kingdom of Naples, though insecurely, since the Spaniards who held Sicily and Calabria continually harassed him, but he was in firm possession of Milan and its territories; he was on good terms with Venice and for a consideration had taken the city states of Florence, Siena and Bologna under his protection. He had an alliance with the Pope, who had granted him a dispensation to put away his barren and scrupulous wife so that he might marry Anne of Brittany, the widow of Charles VIII, and in return the King had created the Pope's son, Cæsar

7

Borgia, Duke of Valentinois, given him Charlotte d'Albret, sister to the King of Navarre, in marriage, and promised to supply troops to enable him to recover the lands, lordships and dominions of the Church, possession of which she had lost.

Cæsar Borgia, known now throughout Italy as Il Valentino from the Duchy that Louis XII had bestowed upon him, was still well under thirty. His mercenary captains, of whom the most important were Pagolo Orsini, head of the great Roman house, Gian Paolo Baglioni, Lord of Perugia, and Vitellozzo Vitelli, Lord of Città di Castello, were the best in Italy. He proved himself a bold and astute commander. By force of arms, treachery and the terror he inspired, he made himself prince of a considerable state, and Italy rang with his exploits. Taking advantage of a favourable opportunity be blackmailed the Florentines into hiring him at a large salary with his men-at-arms for a period of three years; but then, having assured themselves of the protection of King Louis by a further payment in hard cash, they revoked Cæsar's commission and stopped his salary. This enraged him, and presently he took his revenge.

In June of the year with which this narrative is concerned Arezzo, a city subject to Florence, revolted and declared itself independent. Vitellozzo Vitelli, the ablest of Il Valentino's commanders and bitter enemy of the Florentines because they had executed his brother Paolo, and Baglioni, Lord of Perugia, went to the support of the rebellious citizens and defeated the forces of the Republic. Only the citadel held out. The Signory in a panic sent Piero Soderini to Milan to hasten the expedition of the four hundred lancers King Louis had promised them. Piero Soderini was an influential citizen and as Gonfalonier occupied the position of president of the Republic. They ordered their own troops encamped before Pisa, which they had long been trying to subdue, to advance to the rescue, but before they arrived the citadel fell. At this juncture Il Valentino, who was at Urbino which he had recently conquered, sent the Signory a peremptory demand for the dispatch of an ambassador to confer with him. They sent the Bishop of Volterra, Piero Soderini's brother, and Machiavelli accompanied him as his secretary. The crisis was resolved, for the French King sent a strong force to fulfil his obligation towards Florence, and Cæsar Borgia, yielding to the threat, recalled his captains.

But his captains were themselves lords of petty states, and they could not but fear that when they had served his purpose he would crush them as ruthlessly as he had crushed other lords of other states. They received information that he had made a secret arrangement with Louis XII by the terms of which the King was to provide a contingent to assist him first in the capture of Bologna and then in the destruction of the captains, whose territories it would be convenient for him to incorporate in his own dominions. After some preliminary discussion they met at a place called La Magione, near Perugia, to consider how best to protect themselves. Vitellozzo, who was ill, was carried to the meeting on a litter. Pagolo Orsini came accompanied by his brother the Cardinal and his nephew the Duke of Gravina. Among others who attended were Ermek Bentivoglio, the son of the Lord of Bologna, two Baglionis from Perugia, the young Oliverotto da Fermo, and Antonio da Venafro, the right-hand man of Pandolfo Petrucci, Lord of Siena. Their danger was great and they agreed that for their own safety they must act, but the Duke was a dangerous man and they knew that they must act with prudence. They decided for the present not to break with him openly, but to make preparations in secret and attack only when they were ready. They had in their pay a considerable body of troops, horse and foot, and Vitellozzo's artillery was powerful; they sent emissaries to hire several thousand of the mercenaries that then swarmed in Italy, and at the same time agents to Florence to ask for aid, for the Borgia's ambition was as great a threat to the Republic as to them.

It was not long before Cæsar heard of the conspiracy, and on his side he summoned the Signory to provide him with the troops which he declared they had engaged to let him have in case of need and requested them to send him an envoy empowered to treat with him. This was how it came about that Machiavelli was on his way to Imola. He went with misgiving. The Signory had dispatched him because he was a man of no official consequence, with no authority to make an agreement, who could only refer back to Florence and at every step must await his government's instructions. It was invidious to send such an emissary to one who, though a bastard of the Pope, in official documents styled himself Duke of Romagna, Valencia and Urbino, Prince of Andria, Lord of Piombino, Gonfalonier and Captain-General of the Church. Machiavelli's instructions were to inform him that the Signory had refused the conspirators' request for help, but that if he wanted either men or money he must apprise the Signory and await their reply. His business was to temporize, for such was the consistent policy of the Republic. The Signory could always find excellent reasons for doing nothing. If they got into too tight a corner they would untie the strings of their money-bags and disburse as small a sum as was acceptable. His business was to allay the impatience of a man unused to procrastination, to make no promises that had substance, to cajole a suspicious man with specious words, to use craft against craft, to counter deceit with deceit, and to discover the secrets of one who was notorious for his dissimulation.

Although he had but briefly seen him at Urbino, Machiavelli had been deeply impressed by him. He had heard there how the Duke Guidobaldo di Montefeltro, confiding in Cæsar Borgia's friendship, had lost his state and barely escaped with his life; and though he recognized that Il Valentino had acted with shocking perfidy he could not but admire the energy and adroit planning with which he had conducted the enterprise. This was a man of parts, fearless, unscrupulous, ruthless and intelligent, not only a brilliant general but a capable organizer and an astute politician. A sarcastic smile played upon Machiavelli's thin lips and his eyes gleamed, for the prospect of matching his wits with such an antagonist excited him. He began in consequence to feel much better and was no longer conscious of his queasy stomach; he was able indeed to look forward without displeasure to eating a snack at Scarperia, which was about half-way between Florence and Imola, and where he had decided to hire post horses. They had ridden as fast as was reasonable, for he wanted to get to Imola that day, and the horses, carrying not only their riders, but a good deal of baggage as well, could hardly be expected without hurt to themselves to go so far without more rest than he could afford to give them. He proposed to go on with Piero, leaving the two servants to follow next day with his own horse and Piero's pony.

They stopped at the Albergo della Posta and Machiavelli, dismounting, was glad to stretch his legs. He enquired what food could be prepared without delay and was not dissatisfied when he learnt that he could have macaroni, a dish of small birds, sausage from Bologna and a pork chop. He was a good trencherman and he devoured the meal that was set before him with enjoyment. He drank the strong red wine of the country and felt all the better for it. Piero ate as copiously as his master, and when they got into the saddle again and set out, he felt good and happy, so happy indeed that he began to hum one of the popular songs that ran about the streets of Florence. Machiavelli pricked up his ears.

'Why, Piero, your uncle never told me you had a voice.'

Piero let it out with complacency and sang an ascending scale.

'A pretty tenor,' Machiavelli said with a warm and friendly smile.

He reined in his horse to a walk, and Piero, accepting this as an invitation, broke into a well-known air, but the words were some that Machiavelli had written himself. He was pleased, but did not fail to reflect that the boy sang them to ingratiate himself with him. It was a neat device and he did not disapprove of it.

'How did you learn those words?'

'Uncle Biagio wrote them out for me and they fitted the tune.'

Machiavelli made no reply and broke again into a canter. It occurred to him that it would be worth while to find out what he could about this boy whom he had taken, certainly, to oblige his friend Biagio, but whom also he had the intention of making good use of; so during the rest of the journey, when hilly country obliged them to walk the horses, he set out to do this. No one could be more affable, interesting and amusing than he when he chose, nor so subtle, and Piero would have had to be more worldly-wise than at his age he could be to discover that the friendly, careless questions put to him were designed to make him discover himself naked as when he was born. Piero was neither shy nor self-conscious, he had indeed the assurance of youth, and he answered frankly and ingenuously. To talk about himself seemed a very pleasant way of passing time that was beginning to grow tedious. Marsilio Ficino, the famous old scholar, had died only three years before; he was Biagio's father-in-law and had directed the young boy's studies. It was on his advice that Piero had acquired a sound knowledge of Latin and though against his will a smattering of Greek.

'It is one of the misfortunes of my life that I never

learnt it,' said Machiavelli. 'I envy you for having read the Greek authors in the original.'

'What good will that do me?'

'It will teach you that happiness is the good at which all men aim, and that in order to attain it you need nothing but good birth, good friends, good luck, health, wealth, beauty, strength, fame, honour and virtue.'

Piero burst out laughing.

'It will also teach you that life is uncertain and full of tribulation, from which you may conclude that it is only reasonable to snatch what pleasure you can while you are of an age to enjoy it.'

'I didn't need to learn the tenses of Greek verbs to know that,' said Piero.

'Perhaps not, but it is reassuring to have good authority for following one's natural inclinations.'

By well-directed questions Machiavelli learnt who the boy's friends were in Florence and what life he had led there, and by flattering attention to the opinions on one subject and another that he inveigled him into pronouncing he gained presently a fair impression of Piero's capacity and character. He was inexperienced, of course, but quick-witted, more so than his Uncle Biagio, who, though good and honest, was of mediocre intelligence; he had the high spirits of his youth, a natural wish to enjoy himself, and an adventurous temper; though ingenuous and in a way simple, he was not over-scrupulous, a trait to Machiavelli's mind of no disadvantage, for it meant that he would not be hindered by a too delicate conscience if he were wanted to do something that was a trifle less than honourable; he was strong and active and there was no reason to suppose that he lacked courage; his open face, his air of frankness, his engaging manner might all turn out to be valuable assets; it remained to discover whether he knew how to keep his own counsel and whether he could be trusted. It required only a little time to find out the first, and as to the second Machiavelli had no intention of trusting him or anyone else more than need be. In any case the boy was clever enough to know that it could only be to his benefit to gain the good opinion of his master. A good word from Machiavelli could assure his future; a bad report would entail his dismissal from the service of the Republic.

5

They were nearing Imola. It was situated on a river in a fertile plain, and the surrounding country showed none of the ravages of war, since it had capitulated on the approach of Cæsar's forces. When they were about two miles away they met seven or eight horsemen and Machiavelli recognized among them Agapito da Amalia, the Duke's first secretary, whose acquaintance he had made at Urbino. He greeted Machiavelli warmly, and on learning the errand on which he was found, turned back and accompanied him to the city. The Signory had sent a courier a day before to inform their agent at the Duke's court of their envoy's arrival and the courier was waiting for him at the city gate. It had been a long ride and Agapito asked Machiavelli whether he would not like to refresh himself and rest before presenting his credentials to the Duke. Though the army was encamped outside the walls, the small city, now Il Valentino's capital, was crowded with his personal staff, the members of his court, agents of other Italian states, merchants with necessities or luxuries to sell, solicitors of favours, sycophants, spies, actors, poets, loose women, and all the rag tag and bobtail that followed a victorious condottiere in the hope of making money by fair means or foul. The result was that lodging was hard to get. The city's two or three inns were chock-a-block and men were sleeping three, four and five in a bed. But the Florentine agent had made arrangements for Machiavelli and his servants to be put up in the Dominican monastery and it was thither that the courier now suggested conducting him. Machiavelli turned to Agapito.

'If His Excellency can receive me I should prefer to see him at once,' he said.

'I will ride on and find out if he is at liberty. This officer will lead you to the Palace.'

Leaving the man he had indicated behind, Agapito trotted off with the rest of his party. The others walked their horses through the narrow streets till they came to the main square. On the way Machiavelli asked the officer which was the city's best inn.

'I don't fancy the fare those good monks of the monastery will provide and I have no wish to go supperless to bed.'

'The Golden Lion.'

Machiavelli addressed himself to the courier.

'When you have deposited me at the Palace go to the Golden Lion and see that an ample meal is prepared for me.' Then to Piero: 'Attend to the stabling of the horses. The courier will show you the way to the monastery and you will leave the saddle-bags in charge of Antonio.' This was one of his two servants. 'Then you and the courier will come to the Palace and wait for me.'

The Palace, a large, but unpretentious building, for Caterina Sforza who had built it was a thrifty woman, took up one end of the square, and here Machiavelli and the officer, dismounting, were admitted by the guard. The officer sent a soldier to tell the first secretary they were there. In a few minutes he came into the room in which Machiavelli was waiting. Agapito da Amalia was a swarthy man, with long black hair and a small black beard, with a pale skin and sombre, clever eyes. He was a gentleman, with good manners, suave of speech and with a candid air which deceived many into thinking less of his abilities than was wise. He was devoted both

15

to the person and the interest of the Duke, for Il Valentino had the gift of attaching to himself those whose loyalty was necessary to him. He told Machiavelli that the Duke would receive him at once. They ascended a fine flight of stairs and Machiavelli was ushered into a handsome apartment, the walls painted in fresco, with a large stone fireplace on the hood of which were carved the arms of the intrepid, but unfortunate Caterina Sforza whom Cæsar Borgia now held prisoner in Rome. A bright fire of logs blazed on the hearth, and the Duke stood with his back to it. The only other person in the room was Juan Borgia, Cardinal of Monreale, the portly, shrewd nephew of Pope Alexander. He was seated in a carved, high-backed chair toasting his toes at the fire.

Machiavelli bowed to the Duke and the Cardinal, and the Duke, coming towards him graciously, took his hand and led him to a chair.

'You must be cold and tired after your long journey, Secretary,' he said. 'Have you eaten?'

'Yes, your Excellency, I ate on the way. I offer you my apologies for presenting myself as I am, in my riding clothes, but I did not wish to delay telling you what I have to say on behalf of the Republic.'

He then presented his letter of audience. The Duke gave it a brief glance and handed it to the Secretary. Cæsar Borgia was a man of striking beauty, of more than common height, with broad shoulders, a powerful chest and a slim waist. He was dressed in black, which emphasized his vivid colouring, and besides a ring on the index finger of his right hand, his only ornament was the collar of St. Michael, the order which King Louis had conferred upon him. His hair, of a rich auburn and carefully dressed, was worn long and reached his shoulders; he had a moustache and a short beard trimmed to a point. His nose was straight and delicate and his eyes, under well-marked brows, were fine and bold; his well-shaped mouth was sensual; his skin clear and glowing. His gait was stately, yet graceful, and in his bearing was something of majesty. Machiavelli asked himself how it came about that this young man, the offspring of a Roman woman of the people and a fat, hook-nosed Spanish priest who had bought the papacy by shameless simony, had acquired the demeanour of a great prince.

'I requested your government to send me an envoy because I wish to know exactly how I stand with the Republic,' he said with deliberation.

Machiavelli delivered the discourse he had prepared, but though the Duke listened Machiavelli could not but see that he looked upon the assurances of good will to which on the Signory's instructions he gave utterance as no more than fine phrases. There was a moment's silence. The Duke leant back in his chair and with his left hand fingered the order on his breast. When he spoke it was with a certain coolness.

'My dominions border upon yours along an extended frontier. I am bound to take every means in my power to safeguard them. I know only too well that your city is ill-disposed to me. You have tried to embroil me with the Pope and the King of France. You couldn't have treated me worse if I were a murderer. Now you must choose whether you will have me as a friend or as an enemy.'

His voice was musical, light rather than deep, and it had a quality, not acid, but cutting, which gave his words an insolence which was not easy to bear. He might have been speaking to a scullion. But Machiavelli was a practised diplomatist and knew how to keep his temper.

'I can assure Your Excellency that there is nothing my government wants more than your friendship,' he answered blandly, 'but they have not forgotten that you allowed Vitellozzo to invade our territories and they are doubtful of its value.'

'I had nothing to do with that. Vitellozzo acted on his own account.'

'He was in your pay and under your command.'

'The expedition was begun without my knowledge and continued without my aid. I will not pretend I regretted it. I didn't. The Florentines had broken faith with me and it was right that they should suffer for it. But when I thought they had been sufficiently punished I ordered my captains to withdraw. It has won me their enmity and they are now conspiring my overthrow.'

Machiavelli did not think it the moment to remind the Duke that he had recalled his commanders only on the peremptory command of the King of France.

'You are to blame for that, just as you are to blame for Vitellozzo's invasion of your territory.'

'We?' cried Machiavelli in frank astonishment.

'Nothing of this would have happened if you hadn't been such fools as to torture and execute Paolo Vitelli. You can hardly be surprised that his brother Vitellozzo should seek his revenge, and because I prevented him from pursuing it to the end he has turned against me.'

It is necessary to explain what the Duke meant by this.

The Florentines had long been engaged on the siege of Pisa, but things had gone badly and the army of the Republic suffered a severe defeat which the Signory ascribed to the incompetence of their Captain-General; so they engaged two condottieri then in the service of King Louis, Paolo and Vitellozzo Vitelli, and gave the chief command to Paolo, a captain of renown. A battle was fought, a breach was effected in the walls and the army was on the point of storming the city when suddenly Paolo Vitelli gave the order to retreat. Though he said he had done this to save further loss of life since he was sure of the city's surrender on conditions, the Signory was convinced that he was playing them false, and sent two commissioners ostensibly to furnish funds but in fact to seize the persons of the two generals. Paolo Vitelli was quartered about a mile beyond Cascina, and the commissioners requested him to meet them there so that they might discuss with him the conduct of the war. They gave him dinner and then, leading him into a secret chamber, arrested him. He was taken to Florence and beheaded, though under torture he would not admit his guilt.

'Paolo Vitelli was a traitor,' said Machiavelli.' 'He had a fair trial and was found guilty. He suffered the just punishment of his crime.'

'Whether he was innocent or guilty is no matter. To execute him was a blunder.'

'It was necessary for our honour to act with energy against enemies of the Republic. It was necessary to show that Florence has the courage to provide for her safety.'

'Why then did you leave his brother alive?'

Machiavelli irritably shrugged his shoulders. It was a sore point.

'Men were sent to fetch Vitellozzo and bring him to Cascina. He suspected a trap. He was ill in bed. He asked for time to dress and somehow managed to escape. The affair was bungled. How can you provide always against the stupidity of the people you have to act through?'

The Duke's laugh was light and gay. His eyes sparkled with good humour.

'It is an error to keep to a plan when circumstances have arisen that make its execution inadvisable. When Vitellozzo slipped through your fingers you should have taken Paolo to Florence, and instead of throwing him into a dungeon housed him in the best apartment of the Palazzo Vecchio. You should have tried him and whatever the evidence declared him innocent. Then you should have restored his command to him, increased his pay, and bestowed on him the highest honours at the disposal of the Republic. You should have convinced him that you had entire confidence in him.'

'With the result that he would have betrayed us to our enemies.'

'That might have been his intention, but for a while

he would have had so to act as to prove that the trust you placed in him was justified. These mercenary captains are avaricious and will do anything for money. You might have made offers to Vitellozzo so handsome that he could not have brought himself to refuse; he would have rejoined his brother, and when you had lulled them into security, with a little ingenuity you could have found a suitable occasion to kill them both swiftly and without trial.'

Machiavelli went red in the face.

'Such treachery would have an eternal blot on the fair name of Florence,' he cried.

'Traitors must be dealt with treacherously. A state is not governed by the exercise of Christian virtues, it is governed by prudence, boldness, determination and ruthlessness.'

At this moment an officer came into the room and in a whisper spoke to Agapito da Amalia. Il Valentino, frowning at the interruption, with impatient fingers drummed on the table at which he sat.

'His Excellency is occupied,' said Agapito. 'They must wait.'

'What is it?' asked the Duke sharply.

'Two Gascon soldiers have been caught looting, Excellency. They have been brought here under guard with the objects they seized.'

'It would be a pity to make the subjects of the King of France wait,' said the Duke, smiling faintly. 'Let them be brought in.'

The officer went out and the Duke amiably addressed himself to Machiavelli.

'You will excuse me if I attend to a little matter of business.'

'My time is at your Excellency's disposal.'

'I trust you had no adventures on the road, Secretary.'

Machiavelli took his cue from the Duke's tone.

'None. I was fortunate to find an inn at Scarperia where I was given a tolerable meal.'

'It is my desire that men should travel in my dominions as safely as it is said they travelled in the Roman Empire of the Antonines. While you are here you will have opportunity to see for yourself that now that I have dispossessed those petty tyrants who were the curse of Italy I have by wise administration done much to render the lives of my people secure and prosperous.'

There was a noise without of shuffling feet, voices were raised, and then, the great doors of the spacious chamber being flung open, a crowd surged in. First came the officer who had come in before, and he was followed by two men who from their respectable dress Machiavelli guessed must be dignitaries of the city. On their heels came two women, one old, the other middle-aged, and with them an elderly man of decent appearance. Then came a soldier carrying a pair of silver candlesticks, and another with an ornamental goblet of silver gilt and two silver platters. They wore the red and yellow uniform of the Duke's own troops. Then, half pushed, half dragged by soldiers entered two men with their hands tied behind their backs. They were shabby in nondescript garments and, standing among the Duke's uniformed men, looked a ruffianly pair. One was a scowling fellow of forty, of powerful physique, with a thick black beard and a livid scar on his forehead, and the other a smooth-faced boy with a sallow skin and shifty, frightened eyes.

'Stand forward,' said the Duke.

The two men were given a shove.

'What is the charge?'

It appeared that the house of the two women had been broken into when they were at mass and the silverware stolen.

'How can you prove these articles were your property?'

'Monna Brigida is my cousin, Excellency,' said one of the two respectable men. 'I know the articles well. They were part of her dowry.'

The other confirmed this. The Duke turned to the elderly man who seemed to be with the two women.

'Who are you?'

'Giacomo Fabronio, Excellency, silversmith. These two men sold me the pieces. They said they had got them at the sack of Forlì.'

'You have no doubt that these are the men?'

'None, Excellency.'

'We took Giacomo to the Gascon camp,' said the officer, 'and he picked them out without hesitation.'

The Duke fixed the silversmith with harsh eyes.

'Well?'

'When I heard that Monna Brigida's house had been broken into and her candlesticks and platters stolen, I became suspicious,' the fellow answered, his face pale and his voice tremulous. 'I went at once to Messer Bernardo and told him that two Gascon soldiers had sold me some silverware.'

'Was it from fear or sense of duty?'

The silversmith for a moment could not find his voice. He was shaking with terror.

'Messer Bernardo is a magistrate, I have done much work for him. If the goods were stolen I didn't want them to be in my possession.'

'What he says is true, Your Excellency,' said the magistrate. 'I went to see the articles and immediately recognized them.'

'They are mine, Excellency,' vehemently cried the younger of the two women. 'Everyone will tell you they are mine.'

'Be quiet.' The Duke turned his gaze on the two Gascons. 'Do you confess that you stole these things?'

'No, no, no,' screamed the boy. 'It is a mistake. I swear on the soul of my mother than I didn't. The silversmith is mistaken. I have never seen him before.

'Take him away. A few turns on the rack will bring out the truth.'

The boy gave a piercing shriek.

'No, not that. I couldn't bear that.'

'Take him.'

'I confess,' gasped the boy.

The Duke gave a short laugh and turned to the other. 'And you?'

The older man threw back his head defiantly,

'I didn't steal them. I took them. It was our right; we had captured the city.'

'A lie. You did not capture the city. It capitulated.'

By the rules of Italian warfare at the time, if a city was taken by storm the soldiers were allowed to loot and keep everything they could lay hands on; but if it had capitulated, though the citizens were called upon to pay a large sum to defray the expense to which the condittieri had been put to gain possession of their city, they saved their lives and their property. The rule was useful, for it made the citizens willing enough to surrender; it was not often that devotion to their prince induced them to fight to the death.

The Duke pronounced sentence.

'My orders were that the troops were to remain without the walls and that any harm done to the persons or property of the citizens should be punished by death.' He turned to the officer. 'Hang them in the square at dawn. Let it be published in the camp what their crime and its punishment were. Have two soldiers stand guard over the bodies till noon and let the town crier inform the population at proper intervals that they can rely on the justice of their prince.'

'What does he say?' asked the terrified boy of his

companion, for the Duke had spoken to the two Gascons in French and to the officer in Italian.

The man did not answer, but looked at the Duke with sullen hatred. The Duke, having heard, repeated the sentence in French.

'You will be hanged at dawn as a warning to others.'

The boy gave a great cry of anguish and fell to his knees.

'Mercy, mercy,' he screamed. 'I'm too young to die. I don't want to die. I'm afraid.'

'Take them away,' said the Duke.

The boy was dragged to his feet, screaming incoherently, tears running from his eyes; but the other, his face distorted with rage, gathered the spittle in his mouth and spat in his face. The pair were hustled from the room. The Duke turned to Agapito da Amalia.

'See that they are provided with the consolations of religion. It would weigh on my conscience if they faced their Maker without having had the opportunity to repent of their sins.'

A faint smile on his lips, the secretary slid out of the room. The Duke, apparently in high good humour, addressed himself to the Cardinal his cousin and together to Machiavelli.

'They were fools as well as knaves. It was an unpardonable stupidity to sell the articles they had stolen in the very town they had been stolen in. They should have hidden them till they came to a much larger city, Bologna or Florence for instance, where they could have disposed of them in safety.'

But he noticed that the silversmith was lingering by the door and seemed to wish to say something.

'What are you doing there?'

'Who is to going to give me back my money, Excellency? I am a poor man.'

'Did you pay a fair price for the articles?' Il Valentino asked suavely.

'I paid what they were worth. The sum the scoundrels asked was ridiculous. I had to make my profit.'

'Let it be a lesson to you. Another time don't buy anything unless you are sure it has been honestly come by.'

'I can't afford to lose so much money, Excellency.'

'Go,' cried the Duke in a tone so savage that the man with a cry scuttled out of the room like a frightened rabbit.

Il Valentino threw himself back in his chair and roared with laughter. Then he turned courteously to Machiavelli.

'I must ask you to pardon the interruption; I think it important that justice should be administered promptly, and I wish the people of the territories under my rule to know that they can come to me if they have been ill-used and be sure to find in me an impartial judge.'

'It is the wisest policy for a prince who wishes to assure his hold on dominions that he has recently acquired,' said the Cardinal.

'Men will always forgive the loss of their political liberty if their private liberty is left undisturbed,' said the Duke casually. 'So long as their women are not molested and their property is safe, they will be reasonably contented with their lot.'

Machiavelli had watched the incident with calm, even with amusement, which he took care not to show, for he was convinced that the whole affair was a piece of play acting. He knew very well that Il Valentino would never dare to hang two subjects of the King of France. In all probability they had already been released, with a gift of money for the trouble they had been put to, and on the following day would be found again in the ranks of the Gascon contingent. Machiavelli guessed that the scene had been arranged so that he could tell the Signory how efficiently the Duke was ruling his new conquests, but more particularly for his reference at the end to

Florence and Bologna. The suggestion that the troops might find themselves there was a threat too plain to be missed by anyone with so shrewd a brain as Machiavelli.

Silence fell. The Duke, gently stroking his neat beard, stared at Machiavelli reflectively. Machiavelli had the feeling that he was making up his mind what sort of a man this was that the Signory had sent to negotiate with him, and not wishing to meet the searching eyes fixed on him he looked down at his hands, as though wondering if the nails wanted cutting. He was perplexed, and being perplexed was uneasy. For it was he that had conducted the business that led to the execution of Paolo Vitelli. Assured of his guilt, he had exercised all his powers of persuasion to convince his nervous and temporizing superiors that action must be taken without delay. It was he that had given the commissioners orders to proceed with energy. It was he that had urged the death sentence notwithstanding the fact that Vitellozzo had escaped. But his activities had been behind the scenes and he could not imagine how Il Valentino was aware of them. The thought crossed his mind that the Duke had dwelt upon the unsatisfactory outcome of the affair only to show that he knew what part Machiavelli had played in it and was maliciously pleased to be able to point out to him that he had handled it incompetently. But that man did nothing without a reason. It was unlikely that he wished to let the Florentine envoy know that he was well-informed of what happened in the Chancery of the Republic: it was more probable that his object was to shake Machiavelli's confidence in himself and so render him more amenable. The idea caused the suspicion of a smile to appear on his lips, and he glanced at the Duke. It looked as though the Duke had been waiting to meet his eyes before speaking.

'Secretary, I desire to confide to you a secret I have told to no living man.'

'Do you wish me to leave you, Cousin?' asked the Cardinal.

'No, I trust in your discretion as much as I trust in the Secretary's.'

Machiavelli, his jaw set, his gaze fixed on the handsome Duke, waited.

'The Orsini have begged me almost on their bended knees to attack Florence. I bear your city no ill will and I have refused. But if the gentlemen of your government want to come to terms with me they must do it before I patch things up with the Orsini. We're both friends of the King of France; surely it's advisable that we should be friends of one another. With our territories adjoining each of us can make things easy for the other; each of us can make things difficult. You depend upon mercenary troops under unreliable captains; I have my own army, well-trained, well-armed, and my captains are the best in Europe.'

'But no more reliable than ours, Your Excellency,' said Machiavelli dryly.

'I have others who are reliable. Who are they, the fools who are conspiring against me? Pagolo Orsini, a fool, Bentivoglio who thinks I have designs on Bologna, the Baglioni who fears for Perugia, Oliverotto da Fermo, and Vitellozzo, who is laid aside by the French sickness.

'They are powerful, and in revolt.'

'All their movements are known to me and when things are ripe I shall act. Believe me, the ground is burning under their feet and it needs more water to put out the fire than such men as they can throw. Be sensible, Secretary. With Urbino in my hands I command Central Italy. Guidobaldo di Montefeltro was my friend, and the Pope intended to give his niece Angela Borgia in marriage to Guidobaldo's nephew and heir. I would never have attacked him unless I had seen the strategic importance of his state. I had to have it in order to carry out my plans, and I could not allow sentiment to interfere with policy. I can offer you security from your enemies. If we were to act together, I with my armies, you with your rich lands and your wealth, and with the spiritual authority of the Pope to support us, we should be the strongest power in Italy. Instead of having to pay hard cash for the favours of the French, they would have to treat with us as equals. The moment has come for you to conclude an alliance with me.'

Machiavelli was startled, but he answered with easy amiability.

'I see the force of your Excellency's arguments. No one could have put them more clearly or more convincingly. It is rare to find a man of action, and a great general such as Your Excellency has shown himself, who possesses so logical a mind and such a gift of expression.'

The Duke with a slight smile made a modest gesture of protest. Machiavelli, his heart in his mouth, for he knew that what he had to say was not what the Duke wanted, went on blandly.

'I will write to the Signory and tell the gentlemen what you have said.'

'What do you mean?' cried Il Valentino. 'The matter is urgent and must be settled at once.'

'I have no power to make an agreement.'

The Duke sprang to his feet.

'Then what have you come here for?'

At that instant the door was opened; it was only Agapito da Amalia coming in after attending to the Duke's order, but it had a startling effect. Machiavelli was not a nervous man, but it shook him strangely.

'I have come because Your Excellency requested my government to send an envoy to treat with him.'

'But an envoy with full powers to treat.'

Until now the Duke had treated Machiavelli with tolerable courtesy, but now, his eyes blazing, he strode up to him. Machiavelli rose and the two men faced one another.

'The Signory is fooling me. They sent you precisely because you have no power to decide anything. Their eternal shilly-shallying exasperates me beyond endurance. How long do they think they can continue to try my patience?'

The Cardinal, who had sat in silence, put in a word to calm the storm, but the Duke harshly told him to hold his tongue. He began to pace up and down the room, storming; he was bitter, brutal and sarcastic; he seemed to have lost all control over himself. Machiavelli, unmoved and far from frightened, watched him with curiosity. At last the Duke flung himself back into his chair.

'Tell your government that I am deeply affronted.'

'The last thing my government would wish is to affront Your Excellency. They instructed me to inform you that the rebels had requested their aid and they had refused.'

'Waiting as usual, I suppose, to see which way the cat would jump.'

There was more truth in this than was pleasant for Machiavelli to hear. His face remained impassive.

'They have no love for the Orsini or for Vitellozzo. They are anxious to be on friendly terms with Your Excellency, and I must press you to be more definite. It is at least necessary that I should be able to tell the Signory precisely what sort of an agreement it is that you desire.'

'The discussion is ended. You force me to come to terms with the rebels. I can reduce them to submission tomorrow by agreeing to the proposal of the Orsini to attack Florence.'

'Florence is under the protection of the King of France,' answered Machiavelli sharply. 'He has promised us four hundred lancers and an ample force of infantry whenever we need them.'

'The French promise much in return for the money they continually demand, but when they have received it seldom keep their promises.'

Machiavelli knew that was true. The Florentines had suffered much from the rapacity and double-dealing of King Louis. He had more than once undertaken at a price to send troops to assist them in their difficulties and then, having received the money, had delayed and delayed, and in the end sent only half the number paid for. The Duke could not have made himself more plain. The Florentines must either accept the alliance he offered them (and everyone in Italy knew what a faithless friend he was), or else he would compose his differences with his discontented captains and together with them attack the Republic. Blackmail! The situation was alarming, and Machiavelli in distress sought for something to say that would at least leave the way open for further negotiations, but the Duke prevented him from speaking.

'What are you waiting for, Secretary? You may withdraw.'

He did not trouble to acknowledge Machiavelli's low bow. Agapito da Amalia accompanied the envoy down the stairs.

'His Excellency is a quick-tempered man and is unused to being crossed,' he said.

'That is a fact which has not escaped my observation,' replied Machiavelli acidly.

6

Piero and the courier were waiting in the guard-room, and when the doors were duly unbarred and unlocked the three of them went out into the square. His attendants conducted Machiavelli to the Golden Lion. They had made much of the fact that the repast they had ordered was for the Florentine envoy, and he ate well and amply. The wine of the country, though not to be compared with the Tuscan wine, was strong, and he drank freely. On reflection he came to the conclusion that his conversation with the Duke was after all not unsatisfactory. Il Valentino's anger seemed to indicate that he was nervous, and his insistence on an immediate alliance with the Republic that he knew his position was perilous. Machiavelli was indifferent to the scant courtesy with which he had been treated. He knew when he started on his mission that he need not expect to be used with consideration. Having done eating and belched his full, he bade the courier show the way to the monastery where he was to lodge. In view of his importance a cell had been vacated for him, but Piero and the courier were to share a straw mattress in a corridor along with a number of transients only too glad to have a roof over their heads. But before going to bed Machiavelli wrote a letter to the Signory in which he described the events of the evening. The courier was to take it back to Florence at the crack of dawn.

'You had better write to Biagio so that he can tell your mother you have arrived here without mishap,' he said to Piero. 'And ask him to send me a Plutarch.'

Machiavelli had brought his Dante with him, and besides that only Livy's *Annals*. When Piero had finished, Machiavelli without ceremony took the letter and read it. He smiled faintly when he read: '*Messer Niccolo was silent throughout the morning, and thinking he was occupied with weighty matters I did not disturb him; but after he had dined he talked with so much wit, clearness and good sense that it seemed to me we had hardly left Scarperia when we were arrived at Imola. He thinks I have a good voice. I wish it had been possible to bring my lute.*'

31

'A very good letter,' said Machiavelli. 'The message you have asked Biagio to deliver to your mother is very fit and proper. And now after this long day let us take a well-earned rest.'

7

Machiavelli needed little sleep and awoke soon after sunrise. He called Piero to help him dress. His riding clothes were packed in the saddle-bags and he put on the black raiment which was his usual wear. He had no intention of remaining at the monastery, for he needed quarters where he could if necessary receive persons in secret, and he knew very well that at the monastery his visitors and his movements would be conspicuous. The courier was already on his way to Florence. With Piero to accompany him, Machiavelli set out for the Golden Lion. Imola was a bright little town and there was no sign that it had not long since changed masters. As they walked through the narrow, tortuous streets they passed a good many people going about their various business, and they looked contented. You received the impression that the tenor of their lives remained unaltered. Now and then pedestrians had to make way for a man on horseback or for a string of donkeys with a load of firewood. A man sauntered by with she-asses, whose milk was good for pregnant women, and announced his presence with the habitual cry; an old crone popped her head out of a window and called him; he stopped, and in a minute she appeared at her door with a beaker. A pedlar of pins and needles, thread and ribands, passed along raucously calling his wares. There were shops in the street in which was the Golden Lion; there was a customer at the saddler's, a man was having his hair cut at the barber's, and a woman was trying on a pair of shoes at the shoemaker's. There was about all an air, not of opulence, but of a comfortable prosperity. No beggars pestered.

They entered the Golden Lion and Machiavelli ordered for himself and Piero bread and wine. Dipping the bread in the wine they made it palatable and then drank what remained of the wine. Thus fortified they went to the barber's and Machiavelli had himself shaved; the barber sprinkled strongly-scented water on his short black hair, and combed it. Meanwhile Piero had been meditatively stroking his smooth chin.

'I think I need a shave, Messer Niccolo,' he said.

'It can wait a few weeks yet,' said Machiavelli, smiling thinly; then to the barber: 'Put some of your scent on his head and run a comb through his hair.'

They were both ready. Machiavelli enquired of the barber where was the house of a certain Messer Bartolomeo Martelli whom he desired to visit. The barber gave them directions, but they were so complicated that Machiavelli asked if he could not get someone to show them the way. The barber went to the door of his shop, and calling an urchin who was playing in the street, told him to conduct the strangers. Their way led through the principal square, the square in which was the palace occupied by the Duke, and since it was market day it was crowded with the stalls of the farmers who had brought into the city for sale fruits and vegetables, chickens, meat and cheese, and with the stalls of chapmen with brass, ironmongery, cloth goods, old clothes and what not. A great throng of people were bargaining, buying, or merely looking, and there was a din of voices. It was a gay and busy scene under the bright October sun. As Machiavelli and Piero entered the square they heard the wail of a brass horn and some of the noise was stilled.

'It's the crier,' yelled the little boy excitedly, and seizing Machiavelli's hand he began to run. 'I have not heard him yet.'

A number of people surged forward, and looking in

the direction they took Machiavelli saw that there was a gallows at the other end of the square and two men were hanging there. It was not a sight he cared to see, and he snatched his hand away. Forgetting his errand the boy raced towards the centre of interest. The crier in a loud voice began to speak, but he was too far away for Machiavelli to hear what he said. He turned impatiently to a stout woman who was standing guard over her stall.

'What has happened?' he asked her. 'What is the crier saying?'

She shrugged her shoulders.

'It's only two thieves who've been hanged. By the Duke's orders the crier comes every half hour till noon and says they've been hanged because they stole the property of citizens. They're French soldiers, they say.'

Machiavelli repressed a start. It could not be what he suspected, but he had to see for himself. He strode forward, squeezing his way through the crowd, jostling and jostled, his eyes fixed on the two hanging bodies. The crier had said his say, and stepping down from the platform on which the gallows had been erected sauntered nonchalantly away. The crowd thinned and Machiavelli was able to get close; there was no doubt about it; though their faces were horribly distorted by the strangling rope, they were the two Gascon soldiers, the man with the scowl and the scar, the boy with the shifty eyes, who had been brought in the night before to be judged and sentenced by the Duke. It hadn't been a comedy then. Machiavelli stood stock still and stared with dismay. His small guide touched his arm.

'I wish I'd been here when they hanged them,' he said regretfully. 'No one knew anything about it till it was all over.'

'It's nothing for little boys to see,' said Machiavelli, hardly knowing that he spoke, for his thoughts were busy.

'It wouldn't be the first time,' the child grinned. 'It's fun to see them dancing in the air.'

'Piero.'

'I'm here, Messere.'

'Come, boy, take us to Messer Bartolomeo.'

For the rest of the way Machiavelli, frowning, his lips closed so tightly that his mouth was no more than a bitter line, walked in silence. He tried to think what had been in Il Valentino's mind. Why should he have hanged two useful soldiers because they had stolen a few bits and pieces of silverware when a flogging would have adequately punished the crime? It was true that human life meant nothing to him, but it was unbelievable that he should be so eager to win the confidence of the people of Imola as to risk the anger not only of the commander of the Gascon troops, but of the troops themselves. Machiavelli was puzzled. He was convinced that his presence at that moment was in some way necessary to the Duke's purpose; otherwise, even if he had troubled to deal with the affair in person, he would have waited till he had finished his important conversation with the Florentine envoy. Did he want to show the Signory that he was independent of the French and, notwithstanding the revolt of his captains, strong enough to risk their displeasure; or was the whole point of the scene the scarcely veiled threat he had made when he told Machiavelli that the soldiers could have safely sold their loot when they were in Florence? But who could tell the workings of that ruthless, crafty brain?

'This is the house, Messere,' said the boy suddenly.

Machiavelli gave him a coin and the urchin with a hop, skip and a jump ran off. Piero raised the bronze knocker and let it fall. There was a delay and Piero knocked again. Machiavelli noticed that the house was of handsome proportions, evidently the abode of a man of substance; and the windows on the second floor, the *piano principale*, were not as might have been expected of oiled paper, but of glass, which showed that he had ample means.

8

Machiavelli did not know Bartolomeo Martelli, but he had been instructed to get in touch with him. He was a person of consequence in the small city, an alderman, and a man of property. He owned land in the immediate neighbourhood of Imola and several houses in the town itself; his father had made money by trade in the Levant and he had himself spent some years of his youth in Smyrna. It was on this account that he had connections with Florence, since the Florentines had always traded with the Near East and many of the citizens were settled in its various cities. Bartolomeo's father had been in partnership with a Florentine merchant of good family and had eventually married his daughter. He was distantly related to Biagio Buonaccorsi, for their maternal grandmothers, long since dead, were sisters; this indeed was one of the inducements Biagio had held out to Machiavelli to persuade him to take young Piero with him. The connection would make it easier for Machiavelli to get on intimate terms with the useful man.

And Bartolomeo might be very useful. He was not only a considerable man in Imola, but it was he who had led the party that brought about the capitulation of the city without a struggle. The Duke, who was always generous with other people's property, had rewarded him with the gift of an estate which carried with it the title of count, a fact Machiavelli had learnt from the loquacious barber, and he had learnt also that Bartolomeo, though he pretended otherwise, was inordinately pleased with his rank. The Duke trusted him, knowing it was to his advantage to be trustworthy, and had employed him on various commercial missions in which he had conducted himself with credit. The Duke was secret, but it was likely that Bartolomeo knew as much about his plans as anybody, and Machiavelli was confident that he would in due course succeed in extracting from him anything he knew. The Signory had a hold on him. He had inherited from his mother two houses in Florence, and if he did not behave an accidental fire might easily destroy one of them; and if this were not a sufficient deterrent means might possibly be found to damage the business in the Levant in which he still had a large interest.

'It is good to have friends,' Machiavelli reflected, 'but it is as well that they should know you can retaliate if they should be led to act otherwise than as friends should.'

The door was opened by a serving man. When Machiavelli, first giving his name, asked for his master, he said:

'The Count is expecting you.'

He led them into a court-yard, up an outside staircase, and into a room of moderate size which a glance showed was used by the master of the house as his office. They waited a minute or two and Bartolomeo blustered in. He greeted his visitors with noisy heartiness.

'I heard of your arrival, Messer Niccolo, and I have been awaiting you with eagerness.'

He was a big corpulent man of about forty, with long hair, receding from his forehead, and a full black beard; he had a red face, shining with sweat, a double chin, and a somewhat imposing paunch. Machiavelli, himself as lean as a rail, did not like fat men; he was used to say that no man could grow fat in Italy without robbing the widow and the orphan and grinding the faces of the poor.

'Biagio Buonaccorsi wrote and told me you were coming. A courier brought the letter yesterday.'

'Yes, a courier was coming and Biagio made use of him. This is Piero Canestrini, son of our good Biagio's sister.'

Bartolomeo gave a ringing laugh, and taking the boy in his arms, pressed him to his paunch and kissed him on both cheeks.

'Then we are cousins,' he cried in a loud, booming voice.

'Cousins?' murmured Machiavelli.

'Did you not know? Biagio's grandmother and my grandmother were sisters. They were both daughters of Carlo Peruzzi.'

'Strange he should never have told me. Did you know this, Piero?'

'My mother never told me.'

Machiavelli only disclaimed knowledge of this fact with which of course he was perfectly acquainted, because it was one of his principles never to let anyone know how much you know except with good reason. He was pleased to see that Piero had taken the cue without a moment's hesitation. A good boy.

Bartolomeo asked them to sit down. There was no fire-place in the room, but a brazier of live charcoal took the chill off the air. He asked after his friends in Florence, which he frequently visited on business, and Machiavelli gave him news of such as he knew. They chatted about one thing and another, and presently the conversation turned upon Piero Soderini who had just been elected Gonfalonier for life.

'He is a good friend of mine, a very worthy and honest man,' said Machiavelli. 'It is at his express desire that I have come to Imola now.'

He thought it well to let Bartolomeo know that he had the confidence of the head of the Republic.

'I am very glad to see you and you may be assured that you can count on my services. I asked Biagio to send a bolt of fine linen, but in the circumstances I suppose you had no opportunity to bring it.'

Biagio, since he was ever ready to do a service, was constantly asked to do commissions for all and sundry, and no one used him more unconscionably than Machiavelli.

'On the contrary,' he answered. 'Biagio made a point of my bringing it, but my servants have it and they will not get to Imola till later in the day.'

'My wife is making me some shirts. She was taught embroidery by the nuns and I have no hesitation in saying that there isn't a woman in Imola to equal her. She is an artist.'

Machiavelli's mind was busy. He was trying to size the man up. Bluff and hearty, plethoric, which suggested that he liked to eat well and drink deep, with a fat laugh and a booming loquacity. It remained to be seen whether the jovial manner and frank cordiality masked an astute and scheming brain. He had the reputation of being a good business man who drove a hard bargain. Machiavelli turned the conversation to Imola and its condition. Bartolomeo was eloquent in praise of the Duke. He had adhered scrupulously to the terms of the capitulation; the sum he had exacted on occupying the city was not unreasonable, and he was proposing to spend much on making it a finer and grander place. For Imola was the capital of his newly-acquired state. He was having plans drawn out for building a new palace for himself, a new house for the merchants to meet at, a hospital for the poor; order reigned in the city, crime had diminished and justice was prompt and cheap. Poor and rich were equal before the law. Commerce was flourishing; bribery and corruption had ceased. The Duke interested himself in the agricultural resources of the country and had given instructions that everything possible should be done to foster them. The troops were stationed outside the city, which was entering upon an era of prosperity and everyone was well satisfied.

'Long may it last,' said Machiavelli pleasantly, 'and what will happen to you if the Duke's captains overthrow him and march into your city with their troops?'

Bartolomeo burst into a bellow of laughter and slapped his thigh.

'They amount to nothing. They know they're powerless without the Duke and they'll come to terms with him. Believe me, it will all blow over.'

Machiavelli could not make up his mind whether Bartolomeo believed what he said, wanted to believe what he said, or was just saying what he wanted Machiavelli to believe. He had still not made up his mind whether the man was stupid or clever. That frankness, that enthusiasm, that guileless air and those smiling, friendly eyes might conceal anything. He changed the conversation.

'You were good enough to say that you would be pleased to be of service to me. Can you tell me where I can find a place to live with Piero and my servants?'

'I wish you had asked me anything but that,' Bartolomeo laughed boisterously. 'What with the Duke's court and all the hangers-on, poets, painters, architects, engineers, to say nothing of the people from his other possessions who are here on business, and the merchants, the vendors of this and that, who've been attracted by the opportunities to make money, there isn't a hole or corner in the city that isn't occupied.'

'I wish to stay here no longer than I need, but I am at the orders of the Signory. I cannot conduct my business in a monastery cell. I must find accommodation for Piero and my servants.'

'I will ask my mother-in-law. She knows more about a matter like this than I do. I will call her.'

He left the room, and on his return after an interval invited his guests to follow him. He led them into a much larger apartment, with handsomely-painted walls and a fireplace. The ladies were seated at work by the fire. They rose when the strangers entered and curtsied in response to their low bows. One of them was a middle-aged woman of a comely presence.

'This is my mother-in-law, Monna Caterina Cappello,' said Bartolomeo. 'And this is my wife.'

She was young enough to be his daughter. Following the fashion of the day her hair, naturally dark, was dyed very fair; and since the swarthy skin of Italian women did not go with this, her face, neck and bosom were heavily coated with a white cosmetic. The contrast of the golden hair with her handsome black eyes was very effective. Her eyebrows were plucked to a thin line. She had a small straight nose and a lovely mouth. She was dressed in a pale grey, with a full skirt, billowing sleeves, and a bodice fitting her slim figure tightly and cut low in a square to show her snowy bosom and the outline of her young full breasts. There was a virginal quality in her beauty and at the same time a ripeness that made a highly attractive combination. Machiavelli, though his face gave no indication of it, felt a queer sensation in what he was pleased to call his heart.

'A very pretty young woman,' he said to himself. 'I should like to go to bed with her.'

While the two ladies brought up chairs for the visitors to sit on, Bartolomeo explained to Monna Caterina Machiavelli's difficulty and then, as an afterthought, added that in Piero he had found a cousin whom he had never seen. Both women gave the boy a smile when the relationship was explained to them, and Machiavelli noticed with pleasure that Bartolomeo's wife had good teeth, small, even and white.

'Would these gentlemen not like some refreshment?' asked Monna Caterina.

She was dressed very like her daughter, but in a darker colour, and since it was not thought proper for a respectable elderly woman to dye her hair or to paint her cheeks she was as nature made her; but she had her daughter's fine black eyes and in youth must have been as beautiful. Machiavelli said they had already breakfasted, but his host insisted that they should at least drink a glass of wine.

'Aurelia, go and tell Nina,' he said to his wife.

The young woman went out. He repeated to his mother-in-law what Machiavelli had told him about his requirements.

'It's impossible. There's not a room to be let in the whole city. But wait. Since Messere is a person of consequence and this young man your cousin, it may be that Serafina would take them. She has always refused to take lodgers; only the other day I told her it was a shame to keep that room empty when people were willing to pay anything to have a roof over their heads.'

Bartolomeo explained that Monna Serafina was the widow of one of his factors in the Levant and the house she lived in belonged to him. Her eldest son was in his office at Smyrna, and she had two children living with her, a boy who was to be a priest and a girl of fourteen. It was on their account, so that they might not be exposed to the danger of bad company, that she had refused to have strangers in her house.

'She could hardly refuse you, my son, if you made a point of it.'

It was odd to hear Monna Caterina address the fat man as her son, for she could not have been more than two or three years older than he.

'I will take you round myself,' said Bartolomeo. 'I'm sure it can be arranged.'

Aurelia came back and was immediately followed by a maid who brought a salver on which were glasses, a bottle of wine and a dish of sweetmeats. Aurelia sat down and resumed her work.

'Messer Niccolo has brought you the linen, dear,' Bartolomeo said, 'so you can get to work on my shirts.'

'God knows you needed some new ones,' said Monna Caterina.

Aurelia smiled, but did not speak.

'Let me show you how beautifully my wife embroiders.'

Bartolomeo went over to Aurelia and took the material on which she was busy.

'No, Bartolomeo, these are women's things.'

'If Messer Niccolo has never seen a woman's shift it is high time he did.'

'I am a married man, Monna Aurelia,' said Machiavelli with a smile that made his thin face not unattractive.

'Look at the beauty of her needlework and the elegance of her design.'

'Is it possible that she draws it herself?'

'Of course. She is an artist.'

Machiavelli made a suitable compliment and the garment was returned to her. She thanked him with a smile of her bright eyes. When they had eaten of the sweetmeats and drunk a glass of wine Bartolomeo proposed that he should take them round to the widow Serafina.

'Her house is just behind this one,' he said.

Machiavelli and Piero accompanied him downstairs, and through a small yard in which was a well with a carved well-head and a chestnut-tree, its leaves now scattered after the first frost of autumn, to a small door that led into a narrow alley.

'Here we are,' said Bartolomeo.

The deserted alley suggested to Machiavelli that visitors could in all likelihood come to see him without being observed. Bartolomeo knocked, and in a minute the door was opened by a thin, tallish woman with a lined face, darkly pale, sullen eyes and grey hair. The look of suspicion she wore changed, when she saw who it was that knocked, into one of effusive welcome. She begged them to enter.

'This is Messer Niccolo Machiavelli, First Secretary of the Second Chancery, and envoy to the Duke from the Florentine Republic, and this youth is my cousin

Piero, nephew of my good friend and relative, Biagio Buonaccorsi.'

Monna Serafina led them into a parlour and Bartolomeo set forth the purpose of their visit. Monna Serafina's face went glum.

'Oh, Messer Bartolomeo, you know I've refused everybody. You see, with two young children in the house. And people one knows nothing about.'

'I know, I know, Serafina, but here are people I vouch for. Piero is my cousin; he will be a good friend to your Luigi.'

The discussion proceeded. Bartolomeo, in his bluff, hearty way, managed to convey to the unwilling woman that the house was his and if he wanted to he could turn her out, and that her elder son was in his employment and depended on his good will for advancement; but it was done in such a friendly, bantering manner as to excite Machiavelli's admiration. The man, simple though he looked, was no fool. Serafina was poor and she could not afford to offend Bartolomeo. With a grim smile she said that she would be happy to do him and his friends a service. It was arranged that Machiavelli should have a room and the use of the parlour, Piero would double up with her son Luigi, and she would put down mattresses for the two servants in the attic. The sum she asked for rent was high, and Bartolomeo remarked on it, but Machiavelli thought it beneath his official dignity to haggle and said that he would be glad to pay it. He knew that nothing more predisposes someone in your favour than to let him rob you a little. There was of course no glass in the windows, but there were shutters to them and oiled paper screens which could be opened entirely or in part to let in air and light. There was a fireplace in the kitchen and the parlour could be warmed by a brazier. Serafina consented to give her own room to Machiavelli and move in with her daughter to a smaller room on the ground floor.

9

This having been settled Bartolomeo left them, and Machiavelli and Piero went back to the Golden Lion to have dinner. They were just finishing when the two servants arrived from Scaperia with the horses and the baggage. Machiavelli told Piero to show them the way to the monastery and fetch the saddle-bags which had been left there.

'Take the bolt of linen to Messer Bartolomeo's and bid the maid take it up to the ladies. She wasn't a bad-looking wench; it might be worth your while to get into conversation with her. Then go back to Serafina's and wait till I come.'

He paused for a moment.

'She's a talkative woman and certainly a gossip. Go and sit with her in the kitchen. She'll be glad of company. Let her talk to you about her children, and talk to her about your mother. Then find out all you can about Bartolomeo, his wife and his mother-in-law. Serafina's under too great an obligation to him not to bear him a grudge; you have a frank, honest face, you're only a boy, if you can gain her confidence she'll pour out her soul to you. It will be good practice for you to learn how with kind words and pretty speeches you can get someone to betray the hatred that is in his heart.'

'But, Messer Niccolo, why are you so certain that she hates him?'

'I'm not certain at all. It may be that she's only a foolish, garrulous woman. The fact remains that she is poor and he is rich, and that she depends on his bounty; the burden of gratitude is very hard to bear. Believe me, it is easier to forgive the offences your enemy does you than the benefits your friend confers upon you.'

He smiled acidly and went his way. He had an appointment with the Florentine agent to meet a fellow-citizen, Giacomo Farinelli by name, who had been exiled with the Medici, and who, being a clever accountant, had been engaged by the Duke. But he was anxious to get back to Florence and have his confiscated property restored to him, and so could be counted on to make himself useful. He confirmed what Bartolomeo had told Machiavelli in the morning. The Duke's new subjects were contented with his rule. The administration was severe, but competent. The people who had groaned under the tyranny of their petty princes enjoyed a freedom from oppression they had not known for a century. By conscription, taking one man from every house in his dominions, the Duke had created an army which was much more reliable than the hirelings of which in general armies consisted. The French men-at-arms and the Gascons might at any time be recalled by their king, the Swiss were always prepared to desert if another power made it worth their while, and the Germans ravaged every district they went through and were a terror to the population. The Duke's soldiers were proud of the red and yellow uniform into which he had put them; they were well paid, well drilled and well armed; and he had succeeded in inspiring them with loyalty.

'And what of the Captains, Vitellozzo and the Orsini?' asked Machiavelli.

There was no news of them. No one knew what they were doing.

'What is the feeling at the Palace?'

'You would say that nothing was the matter,' said Farinelli. 'The Duke is secret and keeps to his apartments. The secretaries give no sign that there is cause for anxiety. I have never seen Messer Agapito in a better humour.'

Machiavelli frowned. He was puzzled. It was evident enough that something was brewing, but though the accountant was very willing to tell all he knew, at the end Machiavelli was obliged to admit that he was no wiser than before. He returned to his lodging, where Piero was waiting for him.

'Did you deliver the linen?' he asked.

'Yes. Messer Bartolomeo was at the Palace. The maid told me to wait while she took it up to the ladies, and when she came down said they wanted to thank me in person for bringing it. So I went up.'

'Then you didn't make friends with the maid as I told you to.'

'There was no opportunity.'

'You might have pinched her or at least told her she was pretty. There was opportunity for that.'

'The ladies were very nice to me. They gave me fruit and cake and wine. They asked me a lot of questions about you.'

'What did they ask?'

'They wanted to know how long you'd been married and whom you'd married and what Monna Marietta was like.'

'And have you talked to Serafina?'

'You were right about her, Messere. If you hadn't come in she'd be talking still. I thought she'd never stop.'

'Tell me.'

When Piero had finished Machiavelli gave him a genial smile.

'You have done very well. I knew I was right, I knew that your youth would appeal to the ageing woman and your simple innocent look make it easy for her to confide in you.'

Piero had found out a great deal. Bartolomeo was in high favour with the Duke. He was one of the first men in the city. He was honest, kindly, generous and devout.

This was his third marriage. His first had been arranged by his parents, and his wife after eight years died of cholera. After a decent interval he married again, but eleven years later his second wife also died. Both had brought him handsome dowries, and both were childless. He had remained a widower for three years and then suddenly married Aurelia. She was a native of Sinigaglia, a port on the Adriatic, and her father was owner and master of a coasting vessel that carried merchandise to the Dalmatian cities. He was lost with his ship in a storm, and his widow was reduced to poverty so that she had to earn her living as a sempstress. She had three daughters, a son having been drowned with his father, but two of them were married. Aurelia was sixteen when accident brought her to the notice of Bartolomeo. He was struck by her virginal beauty, but neither by birth nor fortune was she a proper match for a man of his consequence; but, young though she was, there was in her a ripeness that gave promise of fecundity, and that was a matter of moment to Bartolomeo, for there was nothing in the world he wanted more than a son. During the lifetime of his two wives he had kept likely young women of humble station, but none of these irregular amours had resulted in issue. The fact that Monna Caterina had had six children (two had died in infancy) showed that the stock was fruitful, and by discreet enquiries he discovered that Aurelia's older sisters had already had three or four babies each. They had in fact given birth once a year with the regularity which was proper to a healthy young person of the female sex. But Bartolomeo was cautious. He had married two barren women and did not want to marry a third. Through an intermediary he proposed to Monna Caterina that he should install her and her daughter on a handsome allowance in one of his villas outside Imola, with a promise that he would recognize any child that might be born. He went so far as to permit the intermediary to hint at the possibility of marriage if the child were male. But Monna Caterina whether owing to religious scruples or worldly wisdom refused the offer with indignation. Her dead husband, though no more the master of a small coasting vessel, had been an honourable man, and her two daughters were respectably, if not richly, married. Sooner than see her beloved child the kept woman of a merchant she would put her in a nunnery. Bartolomeo reviewed the marriageable young women in Imola and could think of none who attracted him so much as Aurelia or who seemed more likely to give him the son he yearned for. He was a business man and a sensible one. He knew that if you wanted something enough and could not get it at your own price there was only one thing to do and that was to give the price asked for it. With a good grace he made an offer of marriage. It was promptly accepted.

Bartolomeo was not only a business man, but a shrewd one. Aurelia was twenty years younger than he, and he thought it advisable that she should have someone to keep an eye on her. He invited Monna Caterina to live with him and his bride.

Serafina sniggered.

'The old fool trusts her. But look at her; that isn't a woman who was faithful to her husband. You can tell at once. When her husband was at sea she wasn't so virtuous as all that.'

'She evidently doesn't like Monna Caterina,' said Machiavelli. 'I wonder why. Perhaps she wanted to marry Bartolomeo herself and have him adopt her children. Perhaps merely envy. It may be of no importance, but it is just as well to know.'

The marriage had been happy and Bartolomeo was delighted with his young wife. He gave her fine clothes and fine jewels. She was dutiful, respectful, submissive, in fact all that a wife should be, but though they had been married three years she had not had a baby and showed no sign of having one. It was the great cross of Bartolomeo's life, and now that he had a title to transmit he wanted a son more than ever.

'Did Monna Serafina hint that the beautiful Aurelia might be unfaithful to her old husband?' Machiavelli asked with a smile.

'No. She seldom goes out except to mass, and then only with her mother or the maid to accompany her. According to Monna Serafina she is very pious. She would look upon it as a mortal sin to deceive her husband.'

Machiavelli pondered.

'When you were talking to the ladies about me did you happen to mention that Monna Marietta was pregnant?'

The boy flushed.

'I thought there was no harm.'

'None at all. I'm not sorry they know.'

Machiavelli smiled significantly, but the significance of his smile escaped Piero. It has been said that Machiavelli had not married Marietta for love. He respected her, he appreciated her good qualities, and he approved of her devotion to him. She was a thrifty housekeeper, an important matter to one of his small means, and she never wasted a penny; she would be the mother of his children, and a good mother; there was every reason why he should regard her with indulgence and affection, but it had never entered his mind that he should be faithful to her. Aurelia's beauty had taken his breath away, but it was not only her beauty that had moved him, he could not remember any woman who had so immediately and so violently excited his senses. His very stomach ached with the vehemence of his desire.

'I'm going to have that woman if I die for it,' he said to himself.

He knew a great deal about women and it was not often that he had failed to satisfy his lust. He had no illusions about his appearance; he knew that other men were handsomer than he and that many had the advantage of him in wealth and station. But he was confident in his powers of attraction. He could amuse them, he knew just how to flatter them, he had a way with him that put them at their ease with him, but above all he desired them; they were very conscious of that and it excited them.

'When a woman feels with every nerve in her body that you want her she can resist only if she's passionately in love with another,' he had once told Biagio.

It was impossible to suppose that Aurelia loved her fat husband, a man so many years older than herself, to whom she had been married by her mother because it was a good business proposition. But Bartolomeo must know that there were young men in the city, dissolute fellows attached to the Duke's court, who had noticed that she was beautiful, and he must be on his guard. The serving man had suspicious eyes. He was beetle-browed, a sullen fellow with a great bony nose and a cruel mouth; he might well have been put there to spy on his young mistress. And then there was the mother. Serafina said she had been gay in her youth and it might be true; she had the bold roving eye of the woman who has had adventures, and though it might be that it would be no outrage to her virtue if her daughter took a lover, it was a risk to run. Machiavelli had come to the conclusion that Bartolomeo was a vain man, and he knew that no one can be so vindictive as the vain man who discovers that he has been fooled. It was no easy matter that Machiavelli was undertaking, but that did not disturb him, he had confidence in himself, and the difficulty made that affair more interesting. It was evident that he must cultivate Bartolomeo and lull him into security, and it would be well to get on good terms with Monna Caterina. It had been a sound idea to get Piero to question Serafina and it had given him some notion of the situation. But he had to know more, and then some plan might suggest itself to his fertile mind. He knew it was no use to rack his brain. He must wait for an inspiration.

'Let us go and have supper,' he said to Piero.

They walked to the Golden Lion and having eaten returned to their lodging. Serafina had put her children to bed and was in the kitchen darning a pair of stockings. Machiavelli sent Piero up to the room he shared with her son, and politely asking if he might warm himself for a little by her fire sat down. He had an inkling that Monna Caterina would be over very soon to ask Serafina about him and he wanted her to give a good report of him. He could be very charming when he chose, and now he did. He told her of his mission to the court of France, partly because he knew it would interest her, but more to impress upon her his own importance; he talked of the King and of his minister the Cardinal as though he were hail-fellow well-met with them, and told her scandalous and amusing stories of the gallantries of great ladies. Then he took another line; he told her of Marietta, and how hard it was to leave her when she was pregnant, and how much he wanted to go back to Florence and his happy home. Serafina would have had to be a very clever woman to doubt that he was the good and devoted husband, the plain, honest man he made himself out to be. He listened with sympathetic interest while she told him of her husband's illness and death, the better days she had seen, and the responsibility it was to have two young children to launch into the world. Of course she thought him a delightful, distinguished and kindly man. When he told her that he was delicate, with a digestion that was the torment of his life, and that the food at the Golden Lion didn't agree with him, for he was used to Monna Marietta's simple fare, it was natural enough for Serafina to say that if he wasn't too proud to eat with her and her children she would gladly provide meals for him and Piero. This suited him very well, for it would save money and in other ways be more convenient. He left her with just the impression of himself that he wanted, went up to his room, and by the light of a candle read his Livy till he felt inclined to sleep.

10

Machiavelli lay in bed late next morning. He read one of the cantos of the *Inferno*. Though he knew the noble poem almost by heart it filled him as usual with exaltation; he could never read it without being ravished by the beauty of its language; but at the back of his mind hovered the picture of Aurelia primly at work on her embroidery, and now and then he was obliged to put the book down and indulge in thoughts of some indecency. He wondered how on earth he could arrange to see her again. Of course it might be that on a second meeting she would seem less desirable, and in a way it would be a blessing, for he had enough to do without engaging in a love affair. on the other hand it would be a pleasant distraction from his political labours. His reflections were interrupted by his servant Antonio, who told him that Messer Bartolomeo was below and desired to see him. Sending down a message that he would join him immediately Machiavelli threw on his clothes and went downstairs.

'Forgive me for keeping you waiting, Count, but I was just finishing a letter to the Signory,' he lied easily.

Bartolomeo, with a slight gesture of deprecation at Machiavelli's use of his title, as though to say that it was a trifle of no account, was obviously flattered. He brought news. The strongest fortress in the Urbinate was San Leo; it was perched on a steep, isolated rock and was reputed to be impregnable. It happened that it was undergoing repair, and taking advantage of this a number of armed peasants had rushed the gate and massacred Il Valentino's garrison. The news spread quickly and other villages at once rose in revolt. Il Valentino had flown into a temper when intelligence of this was brought him; it was evident that the rising had been instigated by the conspirators at La Magione, and that could only mean that they had decided to attack him. The Palace was in a turmoil of activity.

'What are the troops the Duke can at present dispose of?' Machiavelli interrupted.

'You'd better come and see for yourself.'

'I doubt whether His Excellency would give me permission.'

'Come with me. I'm going to the camp now. I'll take you.'

It flashed across Machiavelli's mind that Bartolomeo had not come in a friendly way to give him information which in any case could not have been for long kept secret, but had been sent by the Duke expressly to tender this invitation. Like a hunter in the forest who hears a rustling in the undergrowth, Machiavelli was on a sudden alert, but he smiled amiably.

'You must be a powerful man, friend, if you can come and go about the camp at your own free will.'

'No, it isn't that,' Bartolomeo replied, with a semblance of modesty. 'The Duke has put me at the head of the citizens commissioned to see to the provisioning of the troops.'

'You must be making a pretty penny out of it,' said Machiavelli slyly.

Bartolomeo burst into a fat laugh.

'A bare profit, if that. The Duke isn't a man to trifle with. At Urbino the men almost mutinied over the quality of their food, and when the matter was brought to his attention and he discovered that their complaints were justified, he hanged the three commissioners.'

'I can well understand that it makes you careful.'

They rode out to the camp. It was three miles from the city. There were three companies of fifty lancers under Spanish captains, and a hundred lancers, Roman gentleman who had joined the Duke's army for adventure and to win renown. Each lancer was mounted, and had a page on a pony and an infantryman as attendants. There were twenty-five hundred mercenaries; and the Duke's conscripted soldiers, six thousand of them, were expected to arrive in two days. He had sent an agent to Milan to collect five hundred of the Gascon adventurers who were scattered in Lombardy and another to hire fifteen hundred Swiss. His artillery was formidable and in good condition. Machiavelli was interested in military affairs, of which he had gained some experience in the unsuccessful siege of Pisa, and he flattered himself on his knowledge. He kept his eyes open. He asked a lot of questions, both of officers and men, and sorting the answers, accepting what looked like truth and rejecting what was improbable, formed the opinion that the Duke's force was far from negligible.

On getting back to the city he found a message from Agapito da Amalia to say that the Duke desired to see him at eight o'clock that evening. After dinner he sent Piero over to Bartolomeo's house to tell him that he was to have an audience with the Duke that night, and if Bartolomeo would meet him later at the Golden Lion they might drink a cup of wine together; it was possible that he could only get into communication with Aurelia through her husband and therefore must make friends with him. Bartolomeo was a trusting soul, who liked good cheer and good company, and such a proof of confidence as the envoy of the Republic was now offering could not fail to flatter his conceit.

Machiavelli went to his room and had a siesta, then decided that it would be worth his while to have another talk with Serafina. He had a notion that he could get more out of her than Piero had. She had spoken well of Bartolomeo to him, but that might have been from discretion; if he knew anything about human nature she must be less grateful for the benefits the fat man had conferred on her than resentful on account of those he had omitted. Machiavelli thought himself clever enough to induce her to divulge her real feelings.

When he awoke he strolled downstairs as though to go to the parlour and on his way sang, a little more loudly than was necessary, the catch of a Florentine song.

'Are you there, Monna Serafina,' he said as he passed the kitchen door. 'I thought you were out.'

'You have a fine voice, Messere,' she said.

'A thousand thanks. May I come in for a minute?'

'My eldest son has a beautiful voice; Messer Bartolomeo used often to have him over and they would sing together. Messer Bartolomeo is a bass. It is strange that a man so big and strong should have a voice of so little power.'

Machiavelli pricked up his ears.

'My friend Biagio Buonaccorsi, Messer Bartolomeo's cousin, and I are fond of singing together. What a pity I couldn't bring my lute with me! It would have been a pleasure to me to sing some of my songs to you.'

'But my son left his lute here. He wanted to take it with him, but it's a valuable instrument which was given to his father, my poor husband, by a gentleman to whom he had done a service, and I wouldn't let him take it.'

'Will you let me see it?'

'It hasn't been touched for three years now. I dare say some of the strings are broken.'

But she fetched it and put it in Machiavelli's hands. It was a lovely thing of cedar with ivory inlay. He tuned it and proceeded in a low voice to sing. He was not only very fond of music, but had a technical knowledge of it, and he had written the words and himself composed the melody of several songs. As he finished he noticed that tears were in Serafina's eyes. He put down the instrument and had looked at her kindly.

'I didn't wish to make you cry.'

'It reminds me of my boy, so far away and exposed to so many dangers among those heathen people.'

'It'll be good experience for him, and under the protection of Messer Bartolomeo his future is assured.'

She gave him a pinched glance.

'Lazarus must be thankful for the crumbs that fall from the rich man's table.'

Her acid remark assured him that he had not been far wrong in his conjecture.

'The Holy Scriptures assure us that in heaven the position will be reversed,' he answered.

She gave a laugh that was more like a snort.

'He would give half his wealth to have my children.'

'It is strange that none of his three wives should have produced a child.'

'You men, you always think it's the woman's fault. Monna Caterina has her head screwed on her shoulders all right; she knows that if Aurelia doesn't have a baby soon it'll go badly with both of them. No more fine dresses then. No more rings and bracelets. I've known Bartolomeo all his life. He doesn't give much away for nothing. Monna Caterina is wise to worry. She's giving Fra Timoteo money to pray that Aurelia should conceive.'

'Who, pray, is Fra Timoteo?' asked Machiavelli.

'Their confessor. Bartolomeo has promised to give a Virgin and Child when Aurelia has a son. Fra Timoteo is making a pretty penny out of them. He twists them round his little finger, and he knows as well as I do that poor Bartolomeo is impotent.'

Machiavelli had learnt more than he had hoped; a scheme beautiful and simple flashed through his mind and he thought it wise to drop the conversation. He idly plucked the strings of the lute.

'You're right, it's a beautiful instrument. It's a pleasure to play on it. I don't wonder that you were unwilling to let your son take it overseas.'

'You are very sympathetic, Messere,' she said. 'If it gives you pleasure to play, I will lend it you while you're here. I know you'll be careful with it.'

Machiavelli had been wondering how he could induce her to make such an offer: she saved him all further trouble. There was no doubt about it, he had a way with women: it was a pity she was old, haggard and sallow; otherwise he might have permitted himself a little nonsense with her. He thanked her warmly.

'It will be a comfort to me to sing the little songs my wife is fond of. I haven't been married to her long and she is pregnant; it was hard to leave her. But how could I help it? I am a servant of the Republic and I must put my duty before my inclination.'

When, a little later, Machiavelli left her he had persuaded Serafina that he was not only a person of distinction, but a good husband, a sincere friend, and an honest, charming and reliable man.

11

At the appointed time one of the Duke's secretaries, accompanied by men with torches, came to fetch him, and Machiavelli, calling one of his servants to follow, started out for the Palace. The Duke received him with a show of affection that was the more surprising since two nights before he had dismissed him in a passion. He appeared to be in high spirits. He mentioned the fall of the fortress of San Leo in an off-hand way and seemed to have no doubt that he would easily settle the trouble in Urbino. Then in an intimately confidential manner that would have flattered Machiavelli had he been sensible to flattery he told him that he had sent for him to impart some news that would interest the gentlemen of the Signory. He produced a letter he had just received from the Bishop of Arles, the Pope's legate in France, in which the Bishop told him that the King and the Cardinal, his minister, were anxious to please him and knowing that he needed men for his attack on Bologna had given orders to Monsieur de Chaumont at Milan to send him three hundred lancers under Monsieur de Lancres, and on the Duke's demand to march in person on Parma with another three hundred lancers. The Duke showed the letter to Machiavelli so that he could vouch for its authenticity.

The cause of the Duke's good humour was obvious. If he had not marched on Florence after his capture of Urbino it was only because the French had sent a force to protect it, and the only conclusion to be drawn from this was that he could no longer count on their aid. It was the assurance of this that had encouraged the captains to revolt. But if the French, for reasons which could only be surmised, were once more prepared to support him his situation was much improved.

'Now listen to me, Secretary,' he said. 'This letter was written in answer to the request I made for help to attack Bologna. You can see for yourself that I shan't lack strength to cope with these rascals. They couldn't have discovered themselves at a more convenient time. I know now against whom I have to protect myself and who are my friends. I'm telling you this so that you may write to your masters and show them that I'm not bowing before the storm. I have good friends, and among them I should like to count the Signory – if they're disposed to come to terms quickly; but if they're not I'm finished with them for good and all, and even if I were up to my neck in water I wouldn't talk of friendship again.'

Though his words were menacing, he spoke in such a gay and debonair fashion that they hardly seemed offensive. Machiavelli said he would write at once to the Signory to inform them of what the Duke had told him. The Duke bade him good night with cordiality.

When Machiavelli arrived at the inn he found Bartolomeo waiting for him. They ordered mulled wine. Machiavelli, pledging him to secrecy to make what he had to say appear more important, though he guessed that if Bartolomeo did not know it already, he soon would, told him what he had learnt from the Duke. It suited him then to invent a little; he told Bartolomeo that the Duke had spoken most obligingly of him, and when the fat man wanted to know in exactly what terms, Machiavelli had no difficulty in specifying them. Bartolomeo beamed.

'You are already the first man in Imola, Messer Bartolomeo; if the Pope lives and things prosper with the Duke you may well be one of the first men in Italy.'

'I am nothing but a merchant. I do not aim so high.'

'Cosimo de' Medici was nothing but a merchant, and yet he became the master of Florence and his son, Lorenzo the Magnificent, treated on equal terms with kings and princes.'

The expression on Bartolomeo's face showed him that the dart had hit its mark.

'Is it true that your wife is pregnant, Messere?'

'It is a great joy to me. She expects her confinement some time next year.'

'You are more fortunate than I,' sighed Bartolomeo. 'I have had three wives and not one of them has borne me a child.'

'Monna Aurelia is a strong and healthy young woman. It is impossible to believe that she is barren.'

'What other explanation can there be? We have been married three years.'

'Perhaps if you took her to the baths . . .'

'I took her to the baths, and when that failed, we went on a pilgrimage to Santa Maria de la Misericordia at Alvanio, where there is a miraculous image of the Madonna which causes barren women to conceive. It had no effect. You can imagine what a mortification it is to me. My enemies say that I am impotent. That is absurd. Few men are more virile than I am. Why, I have bastards in every village within ten miles of Imola.'

Machiavelli knew that was a lie.

'Would you imagine that anyone could have such bad luck as to marry three barren women?'

'You mustn't despair, my friend. A miracle is always possible and you have surely deserved well of our Holy Church.'

'That is what Fra Timoteo says. He prays for me daily.'

'Fra Timoteo?' asked Machiavelli as though the name meant nothing to him.

'Our confessor. He tells me to have faith.'

Machiavelli called for more wine. By the exercise of judicious flattery, namely by asking Bartolomeo's advice on how he should conduct himself in his difficult negotiations with the Duke, he soon brought him to a more cheerful state of mind. Then he told him a number of highly indecent stories, of which he had a great store and which he told with effect. Bartolomeo laughed with great guffaws and by the time they parted he had decided that he had never known a more entertaining fellow. On his side Machiavelli thought that he had spent his evening to advantage. He was a temperate man, but he had a strong head, and the wine that had made Bartolomeo a trifle tipsy had not affected him at all. When he got back to his room he proceeded to write a long letter to the Signory telling them of his interview with the Duke and what forces he had at his disposal or within easy call. He wrote fluently and without erasures. Then he read what he had written. It was a good letter.

12

Il Valentino was in the habit of working far into the night, and so did not get up early in the morning. His secretaries, kept busy till all hours, took advantage of this to sleep late, and so next morning Machiavelli, with nothing much to do till after dinner, his letter to the Signory dispatched, thought he would take things easily. He read his Livy and made a few notes of the reflections his reading had occasioned and then to pass the time took his borrowed lute. It had a good tone, resonant but sweet, and he had noticed when first he tried it that it suited his light baritone. It was a sunny day and he sat by the open window enjoying the grateful warmth. Somewhere in the not far distance they were burning wood and the smell of it was pleasant in his nostrils. The lane that separated Serafina's house from Messer Bartolomeo's was so narrow that a donkey with panniers could hardly have scraped its way through, and from his window Machiavelli looked down into the tiny court-yard with its well-head and its chestnut-tree. He began to sing. He was in good voice that morning and liking the sound of it went on. Then he noticed that the window in a room opposite was being opened, he could not see by whom, he did not even see the hand that fixed the paper panel, but he had a sudden thrill of exultation, for he was convinced that the unseen person could be none other than Aurelia. He sang two of his favourite songs, love songs both of them, and was in the middle of a third when the window was suddenly closed as though someone had come into the room. This some-what disconcerted him and a suspicion passed through his mind that it might have been the maid interrupted by her mistress who did not want to be found neglecting her work to listen to a stranger singing in the next house. But at dinner-time his well-directed conversation discovered to him that the window that had been opened was that of the nuptial chamber of Bartolomeo and his young wife.

Later on in the day he went to the Palace, but succeeded in seeing neither the Duke nor any of the secretaries. He entered into conversation with various persons who were lounging about apparently with nothing to do and asked them what the news was. They knew nothing, but he received the impression that they knew at least that something had happened. Whatever it was, a secret was being made of it. Presently he ran across Bartolomeo, who told him he had an appointment with the Duke, but he was too busy to see him.

'We're both wasting our time here,' said Machiavelli with his pleasant friendliness. 'let us go to the inn and drink a cup of wine. We might have a game of cards, or if you can play chess, a game of chess.'

'I'm fond of chess.'

On their way to the Golden Lion Machiavelli asked him what everyone at the Palace was so busy about that day.

'I haven't a notion. I can't get anyone to tell me anything.'

By the slight peevishness of Bartolomeo's tone Machiavelli guessed that he was telling the truth. He had a great idea of his own importance and it humiliated him to find that he was not in the Duke's entire confidence.

'I have heard that when the Duke wishes to keep something secret not even those closest to him know about it,' said Machiavelli.

'He's been occupied with his secretaries all day. Messengers have been dispatched one after the other.'

'It's evident that something has happened.'

63

'I know that a courier arrived from Perugia this morning.'

'A courier, or someone disguised as a courier?'

Bartolomeo looked at him quickly.

'I don't know. What do you suspect?'

'Nothing. I was only asking.'

It was but a short walk to the inn. They ordered a flagon of wine and asked for chessmen. Machiavelli was a good player and it did not take him long to discover that Bartolomeo was no match for him, but he amused himself by giving him a hard game and letting himself be beaten in the end. Bartolomeo was puffed up with pride and while they drank their wine pointed out to Machiavelli exactly what mistakes he had made and what his move should have been to counter his opponent's strategy. Machiavelli blamed himself for his want of foresight. On their way back to their respective domiciles Bartolomeo remarked:

'My mother-in-law says she heard someone singing in your house this morning. A very pretty voice. Was that you or my young cousin Piero?'

'Piero's voice is better than mine, but it was I who was singing. I'm flattered that Monna Caterina should not have thought too badly of my efforts. Biagio and I and one or two more used often to while away the time by singing.'

'I sing a very good bass myself.'

'Piero sings tenor. It would be an excellent combination. If you don't object to my humble quarters it would be a great pleasure to me if you would come in when you have nothing better to do, and we'll give our good friend Serafina a little concert.'

Would the fish swallow the fly that was so skilfully cast? There was no sign of it.

'We will certainly do that. It will bring me back my youth. When I was a young fellow in Smyrna we Italians would sing all the time.'

'Patience,' Machiavelli muttered to himself. 'Patience.'

When he got in, taking a greasy pack of cards, he began to play patience, but as he played he turned over in his mind what Bartolomeo had told him and what he had learnt from Serafina. He had a plan, and it was a good one, but to carry it out called for ingenuity. The more he thought of Aurelia the more she inflamed his fancy, and it tickled him to death to think that he could provide Bartolomeo with the child, preferably male, that he so much wanted.

'It is not often,' he reflected, 'that you can do a good action with so much pleasure to yourself.'

It was evident that he must ingratiate himself with Monna Caterina, for without her he could do nothing, but the difficulty was to get on terms with her sufficiently intimate to enable him to enlist her help. She was a woman of voluptuous appearance, and it occurred to him that he might persuade Piero to go to bed with her. Piero was young. At her age she could not fail to be grateful. But he dismissed the notion; it would serve his purpose better if Piero became the maid's lover. But they said that in her time Monna Caterina had been gay. If there was one thing of which Machiavelli was convinced it was that when a woman ceased to be desirable a procuress is born. He thought there was a natural instinct in the sex that led them to enjoy vicariously pleasures that were no longer befitting to their age. And what should she care about Bartolomeo's honour? It was to her interest that Aurelia should have offspring.

And what about this Fra Timoteo? He was their confessor; he was a friend of the house. It might be worth while to see him and find out what sort of a man he was. It might be that he could be put to good use. Machiavelli's meditation was on a sudden disturbed by a tap on the shutter. He looked up but did not move; the tap, low and discreet, was repeated. He went to the window and slightly opened the shutter. A name was muttered.

'Farinelli.'

'Wait.'

'Are you alone?'

'I am alone.'

He went into the passage and opened the door. In the darkness he could see nothing but that someone was standing there. Farinelli, it may be remembered, was the Florentine accountant with whom Machiavelli had made contact the day after his arrival. Huddled in a cape, with a scarf to conceal his face, he slipped in and followed Machiavelli into the parlour. It was lit by a single candle. He sat at the table close to Machiavelli so that he need hardly raise his voice above a whisper.

'I have something important to tell you.'

'Speak.'

'Can I count on the generosity of the Signory if what I say is useful to them?'

'Without doubt.'

'A messenger, riding post, arrived at the Palace today. The rebels have at last signed articles of agreement. They are pledged to stand by Bentivoglio in defence of Bologna, to reinstate the dispossessed lords in their dominions, and not to undertake any separate negotiations with the Duke. They have decided to collect seven hundred men-at-arms, a hundred light horse and nine thousand foot. Bentivoglio is to attack Imola and Vitellozzo and the Orsini are to march on Urbino.'

'That is news indeed,' said Machiavelli.

He was pleasantly excited. Stirring events exhilarated him and he looked forward with the anticipation of a spectator at a play to seeing how the Duke would cope with the danger that confronted him.

'There is one more thing. Vitellozzo has given the Duke to understand that if he can have reliable assurances that no attempt will be made to deprive him of his own state of Castello he will rejoin him.'

'How do you know this?'

'It is enough that I know it.'

Machiavelli was perplexed. He knew Vitellozzo, a sullen, suspicious, moody man, subject to wild rages and to attacks of profound depression. The syphilis from which he suffered had so affected him that sometimes he was hardly sane. Who could tell what wicked plans that tortured brain was contriving? Machiavelli dismissed the accountant.

'I can count on your discretion, Messer Niccolo? My life would be short if it were discovered that I have told you what I have.'

'I know. But I am not one to kill the goose that lays the golden eggs.'

13

From then on things moved quickly. On hearing of the uprising in Urbino the Duke had sent two of his captains, Spaniards both, Don Ugo da Moncada and Don Michele da Corella, to put it down. Making Pergola and Fossombrone their headquarters they ravaged the surrounding territories, sacked the towns and killed most of the inhabitants. At Fossombrone women threw themselves and their children into the river to escape the savagery of the soldiery. The Duke, sending for Machiavelli, told him of these exploits with a great deal of good humour.

'It looks as though the season were not too healthy for rebels,' he said with a grim smile.

He had just received news from an envoy of the Pope at Perugia that on his arrival the Orsini had come to assure him of their loyalty to the Holy Father and to excuse their acts. Machiavelli remembered what Farinelli had told him about Vitellozzo.

'It is difficult to understand what they have done that,' he said.

'Use your brain, Secretary. It can only mean that they're not yet ready and want to gain time by behaving as though an accommodation were still possible.'

A few days later Vitellozzo carried the city of Urbino by assault and the Duke again sent for Machiavelli. Machiavelli expected to find him disconcerted by the bad news, but he did not even mention it.

'I want to confer with you as usual on the matters that concern your government and our common interests,' he said. 'I have received this letter from someone I sent to Siena.'

He read it aloud. It was from the Chevalier Orsini, a bastard of that noble and powerful house, who was in the Duke's service. He had spoken with the leaders of the conspiracy, and they had declared their desire to be on good terms with the Duke and professed their willingness to re-enter his service if he would abandon his attack on Bologna and instead combine with them to invade the Florentine territories.

'You see what confidence I place in you,' he added, when he had finished, 'and what trust I have in the good faith of your government. In return they should place more reliance on me than they have in the past and they can be sure that I shall not fail them.'

Machiavelli did not know how much of this to believe. The Orsini were the bitter enemies of Florence and would welcome the opportunity to restore the exiled Medici to power. It was not unlikely that they had made some such offer. He could only suppose that the Duke had not accepted it for fear of angering the French and was divulging in it in order to put the Republic under such an obligation that the Signory would be willing to give him again the profitable *condotta* he had not long before forced upon them at the sword's point, but which, the danger passed, they had to his vexation withdrawn from him. A *condotta* was the term used for the engagement of a mercenary captain, hence called condottiere, for a period of time. On his salary, settled after a lot of haggling on both sides, he paid his men and made a pretty penny for himself.

Two days later the rebel forces attacked the Duke's army under the joint command of the two Spaniards and defeated it. Don Ugo da Moncada was taken prisoner and Don Michele da Corella, wounded, fled to the stronghold of Fossombrone. It was more than a set-back, it was a disaster. The news was kept secret in Imola, for, as Machiavelli wrote to the Signory, in the Duke's court things which were not to be bruited about were not spoken of; but he had his ways of finding out what was important for him to know, and as soon as the event reached his ears he went to the Palace and requested an audience.

Machiavelli entered the presence with a lively sense of curiosity. He was desirous to see in what state he would find the Duke, hitherto self-confident and imperturbable, now that ruin stared him in the face. He could not but know that he could expect no mercy from his enemies. He was calm and even gay. He spoke of the rebels with disdain.

'I don't want to boast,' he said, 'but I expect the outcome, whatever it is, will show what stuff they're made of and what stuff I'm made of. I know them well, the whole gang of them, and I think nothing of them. Vitellozzo has a great reputation, but all I can tell you is that I've never seen him do a thing that needed courage. His excuse is the French sickness. The fact is, he's good for nothing but to ravage undefended territories and rob those who haven't the guts to stand up to him. A false friend and a treacherous enemy.'

Machiavelli could not withold his admiration for this

man who faced destruction with such an indomitable spirit. His situation was desperate. The Bentivogli, Lords of Bologna, were on his northern frontiers; Vitellozzo and the Orsini, flushed with victory, must be advancing from the south. Attacked simultaneously on two fronts by superior forces he could not escape annihilation. Il Valentino was no friend of Florence and his downfall and death would be a relief to the Republic, but Machiavelli, against his will, had an inclination – it was no more than that – to wish that he might succeed in extricating himself from the strait he was in.

'I have received letters from France,' said the Duke after a pause, 'from which I learn that the King has instructed your government to give me every possible assistance.'

'I have heard nothing of it,' said Machiavelli.

'Well, it is true. You will write to your masters and tell them to send me ten squadrons of cavalry, and you may add that I am ready to make a firm and indissoluble alliance with them from which they will gain all the advantages that may be expected from my help and my good fortune.'

'I will naturally carry out Your Excellency's instructions.'

The Duke was not alone. With him were Agapito da Amalia, the Bishop of Elna, his cousin, and another secretary. There was an ominous silence. The Duke stared at the Florentine envoy reflectively. The silence and those staring eyes would have incommoded a more nervous man than Machiavelli, and even he had to exercise some self-control to maintain an air of composure.

'I've heard from various sources,' said the Duke at last, 'that your government is urging the Lords of Bologna to declare war on me, and that they're doing this either because they wish to ruin me or to make a pact with me on more favourable terms.'

Machiavelli contrived to smile with as much geniality

as his cold and somewhat austere cast of countenance allowed.

'I don't believe it for a moment, Excellency,' he replied. 'The letters I receive from the Signory never fail to contain protestations of friendship for the Holy Father and yourself.'

'I don't believe it either, but protestations of friendship are more convincing when acts conform with them.'

'I am sure my government will do everything in its power to show the sincerity of its intentions.'

'If it is as wise as it is dilatory I am sure it will.'

Within himself Machiavelli shivered. He had never in his life heard such cold ferocity in a man's voice.

14

For some days after this Machiavelli busied himself in gathering information from his agents, from Bartolomeo, from Farinelli and from those about the Duke. He could trust no one completely and he knew that Il Valentino's intimates told him only what they wanted him to know. But the most puzzling fact of it all was the inactivity of the revolting captains. The Duke's troops, which he had been enlisting wherever men were for sale, had not yet arrived, and thought he still held some fortresses in the states that had rebelled, it was impossible to believe that he could withstand a determined assault. Now was the time to attack. Now. Yet they did nothing. Machiavelli was at his wit's end; he could not for the life of him understand what caused them to delay. Then an event occurred that increased his bewilderment: the Orsini sent an emissary to the Duke's court, who arrived one evening and left next day; Machiavelli for all his efforts could not find out the purpose of his visit.

He had by now received the Signory's reply to the

Duke's demand for armed help, and in the hope of getting some inkling of what was happening, he applied for an audience. It was not without trepidation that he went to the Palace, for what he had to tell the Duke was that the Florentines had no troops to send and all they were prepared to offer was an assurance of their benevolence. Machiavelli had seen Il Valentino in a rage and he knew that it was terrible; he braced himself to bear the storm with fortitude. No one could have been more astonished than he when the Duke received the intelligence he brought with indifference.

'I've told you several times and tonight I tell you again that I'm not devoid of resources. The French lancers will be here soon and so will the Swiss infantry. You can see for yourself that I'm engaging troops every day. The Pope has no lack of money, nor the King of men. It may well be that my enemies will regret their treachery.'

He smiled, and his smile was cruel and cunning.

'Would it surprise you to know that they've already made offers of peace?'

Machiavelli repressed a start.

'Messer Antonio da Venafro came on their behalf.'

This was evidently the mysterious visitor of whom Machiavelli had heard. He was the confidant and trusted adviser of Pandolfo Petrucci, Lord of Siena, who by common report was the brains of the conspiracy.

'He made the proposal that we should overthrow the government of Florence, but I answered that your state had never offended me and that I was on the point of signing a treaty with you. 'Don't sign on any account,' he said. 'Let me go back and return and we'll do something worth while.' To which I answered: 'We've gone so far it's impossible to withdraw.' And I tell you once more that though I'm prepared to listen to these people and throw dust in their eyes I'll do nothing against your state unless it forces me to.'

As Machiavelli was taking his leave the Duke in a

very casual fashion dropped a remark which astounded the envoy of the Republic as in all probability he expected it to do.

'I'm expecting Pagolo Orsini at any moment.'

Piero had accompanied Machiavelli to the Palace and was waiting for him in the guard-room with a lantern to light him back to their lodging. Piero had learnt to read his master's face and he saw at a glance that he was in no mood for conversation. They walked in silence. When Machiavelli had taken off his cloak and his headgear he told Piero to bring him ink, quills and paper, and sat down to write to the Signory.

'I shall to go bed,' said Piero.

'No, wait,' said Machiavelli, throwing himself back in his chair. 'I want to talk to you.'

He did not know how much to believe of what the Duke had told him and he thought it might help him with his letter if before writing he put into words what he had in mind.

'I'm confused by this guile, these lies, and the deceit of everyone I have to deal with.'

In no more words than were necessary he repeated to Piero what the Duke had said to him.

'How is it possible for Il Valentino, with his spirit, his good fortune and his great ambition, to condone the acts of men who've not only prevented him from acquiring a state he has cast his eyes on, but have caused him to lose a state he had already acquired? The captains revolted because they wanted to destroy him before he could destroy them. Why have they delayed to attack when they had him at their mercy?'

Machiavelli looked at Piero with frowning eyes, but Piero, very sensibly surmising that the question was rhetorical, made no attempt to answer.

'Now he's strengthened his fortresses and garrisoned important places. Every day more troops are arriving. He's getting money from the Pope and men from the

73

French. And he has the great advantage that he need consult no one but himself. The captains are united only by their hatred and fear of the Duke. Alliances are fragile because the respective parties are more concerned with their particular interests than with their common advantage. Allies cannot act swiftly because every step must be discussed, and the folly, unpreparedness or incompetence of one may cause the disaster of all. They're necessarily jealous of one another, for no one of them wishes any one of the rest to gain so much power that he will be later a danger. The captains must know that emissaries are passing to and fro – you can be sure that Il Valentino has seen to that – and each at the back of his mind must be haunted by the suspicion that he is to be thrown to the wolves.'

Machiavelli nervously gnawed his thumbnail.

'The more I think of it the more I believe that the rebels can no longer do much harm to the Duke, they've missed their opportunity, and in that case they may think it better worth their while to seek a reconciliation.'

Machiavelli gave the boy an angry look for which there was no justification since he had not opened his mouth.

'D'you know what that means?'

'No.'

'It means that with their forces joined to his the Duke will have under his orders a formidable army, and it's inevitable that it will be put to use. No one can afford to pay troops to sit about in idleness. How will it be used? Against whom? That will be decided, I suspect, when Il Valentino and Pagolo Orsini come face to face.'

15

Since no one in Italy was such a fool as to trust anyone else farther than he could see, and a safe conduct was worth no more than the paper it was written on, Cardinal Borgia, the Pope's nephew, put himself in the hands of the Orsini as a hostage, and two days later Pagolo, the head of the house arrived at Imola disguised as a courier. He was a vain, loquacious, effeminate and silly man, middle-aged, plump and baldish, with a round, smooth face, and a fussy, familiar manner. Il Valentino treated him with great distinction and in his honour gave a great banquet followed by a performance of the Menaechmi of Plautus. The two leaders held long conferences, but what they discussed Machiavelli could discover neither for love nor money. Such of the Duke's secretaries as had seemed friendly disposed deliberately avoided him. He had nothing to go on but a smiling remark of Agapito da Amalia's that the negotiations were devised only to keep the enemy from taking action. Neither army in fact moved, and indeed the Bolognese troops withdrew from the places in the Duke's dominions that they had occupied. The suspense soon grew too great for Machiavelli to bear and, taking advantage of a letter he had just received from Florence, he asked the Duke to see him. Il Valentino received him in bed. He listened with his usual good humour to the Signory's protestations of friendship and then entered upon the topic which so much concerned Machiavelli.

'I think we shall come to an agreement,' he said. 'They want no more from me than that the possession of their states shall be secured to them and now we've only got to decide how that can be arranged. Cardinal Orsini is drawing up articles and we must wait and see what they are. So far as you're concerned you can rest assured that nothing will be done contrary to the interests of your masters. I would never allow the slightest harm to be done them.'

He paused, and when he spoke again it was with the smiling indulgence with which you might speak of the whims of a spoilt woman.

'Poor Pagolo is very much incensed with Ramiro de Lorqua. He accuses him of oppressing the people, of peculation, and of maltreating various persons who are under the protection of the Orsini.'

Ramiro de Lorqua was the most trusted of the Duke's commanders. It was he who had conducted the retreat of the routed forces after the battle of Fossombrone and so saved them to fight another day. Il Valentino chuckled.

'It appears that on one occasion a page was bringing him some wine and spilt it, and Ramiro flew into a temper and had him thrown into the fire and burnt alive. For some reason Pagolo took an interest in the boy. I've promised to look into the charges and if they're proved give him satisfaction.'

But then a piece of news arrived which suggested that the revolting captains were far from agreement among themselves: though the more prudent were ready to make peace, the more adventurous were still determined to wage war. Vitellozzo seized the Duke's fortress of Fossombrone and two days later Oliverotto da Fermo took Camerino by storm. This completed the loss of all the territories Il Valentino had won during his last campaign. It looked as though the ruffians were deliberately set upon frustrating the negotiations, and Pagolo Orsini was enraged. But the Duke maintained his equanimity. Bentivoglio and the Orsini were the most powerful of his enemies and he knew that if he came to terms with them the others would have to toe the line. Pagolo went to Bologna. On his return Agapito da Amalia told Machiavelli that an agreement had been reached and only awaited the consent of Pagolo's brother the Cardinal.

Machiavelli was filled with apprehension. If this was a fact, Il Valentino was prepared to forgive the injury the rebels had done him, if they were prepared to forget the fear that had driven them to take up arms, it could only be for one reason, which was that they had agreed to make a joint attack on a third party; and this third party could only be Florence or Venice. Venice was strong and Florence was weak. Her only safeguard was the power of France, but she had bought the protection of France with gold and the coffers of the Republic were empty. What would France do if she were confronted with the brute fact that Cæsar Borgia with his reconciled commanders had invaded the territories of Florence and captured her defenceless cities?

Machiavelli had a poor opinion of the French. Experience had taught him that they were more concerned with present loss and present gain than with future good and future ill. When asked to render a service their first thought was how it could be useful to them, and they kept faith only so long as it served their purpose. The Pope's jubilee had brought enormous amounts of money into the Vatican treasury, and his somewhat high-handed procedure of seizing a cardinal's property on his decease was continually adding to the sums at his disposal; for the mortality of these princes of the church was high; and the malicious indeed whispered that His Holiness found it convenient on occasion discreetly to come to the aid of a dilatory Providence. Thus he had ample funds to appease the anger of King Louis should he take it amiss that his orders had been disobeyed. Il Valentino had a well equipped and well trained army; the King might hesitate to pit his strength against one who after all was a vassal and a friend. The more Machiavelli considered, the more likely it seemed to him that the crafty Louis would accept a situation in which the profit was immediate and the danger, that Cæsar Borgia would grow too powerful, remote. There was every reason for Machiavelli to fear that the Florence he loved with all his heart was doomed.

16

But Machiavelli was not only the diligent and conscientious servant of the Republic, he was also a man consumed with the lusts of the flesh; and while he studied with attention the letters he received from the Signory and wrote almost every day careful and exact reports; while he received in Serafina's house, sometimes openly, sometimes in secret, messengers, spies, agents; while he betook himself here and there, to the Palace, to the market-place, to houses where he had acquaintance to discuss and consult with; while he gathered every scrap of news, every rumour, every piece of gossip so that he could come to conclusions that were at least plausible; he found time to pursue the plan he had devised to seduce Aurelia. But his plan involved spending money, and money was just what he hadn't got. The Florentine government was stingy, his salary was miserable, and he had already spent much of the sum he had been given on leaving Florence. He was extravagant and liked to live well. He had often to pay in advance the messengers who took his dispatches and he had besides to satisfy the various persons about the Duke's court who were prepared for a consideration to give him useful information. There were fortunately Florentine merchants in the city who would advance him money, and he wrote to Biagio urging him to send whatever he could raise by hook or by crook. Then a strange thing happened. Jacopo Farinelli, the accountant, who before had only come to see him at night, muffled-up so that no one should recognize him, appeared at the door in broad daylight and asked to see him. His manner, which hitherto had been furtive and frightened, was now open and cordial. He did not delay to come to the object of his visit.

'I am commissioned by someone who is your friend and who highly esteems your abilities to ask you to accept this small token of his appreciation.'

From the folds of his dress he drew a bag and placed it on the table. Machiavelli heard the clink of coin.

'What is that?' he asked, his lips tightening and his eyes cold.

'Fifty ducats,' smiled Farinelli.

It was a handsome amount. At the moment nothing could have been more useful to Machiavelli.

'Why should the Duke wish to give me fifty ducats?'

'I have no reason to suppose that the Duke is concerned. I was ordered to bring the money to you on behalf of a well-wisher who desired to remain unknown, and you may rest assured that no one but your well-wisher and I will ever know anything of the gift.'

'It appears that both my well-wisher and you take me for a fool as well as a knave. Take your money, return it to him who gave it to you and tell him that the envoy of the Republic does not accept bribes.'

'But it is not a bribe. It is a spontaneous gift offered by a friend in appreciation of your high talents and literary attainments.'

'I do not know how this generous friend can have formed an appreciation of my literary attainments,' said Machiavelli acidly.

'He had an opportunity to read the letters you wrote to the Signory during your legation to France and greatly admired your acuteness of observation, your good sense, your tact and above all the excellence of your style.'

'It is impossible that the person of whom you speak could have had access to the files of the Chancery.'

'I wonder. It is certainly not impossible that someone in the Chancery found your letters interesting enough to copy, and that by some hazard the person of whom I speak gained possession of them. No one knows better than you with what parsimony the Republic pays its officials.'

Machiavelli frowned. He was silent while he asked himself which of the clerks it could be that had sold the letters to the Duke. It was true that they were all ill paid and some were doubtless secret adherents of the Medici. But perhaps there was no truth in what Farinelli said. It was easy enough to invent such a story. Farinelli went on.

'The Duke would be the last man to wish you to do anything against your conscience or to the injury of Florence. What he wants is to your mutual benefit, the Republic's and his. The Signory has confidence in your judgement and all he would have you do is to put his case in such a way as to appeal to the common sense of intelligent men.'

'You need say no more,' said Machiavelli, his thin lips curling into a sarcastic smile. 'I have no use for the Duke's money. I shall continue to advise the Signory according to the best interests of the Republic.'

Farinelli stood up and replaced the bag of gold from where he had taken it.

'The Duke of Ferrara's agent was not too proud to accept a present from His Excellency when it was a question of deciding his master to send a detachment to His Excellency's help. If Monsieur de Chaumont hastened the departure of the French troops from Milan it was because the King's orders were supplemented by a handsome present from the Duke.'

'I am well aware of it.'

When Machiavelli was once more alone he laughed

out loud. Of course the possibility of accepting the money had never for an instant occurred to him, but he could not help being amused when he thought how devilish useful it would have been to him. But as he laughed an idea on a sudden occurred to him and he laughed again. He was sure he could borrow the money he needed from Bartolomeo, who would be only too glad to oblige him; and it would be a priceless jest to seduce his wife by means of money he had himself provided. Nothing could be prettier. And what a good story it would make to tell when he got back to Florence! He could hear his friends chuckle as he gathered them round him one evening in a tavern and narrated it with all the effect he could contrive.

'Ah, Niccolo, Niccolo, what a good companion! No one can tell a story as he can. What humour, what wit! It's as good as a play to listen to him.'

He had not seen Bartolomeo for two days when he ran across him just before dinner at the Palace to which he had gone for news. After exchanging a few friendly words he said:

'Why don't you come this evening and we'll have a little music?'

Bartolomeo was pleased to say he could think of nothing he would enjoy more. Machiavelli proceeded.

'It's true the room is small and the vaulted ceiling echoes, but we'll have a brazier against the chill and with wine to keep the cold out we shall do very well.'

He had not long finished eating when Bartolomeo's servant brought a letter. He wrote that the ladies of his house didn't see why they should be deprived of a treat, the big room in his house was much better suited for music than Serafina's cold small parlour, it had a fireplace so that they could warm themselves at its cheerful blaze, and if he and cousin Piero would do him the honour to come to supper his happiness would be complete. Machiavelli accepted with alacrity.

'It's as easy as falling off a log,' he said to himself.

Machiavelli had himself shaved and his hair trimmed and he put on his best clothes, a long black damask sleeveless tunic and a tight-fitting jacket with billowing velvet sleeves. Piero had dressed himself up also for the occasion, but his pale blue tunic reached only half-way down his thighs and he wore a purple belt round his waist; his handsome legs were encased in dark blue hose, and his jacket with sleeves less ample than Machiavelli's was dark blue also; a purple cap was perched jauntily on his curly locks. Machiavelli looked at him with approval.

'You should make quite an impression on the little maid, Piero,' he smiled. 'What did you say her name was? Nina?'

'Why do you wish me to go to bed with her?' asked Piero, smiling.

'I like to think that you will not have entirely wasted your time on this trip. And besides, it may be useful to me.'

'How?'

'Because I wish to go to bed with her mistress.'

'You?'

There was so much surprise in Piero's tone that Machiavelli flushed angrily.

'And why not, if you please?'

Piero saw that his master was put out and hesitated.

'You're married and – well, as old as my uncle.'

'You speak like a fool. A woman of sense will always prefer a man in the flower of his age to an inexperienced boy.'

'It never entered my head that she meant anything to you. Do you love her?'

'Love? I loved my mother, I esteem my wife and I shall love my children; but I want to go to bed with Aurelia. There is much you still have to learn, my poor boy. Take the lute and let us go.'

But though Machiavelli was quick-tempered he could not be angry long. He patted Piero's smooth cheek.

'It is very hard to keep secrets from a maid,' he smiled. 'You would be doing me a service if you shut her mouth with kisses.'

They had only to step across the narrow lane, and on knocking were let in by the serving man. Monna Caterina was handsomely gowned in black, but Aurelia wore a rich dress of Venetian brocade; its opulent colours enhanced the whiteness of her breast and the brilliant fairness of her hair. It was with a little sigh of relief that Machiavelli decided she was more beautiful even than he had imagined. She was very, very desirable and it was absurd that she should have for a husband that gross, self-satisfied man who would certainly never see forty again.

After the usual compliments they sat down to wait for supper. The ladies had been working when Machiavelli and Piero came in.

'You see, they've already got busy on the linen you brought me from Florence,' said Bartolomeo.

'You are pleased with it, Monna Aurelia?' asked Machiavelli.

'It's impossible to get material of this quality in Imola,' she said.

She looked at him as she spoke and her great dark eyes resting on him for a moment made his heart beat.

'I'm going to have that woman if I die for it,' he said to himself; but of course he didn't quite mean that; what he meant was that he had never met a harlot with whom he more urgently wanted to go to bed.

'We do the rough work, Nina and I,' said Monna Caterina. 'We measure and cut and sew and my daughter does the embroidery. When it comes to that my fingers are all thumbs and poor Nina's no better than I am.'

'Monna Aurelia never makes two alike,' said Bartolomeo proudly. 'Show Messer Niccolo the design for the shirt you're working on now.'

'Oh, I should be ashamed,' she said prettily.

'Nonsense. I'll show him myself.'

He brought over a sheet of paper.

'Do you see how cleverly she's introduced my initials?'

'It is a masterpiece of elegance and ingenuity,' said Machiavelli with a very good imitation of enthusiasm, for he was in truth entirely indifferent to such things. 'I wish my Marietta had such a charming gift and the industry to make such good use of it.'

'This woman of mine is as industrious as she is good,' Bartolomeo said fondly.

Machiavelli could not but reflect that he was interested neither in her goodness nor her industry. He reflected further that husbands are often mistaken in the virtues they ascribe to their wives.

Supper was served and he exerted himself to be at his best. He knew that he told a story well and his sojourn in France had provided him with a number of spicy tales about the ladies and gentlemen at the King's court. Aurelia assumed a modest confusion when his indecencies grew too obvious, but Bartolomeo guffawed and Monna Caterina, enjoying herself hugely, egged him on. He could not but think that he was proving himself a most agreeable guest. They did full justice to a copious repast, and after a decent interval during which he drew Bartolomeo out to talk about himself, his affairs and his properties, which he did with complacency, Machiavelli suggested that they should try their voices. He tuned his lute and by way of prelude played a gay little tune. Then they settled on a song they all knew. Part singing was a common accomplishment of the day, and with Bartolomeo's bass, Machiavelli's light baritone and Piero's agreeable tenor they acquitted themselves to their mutual satisfaction. Then Machiavelli sang one of

Lorenzo de' Medici's songs and the other two joined in the chorus. As he sang he looked at Aurelia in the hope that she would guess he was singing only to her, and when their eyes met, and she looked down, he flattered himself that she was at least aware of his feelings. That was the first step. So the evening passed. It was a dull life the two ladies led and such a diversion was a rare treat to them. Aurelia's delight was plain in the shining of her splendid eyes. The more Machiavelli looked at them the more sure he was that here was a woman, unawakened still, who was capable of passion. He was prepared to awaken her. But before they separated he had something to say that he had been holding back for the proper moment. He did not think he was a vain man; but he could not help finding the idea ingenious. So when the occasion arose he said:

'You were good enough to say that you would be willing to do me a service, Messer Bartolomeo, and now I am going to take you at your word.'

'I would do a great deal for the envoy of the Republic,' answered Bartolomeo, who had drunk a great deal of wine and was, if not drunk, at least mellow. 'But for my good friend Niccolo I would do anything.'

'Well, the matter is this: The Signory are looking for a preacher to deliver the Lenten sermons in the Cathedral next year and they asked me to enquire whether there was anyone in Imola who could be entrusted with this important duty.'

'Fra Timoteo,' cried Monna Caterina.

'Be quiet, mother-in-law,' said Bartolomeo. 'This is a matter of consequence for men to settle after due deliberation. It may bring glory or discredit to our city and we must be sure to recommend only one who is worthy of the honour.'

But Monna Caterina would not be easily silenced.

'He delivered the Lenten sermons in our own church this very year and the whole city thronged to hear him.

When he described the tortures of the damned strong men burst into tears, women swooned, and one poor creature who was near her time suddenly felt the pangs of childbirth and was carried shrieking from the church.'

'I do not deny it. I am a hard-headed man of business and I sobbed like a child. It is true, Fra Timoteo has eloquence and a fine choice of words.'

'Who is this Fra Timoteo?' asked Machiavelli. 'What you tell me is interesting. The Florentines dearly love to be called to repentance at the proper season; it enables them to cheat their neighbours for the rest of the year with a good conscience.'

'Fra Timoteo is our confessor,' said Bartolomeo, a fact of which Machiavelli was well aware. 'And for my own part I never do a thing without his advice. He is not only a worthy man, but a wise one. Why, only a few months ago I was about to buy a cargo of spices in the Levant and he told me that he had seen St. Paul in a vision who told him that the ship would be wrecked on the coast of Crete, so I did not buy.'

'And was the ship wrecked?' asked Machiavelli.

'No, but three caravels arrived in Lisbon laden with spices, with the result that the bottom fell out of the market and I should have lost money on the transaction, so it came to the same thing.'

'The more you tell me of this friar the more curious I am to see him.'

'You are very likely to find him in the church in the morning, and if not you can ask the brother sacristan to fetch him.'

'May I tell him that I come to him with your recommendation?' Machiavelli asked politely.

'The envoy of the Republic needs no recommendation from a poor merchant in a town which is of small account compared with the magnificent city of Florence.'

'And what do you think of this Fra Timoteo?' Machiavelli went on, addressing himself to Aurelia. 'It is important that I should have the opinion not only of a man of position and discernment like Messer Bartolomeo and of a woman of discretion and experience like Monna Caterina, but also of one who has the enthusiasm, the innocence and the sensitiveness of youth, one to whom the world and its perils are still unknown; for the preacher I would recommend to the Signory must not only call sinners to repentance, but confirm the virtuous in their integrity.'

It was a pretty speech.

'Fra Timoteo can do no wrong in my eyes. I am prepared to be guided by him in everything.'

'And I,' added Bartolomeo, 'am prepared that you should be guided by him. He will never advise anything that is not to your best advantage.'

It had all gone very well and exactly as Machiavelli wished. He went to bed satisfied with himself.

17

Early next morning, being market day, Machiavelli took Piero with him to the market-place and bought two brace of plump partridges. At another stall he brought a basket of the luscious figs which were the speciality of Rimini and were so much prized that they were sent all over Italy. These comestibles he told Piero to take to Messer Bartolomeo and deliver with his compliments. With Imola crowded with strangers food was scarce and high in price so that he knew his present would be welcome. Then he made his way to the Franciscan church attached to the monastery in which Fra Timoteo was a monk. It was not far from Bartolomeo's house. It was a building of some size, but of no architectural merit. It was empty but for two or three women praying, a lay brother, obviously the sacristan, who was sweeping the floor, and a friar who was pottering about the altar of a chapel. Machiavelli with a passing glance saw that he was only pretending to be busy and guessed that this must be Fra Timoteo who had been warned by Monna Caterina to expect him.

'Pardon me, father,' said he, with a polite inclination of his backbone, 'I have been told that you are so fortunate as to have a miraculous Virgin in this church and I have a great desire to light a candle before her altar so that she may assist my dear wife, now pregnant, in the pains of childbirth.

'This is she, Messere,' said the monk. 'I was about to change her veil. I can't get the brothers to keep her clean and tidy, and then they're surprised because the pious neglect to pay their devotions to her. I remember when there were dozens of votive offerings in this chapel for graces received, and now there aren't twenty. And it's our own fault; they have no sense, my brothers.'

Machiavelli chose a candle of imposing dimensions, paid for it extravagantly with a florin, and watched the monk while he fixed it on an iron candlestick and lit it. When this was done Machiavelli said:

'I have a favour to ask of you, father. I have reason to speak privately to Fra Timoteo and I should be grateful if you would tell me how I can find him.'

'I am Fra Timoteo,' said the monk.

'Impossible! It looks as though Providence had a hand in this. It is a miracle that I should come here and in the first person I see find the very person I am looking for.'

'The designs of Providence are inscrutable,' said Fra Timoteo.

The monk was a man of medium stature, of a comfortable, but not disgusting corpulence, which suggested to Machiavelli's cool mind that he was given to fasting no more than the rules of his order demanded but not to the gross vice of gluttony. He had a fine head. It reminded one of a Roman emperor's whose fine features, not yet debased by luxury and unlimited power, bore notwithstanding a suggestion of the cruel sensuality that would lead to his assassination. It was a type not unfamiliar to Machiavelli. In those full red lips, in that bold hook nose, in those fine black eyes he read ambition, cunning and covetousness, but these qualities were masked by a semblance of good nature and simple piety. Machíavelli could well understand how he had gained so great an influence over Bartolomeo and the women of his family. He felt instinctively that this was a man he could deal with; he hated monks; to him they were either fools or knaves, and this one was probably a knave, but he must step warily.

'I should tell you, father, that I have heard a great deal to your credit from my friend Messer Bartolomeo Martelli. He has the highest opinion both of your virtue and your ability.'

'Messer Bartolomeo is a faithful son of the Church. Our monastery is very poor and we owe much to his generosity. But may I know whom I have the honour of addressing, Messere?'

Machiavelli knew that the friar was well aware of this, but answered gravely.

'I should have introduced myself. Niccolo Machiavelli, citizen of Florence and Secretary to the Second Chancery.'

The monk bowed low.

'It is a great privilege to speak with the envoy of that illustrious state.'

'You fill me with confusion, father, I am but a man with all the failings of humanity; but where can we speak in private and at length?'

'Why not here, Messere? The brother sacristan is as deaf as a post and as stupid as a mule and the three or four old women you see are too busy with their prayers to listen to what we are saying and too ignorant to understand it if they did.'

They sat down on two of the praying-stools which were in the chapel and Machiavelli told Fra Timoteo how he had been commissioned by the Signory to find a preacher to deliver the Lenten sermons in the cathedral. The friar's Roman face remained impassive, but Machiavelli felt in him an alertness of attention which confirmed his assurance that he had been informed of the previous night's conversation. Machiavelli apprised him of the Signory's requirements.

'They are naturally nervous,' he said. 'They don't want to make again the mistake they made with Fra Girolamo Savonarola. It is very well that the people should be persuaded to repentance, but the prosperity of Florence depends on its commerce and the Signory cannot allow repentance to disturb the peace or interfere with trade. Excess of virtue can be as harmful to the State as excess of vice.'

'Such, I seem to remember, was the opinion of Aristotle.'

'Ah, I see that you, unlike friars in general, are a man of education. That is all to the good. The people of Florence have agile and critical minds and have no patience with a preacher, however eloquent, who is without learning.'

'It is true that many of my brethren are of a shocking ignorance,' Fra Timoteo replied complacently. 'If I understand you aright you want to know if there is anyone in Imola who is in my opinion worthy of the honour you speak of. It is a matter that needs consideration. I shall have to think. I must make discreet enquiries.'

'You will be doing me a great favour. I know from Messer Bartolomeo and his ladies that you are a man of singular perspicacity and of the highest rectitude. I am confident that you will give me a disinterested opinion.'

'Messer Bartolomeo's ladies are saints. That is the only reason why they think so favourably of me.'

'I live in the house of Monna Serafina just behind Messer Bartolomeo's. If I could persuade you to join us in our modest meal tomorrow evening we could discuss the matter further, and it would give my good Serafina infinite pleasure to have you at her table.'

Fra Timoteo accepted the invitation. Machiavelli went home, but on the way called on Bartolomeo and asked him for a loan. He explained that he was put to great expense at Imola in connection with his mission, and the funds he was expecting from the Signory had not yet arrived. He pulled a long story about the parsimoniousness of the Florence government and complained that in order to maintain the dignity of his position and to meet the cost of information he had to pay money out of his own pocket. But Bartolomeo cut him short.

'Dear Niccolo,' he said in his jovial way, 'you do not have to tell me that in this court one can get nothing without paying for it. For your own sake as well as for that of the Signory I shall be happy to lend you whatever you require. How much do you want?'

Machiavelli was surprised and pleased.

'Twenty-five ducats.'

'Is that all? Wait and I will give it you at once.'

He left the room and in a minute or two came back with the money. Machiavelli regretted that he had asked for so little.

'And when you want more don't hesitate to ask me,' said Bartolomeo, beaming. 'You must look upon me as your banker.'

'A fool and his money are soon parted,' Machiavelli said to himself as he returned to his lodging.

18

Brother Timoteo came to supper. Machiavelli had bidden Serafina to buy the best the city could provide and the friar needed little pressing to eat heartily. Machiavelli saw that his cup was well-filled and when, supper finished, he led him into the parlour so that they might talk undisturbed, he told one of his servants to bring a flagon of wine.

'Now let us get down to business,' he said.

Fra Timoteo told him that he had been giving the subject of their conversation careful thought, and mentioned three monks who had some reputation in the city as preachers. He described their respective merits with candour, but with an ingenuity that Machiavelli could not but admire introduced into his eulogy of each a note of disparagement that effectively overrode his recommendation. Machiavelli smiled blandly.

'You have spoken of these excellent monks with a sincerity and a disinterestedness which are what I should have expected of you, father, but you have left out the name of one whose talents and piety according to all accounts are infinitely superior to theirs.'

'And who may that be, Messere?'

'Fra Timoteo.'

The monk gave a start of well-simulated surprise.

'A good actor,' Machiavelli said to himself. 'A preacher must have histrionic gifts, and if the Signory had really given me the commission to find one I should be half inclined to propose this rascally friar.'

'You are joking, Messere.'

'What makes you think that I should joke on a subject of such importance, father? I have not been idle on my side. I have learnt that in the whole history of Imola no preacher has made such a profound impression as you did in the sermons you delivered this Lent. I am told that you have a remarkable eloquence and I can tell for myself that you have a melodious and a beautiful voice. Your presence is imposing and even in the short while that we have talked together I have discovered that you are intelligent, tactful and cultivated. I am assured that your knowledge of the fathers is only equalled by your classical erudition.'

'You cover me with confusion, Messere. The Signory want a monk of reputation, and I am but a poor friar in a poverty-stricken monastery of a provincial city. I have neither great birth to recommend me nor powerful friends. I thank you from the bottom of my heart for the good opinion you so generously have of me, but I am unworthy of the honour you propose.'

'That is something that those can better judge who know you better than you know yourself.'

Machiavelli was enjoying himself hugely. He appreciated the monk's affectation of modesty and with his sharp eyes delving into his innermost heart discerned the greediness of his ambition. With such a bait to dangle he was certain he could get him to do anything he wanted.

'I think I should be less than honest if I did not tell you that I am a person of no great consequence in the state of Florence. I can only advise; the last word is with the gentlemen of the Signory.'

'I cannot think that they would lightly disregard the advice of their envoy to His Excellency the Duke of Romagna and Valentinois,' said Fra Timoteo with an ingratiating smile.

'It is true that our new Gonfalonier for life, Piero Soderini, is my friend, and I think I may say without vanity that his brother the Bishop of Volterra has some faith in my honesty and good sense.'

This remark led Machiavelli very naturally to tell the monk of the mission to Cæsar Borgia when he had accompanied the Cardinal, then a bishop, to Urbino to protest against the attack Vitellozzo had made on Arezzo; and this as naturally led him to describe his own activities in the war with Pisa and his legation to France. He was careful to minimize his role in these proceedings, and yet managed to suggest to the friar that it was he who had pulled the strings. He talked lightly, amusingly, in a familiar way, of kings and cardinals, princes and generals, and thus delicately led his listener to believe that he had the ear of the great both in Italy and France. Secrets of state were no secrets to him. Only a fool could doubt that he knew much more than he told. Fra Timoteo was dazzled.

'Ah, Messere, you cannot know what it means to me to talk with a man of your intelligence and experience. It is like a glimpse of the promised land. We live in this dull little town and know nothing of the world. There is not a man in Imola of culture or distinction. Our wits, if we have any, grow rusty because there is no occasion to use them. One needs the patience of Job to support the stupidity of the people among whom one is compelled to pass one's life.

'Father, I will admit that from what I know of you and from what I have heard I think it a thousand pities that a man of your capacity should be wasted on this place. It is not for me to remind one of your calling of the Parable of the Talents.'

'I have often thought of it. I have buried my talent in the ground, and when the Master asks me to what use I have put it I shall have no answer.'

'Father, no one can do more for another than give him an opportunity; he must know for himself how to make use of it.'

'Who is going to give an unknown monk an opportunity?'

'I am your friend, Father, and such little influence as I have is at your service. And you will not be entirely unknown when I have mentioned your name to the Bishop of Volterra. It would be unbecoming for a man of your habit to put himself forward; but there is no reason why I should not speak of the matter with our good friend Bartolomeo, and I have little doubt that I can persuade him that it is an idea of his own to write to certain powerful connections of his in Florence.'

Fra Timoteo smiled.

'Our dear Bartolomeo! He is goodness itself, but it cannot be denied that he is a little simple. He does not combine the craftiness of the serpent with the innocence of the dove.'

Thus Machiavelli conducted their colloquy to the point at which he had been aiming. He refilled the empty cups. The brazier gave out a pleasant warmth.

'Bartolomeo is a very worthy creature. It has often struck me as remarkable that business men should be able to conduct commercial transaction with success and yet remain so unversed in the affairs of the world. But I do not esteem him less on that account and I would do a great deal to promote his welfare. You have a strong influence over him, father.'

'He is good enough to attach some small value to my counsels.'

'There at all events he shows a natural good sense. How sad it is that such an excellent and deserving creature should not have been granted the dearest wish of his heart!'

Fra Timoteo looked at him enquiringly.

'You must know as well as I do that he would give half his possessions to have a son.'

'It is an obsession with him; he can talk of nothing else. We have interceded for him with our miraculous Virgin, but to no purpose, and he is angry with us because our prayers have not achieved the desired result; but he is unreasonable. The poor man is sterile.'

'Father, I have a small property not far from Florence called San Casciano, and to augment the poor salary I receive from the Signory I make what money I can by selling timber from my woods and farming my land. I have cows, and it sometimes happens that you get a bull, to all appearance strong and healthy, who for some reason suffers from the same unfortunate disability as our good friend Bartolomeo. Then you kill the bull for butcher's meat and on the proceeds buy another.'

Fra Timoteo smiled.

'It is not practicable to go to such lengths with human beings.'

'Nor necessary. But the theory is sound.'

It took the friar a moment to grasp exactly what Machiavelli meant, and when he did he smiled again.

'Monna Aurelia is a virtuous wife, and she is well guarded, though for different reasons, by her mother and her husband. Bartolomeo is not so stupid as not to know that a young and beautiful wife must be a temptation to the dissolute youth of the city, and Monna Caterina lived in poverty long enough to make her take good care that she shall not lose a comfortable home through the indiscretion of her daughter.'

'And yet it might well be that an indiscretion would turn out to be the height of discretion. Monna Caterina's position would be more secure if she had a little grandson to dandle on her knee.'

'I don't deny it. Now that the Duke has bestowed this property on him, with the title that accompanies it, Bartolomeo is more than ever anxious to have an heir. The ladies of his family have discovered that he is thinking of adopting his two nephews. He has a widowed sister in Forlì, and she is willing enough that he should thus provide for her boys; but she will not be separated from them and makes it a condition that he should take her into his house along with them.'

'It is natural that a mother should not wish to be parted from her children.'

'Very. But the prospect distresses both Monna Caterina and Monna Aurelia. They see that their position would be difficult. Monna Aurelia had no dowry. Bartolomeo is a weak and foolish man; Monna Costanza, the mother of his adopted sons, would undermine the influence of a wife whom his vanity insists on thinking a barren woman, and his sister would in no long time be mistress of the house. Monna Caterina has besought me to dissuade him from a course in which there is so much danger to her daughter and herself.'

'He has consulted you?'

'Naturally.'

'And what advice have you given him?'

'I have temporized. His sister's confessor at Forlì is a Dominican, and if she came here it is likely enough that she would take a confessor from the same order. The Dominicans are no friends of ours. We owe much to the generosity of Bartolomeo, and it would be unfortunate if Monna Costanza took advantage of his disappointment with our efforts to get him to bestow his favours in another quarter.'

'No one could see more clearly than I how difficult your situation is, dear father. The only possible solution is the one I suggest.'

'Has it escaped you that it smacks somewhat of sin, Messere?' said the friar with an indulgent smile.

'A small sin, father, from which a great good may come. You can bring happiness to a worthy man, security to two women whose piety merits your help, and last but not least you preserve for the brethren of your habit the munificence of a generous donor. It would be presumption on my part to recall the Holy Scripture to your memory, but I will venture to suggest to you that if the woman of Samaria had not committed adultery the Founder of our religion would never have had occasion to utter those precepts of tolerance and forgiveness which have been of such inestimable value to the miserable sinners that we are.'

'It is a pretty point, Messere.'

'I am human, father. I will not try to conceal from you that the beauty of Monna Aurelia has excited so violent a passion in me that I must satisfy it or die.'

'I did not imagine that your desire for Bartolomeo's welfare and the peace of mind of his two ladies was prompted only by the goodness of your heart,' said Fra Timoteo dryly.

'Your monastery is poor and you doubtless have many calls upon your charity. I would give twenty-five ducats to be assured of your good will, father.'

Machiavelli saw the glint of greed in the monk's dark eyes.

'When?'

'Now.'

He took the bag of money out of an inner pocket and flung it carelessly on the table. The coins made a pleasant clink against the wooden surface.

'You have acquired my good will by the charm of your conversation and the graciousness of your manner, Messere,' said the monk. 'But I do not see how I can be of service to you.'

'I will ask you to do nothing that can weigh on your conscience. I should like you to arrange it so that I may have a conversation with Monna Caterina in private.'

'I can see no harm in that. But it will get you no farther. Bartolomeo is a fool, but he is too good a business man to take unnecessary risks. When his affairs force him to absent himself his servant is there to protect Monna Aurelia from the importunities of unscrupulous and lascivious men.'

'I am well aware of it. Our good Bartolomeo, however,

has a confidence in you which is as implicit as it is well-deserved. He has taken Monna Aurelia to the baths and he has taken her on pilgrimages to the shrines of saints who are accredited with the blessed gift of ridding women of the curse of barrenness. I suggest to you that if our good Bartolomeo, accompanied by his servant, went to Ravenna and spent a night in prayer and meditation before the sarcophagus which contains the mortal remains of San Vitale, you could guarantee that Monna Aurelia would conceive.'

'San Vitale was evidently a great saint, or a church would not have been built in his honour; but what makes you suppose that his bones have the power to cure men of sterility?'

'The name is eminently suggestive, and Bartolomeo knows no more of the miraculous powers of the saint than you or I. A drowning man will catch at a straw and Ravenna is but twenty miles from Imola. Can you believe that our friend would hesitate to make so short a journey to achieve a result he so much desires?'

'Let me ask you a question in return, Messere. Have you any reason to suppose that Monna Aurelia, a virtuous and timid wife, would respond to your advances? Have you made your desires known to her?'

'I have not exchanged more than a few words with her, but unless she is different from the rest of her sex she is well aware of them. Women are subject to two defects, curiosity and vanity.'

'Venial sins,' said the monk.

'And yet they lead these fair creatures to abandon the narrow path of virtue more often than passion.'

'There is much of which my habit has kept me in happy ignorance.'

'When your eminent merit has raised you to the position it deserves you will learn that you can gain influence over men less by fostering their virtues or encouraging their vices than by humouring their foibles.'

'Your scheme is ingenious. I have little doubt that you could persuade Monna Caterina to help you; she will stop at nothing to prevent Bartolomeo from adopting his nephews; but I know Monna Aurelia too well to believe that she would let herself be persuaded to commit a mortal sin either by her mother or by you.'

'That is possible. There are many things which from a distance seem strange and terrifying, but when you come closer to them appear natural, easy and reasonable. I have no reason to suppose that Monna Aurelia is more intelligent than the majority of her sex. It would be well if you explained to her that when there is in prospect a good that is certain and an evil that is uncertain, it is wrong not to do the good for fear of the evil. The certain good is that she will conceive and so create an immortal soul; the evil is that she may be found out, but with proper precautions the possibility of that is eliminated. And so far as sin is concerned – well, there is nothing in that, since it is the will that sins and not the body. It would be a sin to displease her husband, but in this she can only please him. In all things the end must be considered, and the end here is to fill a seat in Paradise and give a husband his heart's desire.'

Fra Timoteo looked at Machiavelli without replying. It seemed to the Florentine that he was preventing himself from laughing only by an effort of will. The monk looked away and his eyes fell on the bag of gold that was lying on the table.

'I am sure that the Signory was well advised when they sent you on a mission to the Duke, Messere,' he said at last. 'I may condemn your intentions, but I can only admire your subtlety.'

'I am very sensible to flattery,' Machiavelli answered.

'You must give me time to think the matter over.'

'It is always best to trust the impulse of the moment, Father. But if you will excuse me I will go into the yard, for I wish to relieve nature. Your local wine is something of a diuretic, I fancy.'

When Machiavelli returned the monk was sitting as he had left him, but the bag of gold was no longer on the table.

'Monna Caterina will bring her daughter on Friday for confession,' he said, looking at his well-kept hands. 'You will have an opportunity of talking to her while Monna Aurelia is in the confessional.'

19

A happy chance gave Machiavelli an opportunity to pursue his suit which he was quick to seize. Unless obliged to, he did not get up early, and the sun had risen some time when, on the morning after his conversation with Fra Timoteo, he rolled out of bed and got into his clothes. He went into the kitchen where Serafina gave him his frugal breakfast and then out into the yard where he drew water from the well and shudderingly washed his hands and face. Then he went up to his room to fetch such of his papers as he wanted. He raised the window to look at the weather and suddenly saw Nina, the maid, bring a chair and a footstool out on to the roof of Bartolomeo's house. The weather had been cloudy for some time, with occasional showers of rain, but that morning the sun shone brightly from an unclouded sky. He guessed what Nina's actions betokened. Presently Aurelia came on to the roof, swathed in a quilted wrapper, carrying a great straw hat in her hand. He was right. Aurelia had taken advantage of the fine day to dry her hair. She sat in the chair and the maid took the long fair hair in her hands and passed it through the hat, which had no crown but only an immense brim; then, placing the hat on Aurelia's head, she spread the hair all around the brim, so that the sun should shine on it and the dye colour it more brightly.

Machiavelli changed his plans. He left his letters to a more suitable season and taking his lute ascended the stairs to a loggia on the upper storey of Serafina's house. By the time he got there the maid had gone about her business and Aurelia was alone. The wide brim of her hat prevented her from seeing him, and indeed she was certainly too much intent on the process of getting her hair a perfect shade to have thoughts of anything else; but when he began to sing, startled, she raised the brim and looked across the narrow space that divided the two houses. Before Machiavelli could catch her eye she lowered it. As though to himself he sang a little love song. Following the fashion of the time his theme was Cupid and his darts, the cruel wounds his loved one's eyes inflicted, and the happiness that would be his if he could pass one moment without thinking of her. He had Aurelia at his mercy; from coyness she might have wished to withdraw, but the sun was essential to make the dye hold, and he felt it was not in a woman's nature to sacrifice her appearance to her modesty. If there had been any doubt in her mind of his feelings towards her there could surely be none now, but such an occasion might not soon recur, so he thought it just as well to make them unmistakable. He had composed a serenade to a woman called Fenice, which began, *Hail, Lady, from all women set apart*, and which went on to address her as a rare example of earthly beauty, a perfect soul imbued with every loveliness; and it was easy, without interfering with the scansion, to change *O only Fenice* into *O only Aurelia*. Plucking the strings of the lute he spoke the words in a recitative which was not wanting in a certain melodiousness. Aurelia sat still, her face hidden by the wide brim of her hat and the overhanging hair, but Machiavelli had a notion that she was listening intently. That was all he wanted. But he had sung no more than two stanzas when she rang a little bell she had evidently brought to call her maid. Machiavelli paused. Nina appeared; Aurelia said something to her and rose from her chair, which the maid took to another part of the roof; Aurelia moved over and the maid sat down on the footstool. The two women began to talk and Machiavelli guessed she was going to keep her there till he withdrew. He was not dissatisfied. He went down to his room, got his papers out of the box in which he kept them locked, and was soon immersed in a letter he was writing to the Signory.

So far so good.

20

He was not in the habit of attending the services of the Church, and on Friday waited till vespers were over and the small congregation coming out before entering the sacred edifice. He was just in time to see Fra Timoteo go into the confessional. In a moment Aurelia followed him. Monna Caterina was sitting by herself in one of the chapels. Machiavelli joined her. She did not seem surprised to see him, and he thought it not unlikely that the monk had spoken to her and she was expecting him. Anyhow he could see no object in beating about the bush. He told her that he had fallen passionately in love with her daughter and asked her to plead his cause with her. Monna Caterina seemed amused rather than indignant. She informed him that he was not the first who had attempted her daughter's virtue, but none had succeeded.

'I brought her up very strictly, Messer Niccolo, and since the night I put her to bed, an innocent virgin, with Messer Bartolomeo, she has been a faithful and dutiful wife to him.'

'If I am rightly informed she has never had the opportunity to be anything else.'

Monna Caterina gave a low, somewhat bawdy laugh.

'Messer Niccolo, you have lived long enough to know that when a wife wishes to deceive her husband no precautions he may take can stop her.'

'All history bears you out, Monna Caterina, and I perceive from what you say that you are a woman with whom one can speak frankly.'

She turned her head a little and looked at him earnestly.

'Messer Niccolo, I have had great misfortunes in my life. I have been tossed on stormy seas and now that I am safe in harbour I have no wish to expose myself again to the fury of the elements.'

'I can well understand it, but are you so sure that your anchor is firm and your mooring taut?'

Monna Caterina did not answer and Machiavelli was conscious of the uneasiness of her silence. He went on.

'Am I not right in thinking that if Monna Aurelia does not soon produce the heir Bartolomeo craves he has it in mind to adopt the two sons of Monna Costanza?'

Once again Monna Caterina made no reply.

'You have too great an experience of the world, Madonna, to make it necessary for me to tell you what your position and that of your daughter would be in such a case.'

Two tears trickled down Monna Caterina's cheeks. Machiavelli patted her hand in kindness.

'Desperate situations demand desperate remedies.'

She shrugged her shoulders despondently.

'Even though I should be able to overcome Aurelia's fears, the opportunity would be lacking.'

'Am I displeasing to your daughter?'

'You make her laugh,' smiled Monna Caterina, 'and a jest will as often gain a woman's favours as a handsome face.'

'You are a woman after my own heart, Madonna. Should the opportunity present itself so that what we both wish could be effected without danger, may I count on your help?'

'It is not only my daughter's fears that must be overcome, but also her scruples.'

'Such of them as you will not have been able to dispel by the exercise of your common sense we can safely leave to be dealt with by the excellent Fra Timoteo. He does not like the Dominicans.'

Monna Caterina gave a low laugh.

'You are a charming man, Messer Niccolo. If I were still desirable and you desired me, I would refuse you nothing.'

'The old cow,' Machiavelli said to himself, but he pressed her hand and aloud answered: 'If I were not so passionately in love with your daughter I should not hesitate to take you at your word.'

'There is Aurelia.'

'I will leave you.'

Slipping out of the church, he went to a silversmith and there bought a chain, only of silver gilt, certainly, for he had not the money for a gold one, but of very pretty workmanship. Next morning he sent Piero to buy a basket of the luscious figs which Monna Caterina had told him she liked so much, and putting the chain at the bottom of the basket told Piero to take it to her. He was to say that the figs were a gift from Machiavelli and to add that underneath them she would find something that he begged her to accept as a mark of his esteem. He felt that he and Monna Caterina understood one another perfectly, but he knew that nothing confirms an understanding like a little present.

21

Some days later Bartolomeo suggested that they should repeat the evening of good cheer and singing which had been so enjoyable. They did so. Things went off as before, with pleasant conversation and some good music; Aurelia, never very chatty, was more silent than usual, but Machiavelli was conscious that when he was talking in his sprightly way to the others she looked at him appraisingly. He was pretty sure that she and her mother had discussed him and his desires, and these enquiring glances of hers meant that she was wondering what he would be like in the capacity of a lover. He knew that it was not his good looks that made his success with women, but his agreeable discourse, his wit and his easy manner. He put his best foot forward. He knew that women appreciated neither irony nor sarcasm, but simple jokes and funny stories. He was amply provided with both. The laughter with which his sallies were greeted excited him and he flattered himself that he had never been more amusing. He took care, however, to show that he was not only a jester, but a good-natured man, kindly and easy to get on with, one in whom you could have confidence and whom it would not be hard to love. Was it only his fancy that when from time to time he caught Aurelia's eyes he saw in them a smiling tenderness that suggested she was not indifferent to him? He had seen that look before in women's eyes. They were strange creatures: they had to bring sentiment in and thus tiresomely complicate a pleasure which a merciful Providence had provided for human beings in compensation for the expulsion of their first parents from the Garden of Eden. But sometimes it was convenient that they should have this foible. He gave a passing thought to Marietta, who had married him by arrangement with her parents and now so doted on him that she could hardly bear him out of her sight. She was a good woman and he had a real affection for her, but she couldn't expect him to be tied to her apron strings.

The affairs of his mission kept Machiavelli so busy

that for several days after this he was obliged to devote his whole time to them; but through Piero he sent Aurelia a flask of attar of roses which he had bought at a cost he could ill afford from a merchant who had recently come from the Levant. It was a good sign that she did not refuse it. He congratulated Piero on the tact and skill with which he had managed to convey it to her without anyone's knowing, and gave him a scudo so that he could prosecute his suit with Nina.

'How are you getting on, my boy?' he asked.

'I don't think she dislikes me,' said Piero. 'She's frightened of that servant of theirs. He's her lover.'

'I suspected that, but don't be discouraged; if she wants you she'll find ways and means to arrange things.'

Then came a rainy afternoon. Bartolomeo sent round to ask Machiavelli if he could spare the time to come to his house and play chess. Machiavelli decided that what work he had to do could be done later, and went. Bartolomeo received him in his study. Though there was no fireplace a brazier warmed it not inadequately.

'I thought we could play more conveniently here than in company with a pair of chattering women,' said Bartolomeo.

Machiavelli had gone in the hope of seeing Aurelia and was somewhat put out, but he answered civilly enough.

'Women will talk, and chess is a game that demands concentration.'

They played, and perhaps because Machievelli's attention was divided, Bartolomeo to his delight beat him without difficulty. He called for wine, and when it had been brought and Machiavelli was setting up the pieces for another game, he leant back in his chair and said:

'It was not only for the pleasure of playing chess with you that I asked you to be good enough to come here, dear Niccolo. I want to ask your advice.'

'It is at your service.'

'Have you ever heard of San Vitale?'

A faint sigh of satisfaction escaped Machiavelli's lips. Fra Timoteo had not failed him.

'Strange that you should ask that! You're speaking of the church at Ravenna? The saint's bones are buried there. Everyone in Florence was talking about him not so very long ago.'

'In what connection?'

'There is no limit to the folly of mankind, and our good Florentines, who pride themselves on their lively intelligence, are of a credulity beyond belief.'

He saw that Bartolomeo was all agog and he thought, I will keep him on tenterhooks.

'What is it that you refer to?'

'The story is so absurd that I am really ashamed to tell it. Within the limits set by our Holy Church my fellow-citizens have a healthy scepticism, and are disinclined to believe in anything that they cannot see, smell or touch for themselves.'

'That is what makes them the good business men they are.'

'Maybe. But how surprising that now and then they fall prey to the most absurd superstition! To tell you the truth I can't bring myself to tell you a story that shows them in such a ridiculous light.'

'I am almost a Florentine myself and now I shall never rest till I hear it. It is always a pleasure to listen to you and on such a cheerless day it is well to laugh.'

'Well, the facts are these: Giuliano degli Albertelli, a citizen of Florence, is a man of property, a man in the flower of his age, with a fine house in the city and a beautiful wife to whom he is greatly attached. He should have been a happy man, but he had no child, and this was a bitter grief to him because he had quarrelled desperately with his brother and could not endure to think that this man and his brood of squalling brats should one day inherit all he possessed. He took his wife to the baths, he took her on pilgrimages to various holy places, he consulted doctors and the old women who pretend to have secret herbs to make women conceive, but nothing served.'

Bartolomeo, breathing heavily, listened as though his life depended on it.

'Then it happened that a monk who had been on a pilgrimage to the Holy Land told him that on his way home he had stopped at Ravenna where there was the church of San Vitale, and the saint had the miraculous power of making sterile men fertile. Though his friends sought to dissuade him, Giuliano insisted on visiting the shrine, and you can image how everyone laughed when he set out on the journey. Lampoons were written and passed from hand to hand. When he came back men had to turn away to prevent themselves from bursting into laughter before his face. Nine months to a day from the date of his return his wife was delivered of a nine-pound son. It was Giuliano who laughed then. All Florence was confounded and the pious cried out that it was a miracle.'

The sweat glistened on Bartolomeo's brow.

'If it wasn't a miracle what was it?'

'Within these four walls, dear friend, I will tell you that I think the time of miracles has passed, doubtless because owing to our sins we are no longer worthy of them, but I must confess that this occurrence has greatly shaken me. I can only repeat after you, if it wasn't a miracle, what was it? I have given you the facts and it is for you to make what you can of them.'

Bartolomeo took a long draught of wine. Machiavelli decided to offer another candle at the shrine of Fra Timoteo's wonder-working Madonna: his invention had served him well.

'I know I can trust you, dear Niccolo,' said Bartolomeo after a pause. 'I am a judge of human nature and I am sure that you are a man of discretion. It was not for nothing that I asked you if you had ever heard of San Vitale, but I never expected you to confirm so promptly the information I have received.'

'You talk in riddles, friend.'

'You are well aware that I too have a great desire for a son to whom I can leave my fortune, my lands and houses, and who will inherit the property and the title which the Duke has granted me. I have a widowed sister who has two sons and having no child of my own I have had it in mind to adopt them. Though it is to their advantage she will not consent to be parted from them; she insists on our all living here together. But she shares with me the masterful character which has made me the man I am, and I can see little peace for me in a house inhabited by three jarring women. It would be the scene of incessant quarrels.'

'That I can believe.'

'I shouldn't have a moment's peace.'

'Your life would be a torment. They would tear you limb from limb.'

Bartolomeo gave a deep sigh.

'And it is on this question that you want my advice?' asked Machiavelli.

'No. I was discussing my difficulties with Fra Timoteo only yesterday and strangely enough he spoke to me of San Vitale. I do not for a moment believe that I am at fault in this matter, but if the saint's relics have the miraculous property reported, it might be worth while to go to Ravenna. I have some business to transact there, so that even if my main object were not achieved my journey would not be wasted.'

'In that case I don't see why you hesitate. You have everything to gain and nothing to lose.'

'Fra Timoteo is a good and saintly man, but he knows nothing of the world. It seems strange to me that if the saint has the power he is reputed to have his celebrity should not have been bruited abroad.'

For a moment Machiavelli was floored, but only for a moment.

'You forget that men are unwilling to admit that they suffer from a deficiency which they prefer to ascribe to their wives. You may be sure that the men who have availed themselves of the saint's intercession go in secret and take care never to divulge by what means their wives have been able to conceive.'

'I hadn't thought of that. But don't forget this, if it were ever known that I had gone and my pilgrimage were not blessed with a happy event I should be a laughing-stock in this city. It would be an admission of impotence.'

'But how could it be known? Has Fra Timoteo not told you what you must do? According to Giuliano you must spend the night in prayer and meditation before the relics of the saint.'

'But how is that possible?'

'For a gratuity the sacristan will let you remain when he locks up the church for the night. You will attend the first mass in the morning and then break your fast. Having done that, in your case, you will attend to your business and after that ride home to your expectant wife.'

Bartolomeo gave his friend a smile.

'Then you would not think me too great a fool if I made the experiment?'

'My dear, the ways of Providence are inscrutable. I can only tell you what happened to Giuliano degli Albertelli. Whether it was a miracle or not, who am I to say?'

'It is my last hope,' said Bartolomeo. 'I will try it. It succeeded with Messer Giuliano; there is no reason why it should not succeed with me.'

'None,' said Machiavelli.

22

During the following week Machiavelli's emotions were as various as the colours of a crazy quilt. At one moment he was hopeful, at another despondent; he passed from happy anticipation to angry disappointment; now he was in a fever of excitement, then in the depths of despair. For Bartolomeo could not make up his mind. He was at once eager and loath to go. He was like a man who is tempted to risk his money on an off chance and is torn between his fear of losing it and his greed for gain. One day he would decide to make the journey and the next decide not to. Machiavelli's digestion was always delicate and this uncertainty gravely affected it. It would be too cruel if, everything being arranged, he were so indisposed that he could not take advantage of the opportunity he had taken such pains and spent so much money to create. He had himself bled, he took a purge, he ate nothing but slops. And to make things worse he had more work to do than ever; negotiations between the Duke and his rebellious commanders were coming to a head, and Machiavelli had to write constant letters to the Signory, see agents, spend hours at the Palace to pick up news, and visit influential persons who were come to Imola on behalf of their respective states. But at the last moment fortune smiled upon him. A letter reached Bartolomeo from his factor in Ravenna to say that if he did not immediately clinch the deal which he had been for some time negotiating another offer would be accepted. This decided him.

Machiavelli's pains vanished. On the day after his conversation with Bartolomeo he had seen Fra Timoteo and the monk had agreed to give Bartolomeo the instructions which Machiavelli suggested. To ingratiate himself with Aurelia he went to one of the merchants whom the chance of easy money had attracted to Imola and bought a pair of scented gloves stitched with gold thread. They cost a great deal of money, but this was not an occasion on which he could stint. He sent them by Piero, telling the boy to ask for Monna Caterina so that the servants might think no more than that he had a message to give her from his master; and at the same time he bade him tell her that he wished to talk with her and would meet her in the church at whatever hour suited her. He was elated when Piero came back and told him that Monna Caterina had called her daughter in and she had been delighted with the costly present. Gloves of that kind were greatly prized, and the Marchioness of Mantua had thought such a gift not unworthy of the acceptance of the Queen of France.

'How did she look?' asked Machiavelli.

'Monna Aurelia? She looked pleased.'

'Don't be stupid, boy. Did she look beautiful?'

'She looked as she always looks.'

'Fool! When will Monna Caterina be at the church?'

'She is going to vespers this afternoon.'

Machiavelli was well pleased when he returned from his interview with her.

'What a noble animal is man,' he reflected, as he walked home. 'With audacity, cunning and money there is practically nothing he cannot do.'

At first Aurelia had been frightened and firmly refused to listen to the proposal, but little by little she had allowed herself to be convinced by Monna Caterina's arguments. They were indeed unanswerable, Machiavelli thought, and that was natural since he himself suggested them. They were strengthened by the gentle, yet firm admonitions of Fra Timoteo. Aurelia was a sensible girl and she could not but admit that it was unreasonable to jib at a small evil when a great good might come of it. The long and short of it was that if Bartolomeo were safely out of the way she was prepared to accede to Machiavelli's wishes.

Having made up his mind Bartolomeo saw no reason to delay and so, accompanied by his servant and a groom, he set out for Ravenna at noon on the following day. Machiavelli with his usual politeness went to bid him goodbye and wish success on the expedition. Nina, the maid, was sent home to spend the night with her parents, and when she had gone Machiavelli dispatched Piero to Bartolomeo's house with a basket in which were fish fresh from the river, a pair of fat capons, sweetmeats from the confectioner's, fruit, and a demi-john of the best wine the city could produce. The plan was that Machiavelli should wait till three hours after sunset, nine o'clock, by which time Serafina would be in bed and asleep, and then present himself at the little door of the yard. Monna Caterina would let him in and they would have supper. At a convenient moment she would retire to her own bed-chamber and Machiavelli would be left with the object of his affections; but she made him promise that he would leave the house well before dawn. When Piero returned, having delivered the basket, he brought a last message from Monna Caterina. She would be waiting at the door as the church clock struck the hour. To make sure it was he, he was to knock twice quickly, wait a moment, knock once, and then after another brief pause again knock twice. The door would be opened and he was to step in without a word.

'What it is to have to do with a woman of experience,' said Machiavelli. 'She leaves nothing to chance.'

He told one of his servants to bring a pail of hot water to his bedroom and he washed himself all over. It was a thing he hadn't done since the night before his marriage to Marietta. He remembered that he had caught cold as the result and as was only natural had given his cold to Marietta. Then he scented himself with perfume he had bought at the same time as he bought the attar of roses for Aurelia. He put on his best clothes. Since he did not want to spoil his appetite for the excellent supper he looked forward to, he refused to partake of the modest meal Serafina had prepared on the excuse that he was going to sup at the inn with the agent of the Duke of Ferrara. He tried to read, but was too excited to read with attention. He strummed a little on the lute, but his fingers served him ill. He thought for a while of that dialogue of Plato's in which he proves to his own satisfaction that pleasure, being mingled with pain, is an imperfect good. There was something in it, but there were moments when meditation on eternal things was but an insipid resource. He laughed in his heart when he passed in review the difficulties of his undertaking and the ingenuity of his devices to overcome them. It would have been a false modesty unworthy of him not to acknowledge that he had been wonderfully clever. He didn't know anyone who could so skilfully have worked on the passions, foibles and interest of the parties concerned as to bend them to his will. The church clock struck eight. He called Piero, thinking to pass the long hour ahead by playing draughts; ordinarily he could beat him easily, but tonight he was careless and Piero won game after game. It seemed as though the hour would never end, and then on a sudden the clock began to strike. Machiavelli sprang to his feet, flung his cloak round him and opened the house door on to the darkness of the night. He was about to step out into the alley when he heard the tread of feet on the cobbles. He closed the door partly and stood just within to wait till the men, whoever they were, had passed. But they didn't pass, they stopped at his door and one of them knocked; since it was not latched the knock pushed it back and the flare of the torches two of the men carried discovered Machiavelli in the passage.

'Ah, Messer Niccolo,' said a man whom Machiavelli

immediately recognized as one of the Duke's secretaries. 'We were coming to fetch you. And you, you were just coming to the Palace? His Excellency desires to see you. He has important news for you.'

For once Machiavelli lost his presence of mind. He could not think of any excuse to make. Had he not been caught thus, ready to go out, he could have sent a message to say that he was sick in bed and could not come, but how could he say that now? The Duke was not a man to whom you could say that you had other things to do, and besides, if he had important news to tell, it was essential that he should hear them. It might very well be that they concerned the safety of Florence. His heart sank.

'Wait a moment and I will tell my boy that he need not accompany me.'

'It is quite unnecessary. Men will be sent to bring you safely back.'

Machiavelli went into the parlour and closed the door behind him.

'Listen, Piero. The Duke has sent for me. I will make the interview short by telling the Duke I have the colic. Monna Caterina must be waiting. Go to the door and knock in the way she told you. Tell her what has happened and say I will come as soon as possible. Ask her to let you wait in the yard so that you can open for me when I knock.'

'Very well.'

'And say that I am distressed, mortified, miserable, woebegone and exasperated. I shall be back in half an hour.'

With that he joined the men who had come for him and went to the Palace. He was taken into an ante-room and the secretary left him saying he would inform the Duke of his arrival. Machiavelli waited. Minutes went by. Five, ten, fifteen. Then the secretary returned to say that the Duke sent his excuses, but a courier had just arrived from the Pope with letters and he was closeted with the Bishop of Elna and Agapito da Amalia to consider them. He would send for Machiavelli as soon as he was ready. Once more Machiavelli was left alone. His patience was sorely tried. He fidgeted, he tossed from side to side in his chair, he bit his fingers, he walked up and down. He fretted, he chafed, he fumed, he raged. At last, in desperation, he flung out of the room and sought out the secretary who had come for him and in icy tones asked him if the Duke had forgotten he was there.

'I have the colic,' he said. 'If the Duke cannot see me I will go home and return tomorrow.'

'It is an unfortunate accident. Surely His Excellency wouldn't keep you waiting except for matters of the greatest urgency. I believe he has something to say to you that is of vital interest to the Signory. Please have patience.'

Mastering his vexation as best he could Machiavelli threw himself into a handy chair. The secretary engaged him in conversation, and though Machiavelli answered in monosyllables and was evidently not paying attention to what he said, would not be discouraged. It was only by a great effort that Machiavelli prevented himself from telling the chatter-box to hold his silly tongue. He kept on saying to himself: if they'd only come one minute later they wouldn't have found me. At last Agapito da Amalia himself came and said the Duke was ready to receive him. Machiavelli had been kept waiting an hour. He gave a sardonic smile as he thought of Piero standing inside the door shivering in the yard. It was some small consolation that he was not the only one to suffer.

The Duke was with his cousin the Bishop of Elna. He was gracious, but wasted no time on compliments.

'I have always been frank with you, Secretary, and I wish now to put my position quite plainly. I am not satisfied with the declaration of good will which at the

Signory's direction you convey to me. The Pope may die any day, and if I want to keep my states I must take measures to secure myself. The King of France is my ally and I have an armed force; but that may not be enough and so I wish to make friends of my neighbours. These are Bologna, Mantua, Ferrara and Florence.'

Machiavelli thought this was no time to repeat his assurances of the Republic's good will, so wisely he held his tongue.

'So far as Ferrara is concerned I have acquired the Duke's friendship by his alliance with Monna Lucrezia, my beloved sister, the enormous dowry the Pope gave her, and the benefits we have conferred on his brother the Cardinal. So far as Mantua is concerned, we are arranging two things; one is to give the Cardinal's hat to the Marquis's brother, for which the Marquis and his brother will deposit forty thousand ducats; and the other is to give my daughter in marriage to the Marquis's son, whereupon the forty thousand ducats will be returned as her dowry. I need not point out to you, Secretary, that mutual advantage is the most solid basis of enduring friendship.'

'I would not dispute it, Excellency,' smiled Machiavelli. 'And Bologna?'

The Lord of Bologna, Giovanni Bentivoglio, had joined the rebellious captains, and though his army had withdrawn from the Duke's frontiers it remained on war footing. Il Valentino stroked his well-kept, pointed beard and smiled maliciously.

'I have no wish to seize Bologna, but only to assure myself of that state's co-operation. I would sooner have Messer Giovanni my friend than drive him out of a state which I might not be able to hold and which might prove my ruin. Besides which, the Duke of Ferrara refuses to give me aid unless I come to an agreement with Bologna.'

'Messer Giovanni has signed the articles of association with the rebels.'

'For once your information is at fault, Secretary,' the Duke answered good-naturedly. 'Messer Giovanni is of the opinion that the articles do not safeguard his interests and has refused to agree to them. I am in communication with his brother the Protonotary and things are proceeding to our mutual satisfaction. When we come to an agreement the Protonotary will receive a Cardinal's hat, or if he prefers to relinquish Holy Orders the hand of my cousin, the sister of the Cardinal Borgia. The forces of our four states, supported further by the King of France, will be formidable, and then your masters will have more need of me than I have of them. I don't say that I bear them ill will, but circumstances alter cases, and if I am not bound to them by a definite pact I shall feel myself at liberty to act as appears best to me.'

The velvet glove was off and the mailed fist was bared. Machiavelli allowed himself a moment's reflection. He was aware that Agapito and the Bishop of Elna were watching him intently.

'What exactly would Your Excellency have us do?' he asked as nonchalantly as he could. 'I understand that you have already come to terms with Vitellozzo and the Orsini.'

'Nothing has been signed yet and as far as I'm concerned I'd just as soon nothing were signed. It is not my policy to crush the Orsini: if the Pope dies I must have friends in Rome. When Pagolo Orsini came to see me one of his complaints was the behaviour of Ramiro de Lorqua; I promised to give him satisfaction and I shall be as good as my word. Vitellozzo is another matter. He is a snake and he has done everything he could to prevent my settling my differences with the Orsini.'

'Perhaps it would be better if Your Excellency were more explicit.'

'Very well. I desire you to write to your masters that it may very well be that the King of France will order them to restore to me the *condotta* which they withdrew without rhyme or reason and they will be obliged to obey. It is surely better for them to do this willingly than by compulsion.'

Machiavelli paused to collect himself. He knew that every word he said was fraught with danger. When he spoke it was in as ingratiating a manner as he could assume.

'Your Excellency acts with prudence in assembling his forces and making friends; but so far as the *condotta* is concerned, Your Excellency can't be classed with hireling captains who have nothing but themselves and a few troops to sell. Your Excellency is one of the powers of Italy, and it would be more suitable to make an alliance with you than to engage you as a mercenary.'

'I should look upon such an engagement as an honour,' the Duke answered suavely. 'Come now, Secretary, surely we can arrange something that will be to our common advantage. I am a professional soldier, bound to your state by ties of friendship; it is a slight your masters put upon me in refusing my request. I don't believe that I'm mistaken in thinking that I could serve them as well as anyone else.'

'I venture to point out that there would be no great safety for my government when three-quarters of its troops were in the hands of Your Excellency.'

'Does that mean that you doubt my good faith?'

'Not at all,' said Machiavelli with a fervour he was far from feeling. 'But my masters are prudent and they must be circumspect. They cannot afford to take a step which they might have reason to regret. Their chief desire is to be at peace with all men.'

'You are too intelligent not to know, Secretary, that the only way to assure peace is to be prepared for war.'

'I have no doubt that my government will take such steps as they deem necessary.'

'By taking other captains into their service?' the Duke asked sharply.

This was the opportunity Machiavelli had been looking for. He knew that Il Valentino was subject to sudden attacks of rage, and having vented it would scornfully dismiss the object of wrath. Machiavelli was too eager to get away to care if he angered him.

'I have every reason to believe that such are its intentions.'

To his astonishment the Duke laughed. He rose from his chair and stood with his back to the fire. He answered with complete good humour.

'Are they under the impression that it is possible to remain neutral in the unsettled conditions that now prevail? Surely they have more sense. When two neighbouring states go to war, the one that has counted on your help because of its intimate relations with you will consider you under an obligation to share its fortunes, and when you fail to do so, will bear you a grudge: the other will despise you for your timidity and lack of spirit. To the one side you are a useless friend and to the other an enemy little to be feared.

'The neutral is in such a position that he can help one party or the other; and in the end he is forced into such a situation that he is obliged against his will to join in the fray which he was unwilling at the beginning to enter boldly and with a good grace. Believe me, it is always wiser to take one side or the other without hesitation, for one or the other of them will be victorious and then you will fall prey to the winner. For who will come to your rescue? You can give no reason why anyone should protect you and will find no one to do it. The victor has no use for friends he can't trust, and the vanquished will do nothing for you, even if he could, because you wouldn't come to his help when your forces might have saved him.'

Machiavelli had no wish at the moment to listen to a disquisition on neutrality and he only hoped that by then the Duke had said his say. But he hadn't.

'Whatever the risks of war, the risks of neutrality are greater. It renders you an object of hatred and contempt, and sooner or later you will fall victim to the first person who thinks it worth his while to destroy you. If on the other hand you come out vigorously on one side and that side wins, even though its power is so great that you may have cause to fear it, you have put it under an obligation and attached it to yourself by bonds of friendship.'

'And it is Your Excellency's experience that men's gratitude for past benefits is so considerable that they will hesitate to exercise their power at your expense?'

'Victories are never so decisive that the victor can afford to alienate his friends. It is to his best interest to treat them with justice.'

'And supposing the side you have taken loses?'

'Then you are all the more valuable to your ally. He helps you to the best of his ability and you are the companion of fortunes that may rise again. So, whichever way you look at it, neutrality is folly. That is all I have to say to you. You will be wise to repeat to your masters the little lesson in statemanship that I have thought well to give you.'

With these words the Duke sank into a chair and held out his hand to the blazing fire. Machiavelli, bowing, was about to withdraw when the Duke turned to Agapito da Amalia.

'Have you told the Secretary that his friend Buonarotti is delayed in Florence and will not be arriving for some time?'

Agapito shook his head.

'I know no such person, Excellency,' said Machiavelli.

'Surely. The sculptor.'

The Duke was looking at him with smiling eyes and Machiavelli on a sudden guessed of whom he was speaking. He had written to his friend Biagio for money and had received an answer from him to say that he was sending it by Michelangelo, a sculptor. The name meant nothing to him. But the Duke's remark suggested that his effects had been searched, evidently with the connivance of Serafina, and he congratulated himself on having put his important correspondence in a safe place; he had kept in his lodging only papers of little consequence, but among them was Biagio's letter.

'There are many stone-cutters in Florence, Excellency,' he said coolly. 'I cannot be expected to know them all.'

'This Michelangelo is not without talent. He made a Cupid in marble and buried it in the ground so that when it was dug up it was taken for an antique. Cardinal di San Giorgio bought it, but when he discovered the fraud returned it to the dealer and in the end it came into my hands. I have sent it as a present to the Marchioness of Mantua.'

Il Valentino spoke in a jesting way and Machiavelli for a reason obscure to him received the impression that he was being made a fool of. He had the irascibility of the highly sensitive man he was, and his impatience overcame him. He was quite willing to affront the Duke if only he could secure his freedom to keep his appointment.

'And does Your Excellency propose to order from him a statue to rival the one Leonardo made for the Duke of Milan?'

The shaft quivered through the air, and the secretaries, startled, glanced at the Duke to see how he would take it. The great equestrian statue of Francesco Sforza, thought by many to be Leonardo's masterpiece, had been destroyed by the soldiery when Marshal Trevulzio captured the city; and Francesco's son, Lodovico il Moro, who had commissioned it, a usurper like Cæsar Borgia himself, driven from his city, was now a prisoner in the castle of Loches. Machiavelli's remark was well designed to remind Il Valentino how dangerous his position was and to what depths he might fall if his good fortune deserted him. The Duke laughed.

'No, I have more important work for this fellow Michelangelo to do than to make statues. The defences of this city are useless and I'm going to let him draw plans for its fortification. But you were speaking of Leonardo; I should like to show you some drawings he has made of me.'

He made a sign to one of the secretaries who left the room and soon returned with a portfolio which he handed to the Duke. He showed the drawings to Machiavelli one after the other.

'Unless you had told me they were portraits of Your Excellency I should never have known it,' said he.

'Poor Leonardo, he has no great gift for catching a likeness. But as drawings I am assured they are not without merit.'

'That may be, but I think it a pity that with his gifts he should waste his time painting pictures and making statues.'

'I can assure you that he will not do so while he is in my service. I sent him to Piombino to drain the marshes and lately he has been at Cesena and Cesenatico to cut a canal and make a harbour.'

He handed the drawings back to the secretary, and with a graciousness which Machiavelli noted acidly was no less regal than that of the King of France, dismissed him. Agapito da Amalia accompanied him out of the Duke's study. During the month he had been at Imola Machiavelli had taken pains to gain the Chief Secretary's confidence. He was related to the great Roman family of the Colonna, the bitter rivals of the Orsini, and so might be supposed to have a certain friendliness for the Florentines whose enemies they were. From time to time he had given Machiavelli information which he accepted as true or false according to his judgment of its likelihood. As now they passed through the presence chamber which was used on ceremonial occasions he took Machiavelli's arm and said:

'Come into my room. I have something to show you that will interest you.'

'It is late and I am sick. I will come tomorrow.'

'As you will. I wanted to show you the articles of agreement between the Duke and the rebels.'

Machiavelli's heart stood still. He knew that the document had arrived at Imola and he had in vain used every method he could think of to get a sight of it. It was of extreme importance to the Signory to know what the terms of the pact were, and they had written to complain of his negligence. It was useless for him to tell them that he sent them all the facts as he discovered them, but that in the Duke's court secrets were well kept and none knew what the Duke meant to do until he did it. At that moment a clock struck: he had kept Aurelia waiting for two hours. The fish fry would be ruined and the fat capons roasted to a cinder, and he was hungry, for he had eaten nothing since before noon. It was said that love and hunger were the two most deep-rooted instincts of man, and who could be blamed for yielding to them? Machiavelli sighed: the safety of Florence was at stake; her liberty in danger.

'Come then,' he said.

He thought bitterly that never had a man been called upon to sacrifice so much for the good of his country.

Agapito led him up a flight of stairs, unlocked a door, and ushered him into a small room, with a bed along one wall, which was dimly lit by the flame of an oil lamp. From it he lit a tallow candle and offered Machiavelli a chair, then he sat down himself, at a table littered with papers, and leaning back, crossed his legs comfortably. He had the appearance of a man to whom time was no object.

'I could not give you a copy of the articles before for a reason I will tell you, and for the same reason I did not give one to the agent of the Duke of Ferrara or to anyone else. The Duke and Pagolo Orsini drew up a draft which was agreeable to them both and the Lord Pagolo took it away to show it to the captains with the understanding that if they agreed to it he would do likewise on behalf of the Duke, who gave him his power of attorney. But when he had started the Duke examined the document again and it seemed to him that an article should have been included which took into account the interests of France.'

Machiavelli had been listening with impatience, for he wanted to see the agreement, if possible get hold of it, and be gone; but now he gave the speaker all his attention.

'The article was duly drawn up and the Duke ordered me to ride after the Lord Pagolo and tell him that unless it was accepted he wouldn't sign. I caught him up and he flatly refused to accept it, but after some discussion he said that he would take it to the others, but he didn't think they would accept it either. And so I left him.'

'What is the point of the article?'

There was laughter in Agapito's voice when he answered.

'If it is accepted it opens a window through which we can slip out of the agreement, and if it is not accepted it unlocks a door through which we can stride with our heads in the air.'

'It looks as though the Duke had more desire for revenge on those who have endangered his state than for peace.'

'You may be quite sure that the Duke will never allow his desires to interfere with his interests.'

'You promised to show me the agreement.'

'Here it is.'

Machiavelli read it eagerly. By its terms the Duke and the rebels were thenceforward to live in peace, concord and union: they were to retain their commands under him with the same pay as before and as a sign of good faith each one of them was to deliver into his safekeeping one of his legitimate sons as a hostage; but they stipulated that not more than one of the captains at a time should encamp with the Duke, and then for no longer than suited him. On their side they agreed to restore to him Urbino and Camerino and in return he undertook to defend their states against anyone, with the exception of His Holiness the Pope or His Majesty the King of France, who attacked them. This was the clause that Il Valentino had insisted on and which, as Agapito had said, even a child might see made the treaty worthless. Bentivoglio of Bologna and Petrucci of Siena were signing a separate agreement with the Pope. With a frown Machiavelli read the document a second time.

'How can they expect the Duke to forgive the injuries they have done him?' he exclaimed when he had finished. 'And how can the Duke be expected to forget the perils in which they have put him?'

'*Quem Jupiter vult perdere dementat prius,*' quoted Agapito with a cheerful smile.

'Will you allow me to take this document away to make a copy of it?'

'I couldn't let it out of my hands.'

'I promise to return it tomorrow.'

'It's impossible. The Duke may ask for it any minute.'

'The Duke never ceases to assure me of his sincere friendship for Florence. It is of the greatest importance that my government should be made acquainted with this agreement. Believe me, you will not find them ungrateful for any service you are able to render them.'

'I have been concerned with affairs of state too long to count on the gratitude of princes or governments.'

Machiavelli continued to press him and at last he said:

'You know that I would do a great deal to oblige you. My respect for your intelligence is only equalled by my admiration for your integrity. I do it with misgiving, I will allow you to make a copy of the agreement here.'

Machiavelli gasped. It would take him half an hour to do this and time was passing. Was ever lover placed in such a predicament? There was nothing to do but to submit. Agapito gave him his place at the table, a sheet of paper and a new quill. He lay down on the bed while Machiavelli scribbled away as fast as his task would let him. As he wrote the last line he heard the night watchman cry out the hour of the night and immediately afterwards the church clock struck. Midnight.

Agapito went downstairs with him and when they came to the court round which the Palace was built called for two men of the guard to light Machiavelli back to his lodging. A chill rain was falling and the night was raw. When they arrived at his house Machiavelli dismissed the soldiers with a gratuity and unlocked the door. He waited within till he could no longer hear their steps and, locking up behind him, slipped out again. He crossed the alley and gently knocked in the prearranged manner. There was no reply. He knocked again. Twice, a pause, once, a pause and then twice more. He waited. A bleak wind blew down the narrow alley, gusts of rain splashed his face, and though he was well wrapped up, with a muffler to keep the noxious air of night out of his lungs, he shivered in the cold. Was it possible that the women had grown tired of waiting? But where was Piero? He had told him to stay in the yard till he came, and Piero had never failed him before. Piero must have explained why he was delayed, and after all, though for different reasons, it was as essential to them, those two women, as it was urgent to him, that the opportunity should not be lost. On the walk from the Palace he had noticed on passing the front of the house that no light showed, and it occurred to him now that it would be well to see if there as a light at the back. After knocking once more, again to no purpose, he went back into his own house and up to his bedroom, since from there he could see into the yard of Bartolomeo's house and the windows that faced it. Nothing. He looked into impenetrable darkness. It might be that Piero had gone in for a moment to drink a cup of wine and to warm himself and by now was back at his post. Machiavelli went out again into the cruel night. He knocked, he waited, he knocked, he waited, he knocked, he waited. His feet and hands were like ice; his teeth were chattering.

'I shall catch my death of cold,' he mumbled.

Suddenly he was swept by a gust of anger and he was on the point of thundering on the door with both his fists. But prudence restrained him; he would be no further advanced if he aroused the neighbours. At last he was forced to conclude that they had given him up and were gone to bed. He turned away, and miserably let himself into his own house. He was cold, hungry and bitterly disappointed.

'If I don't catch my death of cold, I really shall have the colic tomorrow.'

He went into the kitchen to find something to eat, but Serafina bought the day's food every morning and if there was anything left over kept it under lock and key, so he found nothing. The brazier had been taken out of the parlour, which was cold as death, but Machiavelli had not even the solace of going to bed; he had to sit down and write a report of his conversation with the Duke. It took him a long time, because he had to write the most important parts in cypher. Then he had to make a fair copy of the articles of agreement to enclose in his letter. He did not finish till the small hours of the morning. The missive was urgent and he could not afford to wait till he found a casual messenger who could be trusted to deliver a letter for a gold florin or two, so he clambered upstairs to the attic where his two servants slept, woke them and told the more reliable of the two to get his horse saddled and be ready to ride out of the city as soon as the gates were opened. He waited till the man was dressed, let him out of the street door, and then at last went to bed.

'And this should have been a night of love,' he muttered savagely as he pulled his nightcap well over his ears.

23

He slept restlessly. He woke late in the morning and found his worst fears realized. He had caught cold and when he went to the door to shout for Piero his voice sounded like an old crow's. Piero appeared.

'I'm sick,' he groaned. 'I've got fever. I think I'm dying. Get me some hot wine and something to eat. If I don't die of fever I shall die of starvation. Bring a brazier. I'm chilled to the bone. Where the hell did you get to last night?'

Piero was about to speak when Machiavelli stopped him.

'Never mind about that. Later, later. Get me some wine.'

He felt a little better when he had drunk and eaten. He listened sullenly when Piero explained that he had waited in the yard for more than an hour as Machiavelli had told him to do. He had waited though the pouring rain soaked him to the skin. He had waited though Monna Caterina begged him to come in.

'Did you tell them what had happened?'

'I said exactly what you told me to say, Messere.'

'What did they say?'

'They said it was a pity.'

'They said it was a pity?' croaked Machiavelli wrathfully. 'My God! And to think that the Almighty created woman to be a helpmate to man. They said it was a pity. What would they have said to the death of Hector and the fall of Troy?'

'At last they forced me to take shelter. My teeth were chattering. They said we could hear your knock from the kitchen. They made me take off my coat and dry myself by the fire.'

'And the fish and the capons?'

'We kept them hot a long time and at last Monna Caterina said they'd only spoil so we'd better eat them. We were hungry.'

'I was starving.'

'We left something for you. Some fish and half a chicken.'

'Considerate.'

'We heard the clock strike once and we heard it strike a second time and Monna Aurelia went to bed.'

'She did what?' Machiavelli spluttered.

'We tried to get her to wait a little longer. We said you'd be coming in a minute. She said that two hours was enough to wait for any man. She said that if business meant more to you than pleasure there wasn't much pleasure to be expected from any intimate relations with you.'

'A *non sequitur*.'

'She said that if you loved her as much as you pretended you'd have found some excuse to break off your interview with the Duke. We reasoned with her.'

'As if one could reason with women!'

'But she wouldn't listen. So Monna Caterina told me it was no good my waiting, she gave me another drink of wine and sent me away.'

It occurred to Machiavelli then that Piero had no key to get in with.

'Where did you spend the night?'

The boy gave him an arch, complacent smile.

'With Nina.'

'You spent your night more profitably than I did then,' said Machiavelli grimly. 'But I thought she'd gone to stay with her parents.'

'That's what she told Monna Caterina. We'd arranged it beforehand. She got La Barberina to let her have a room in her house and I was to join her as soon as I could get away.'

La Barberina was a procuress with a well-established and respectable business in Imola. For some minutes Machiavelli was silent. He was not a man to accept defeat.

'Listen, Piero,' he said when he had well considered, 'that old fool Bartolomeo will be back before night. We must act quickly. Let us not forget that when Jupiter wished to gain the favours of the beautiful Danae he approached her in the likeness of a shower of gold. Go to the merchant Luca Capelli where I bought the gloves I sent to Monna Aurelia and get him to let you have the scarf in blue silk with the silver embroidery that he showed me. Say I'll pay for it as soon as the money I'm expecting from Florence arrives. Then take it and ask to see Monna Caterina; give her the scarf for Aurelia and tell her that I'm dying of love and the cold I caught waiting at the door, but that as soon as I'm better we'll meet and I will devise a new plan to satisfy Monna Aurelia's desires and my own.'

He waited impatiently for Piero to execute the commission and return with a report of his reception.

'She likes the scarf,' said Piero. 'She said it was pretty and asked how much it cost. When I told her she liked it still more.'

'Very natural. What else?'

'I told her that it had been impossible for you to get away from the Palace and she said it didn't matter at all and not to give it another thought.'

'What!' cried Machiavelli, outraged. 'Really women are the most irresponsible creatures in the world. Doesn't she see that her whole future is involved? Did you tell her that I stood out in the rain for an hour?'

'Yes. She said it was very imprudent.'

'Who expects a lover to be prudent? You might as well ask the sea to be calm when it is assailed by the angry winds of heaven.'

'And Monna Caterina said she hoped you'd take care of yourself.'

24

Machiavelli was laid up for several days, but by dint of purging and blood-letting recovered, and the first thing he did then was to seek out Fra Timoteo. He told him the tragic story. The monk was sympathetic.

'And now,' said Machiavelli, 'let us put our heads together and think out some way to get rid of our good Bartolomeo again.'

'I have done my best, Messere; I can do no more.'

'Father, when our illustrious Duke attacked the city of Forlì he was repulsed, but he did not for that reason raise the siege; he used every stratagem his intelligence suggested and eventually brought about its surrender.'

'I have seen Messer Bartolomeo. He did exactly what I told him to do and he is persuaded that the intercession of San Vitale was efficacious. He is convinced that Monna Aurelia conceived on the night of his return from Ravenna.'

'The man is a fool.'

'Though a religious I am not so ignorant as to be

unaware that a certain time must elapse before it can be known whether he is right or wrong.'

Machiavelli felt some irritation. The friar was proving less helpful than he had expected.

'Come, come, Father, do not take me for a fool too. Whatever miraculous powers the saint's relics may possess we know that to make a sterile man fertile is not one of them. I invented the story myself and you know as well as I do that there isn't a word of truth in it.'

Fra Timoteo smiled blandly and there was unction in his voice when he replied.

'The operations of Providence are mysterious, and who can know the ways of the Eternal? Have you never heard the story of St. Elizabeth of Hungary? Forbidden by her cruel husband to succour the necessities of the needy, she met him in the street one day when she was carrying bread to the poor. Suspecting that she was disobeying his orders, he asked her what she had in her basket and in her fright she told him it was roses. He snatched the basket from her and when he opened it found that she had told the truth: the loaves of bread had been miraculously turned into sweet-smelling roses.'

'The story is edifying,' said Machiavelli coldly, 'but the point escapes me.'

'May it not be that San Vitale hearing in Paradise the prayers that the pious Bartolomeo addressed to him was moved by the simple faith of this good man and performed for him the miracle which you had assured him it was in the saint's power to do? Does not Holy Scripture tell us that is we have faith we can move mountains?'

If Machiavelli had not possessed great self-control he would have given rein to his anger. He knew very well why the monk was refusing his further aid. For twenty-five ducats he had done what he had agreed to do and it was not his fault if the plan had miscarried. He wanted more money, and Machiavelli had no money to give him. The chain he had given Monna Caterina, the gloves, the attar of roses he had bought for Aurelia, had taken all his spare cash; he owed money to Bartolomeo, he owed money to several merchants, the money he was receiving from the Signory only sufficed for his current expenses. He had nothing to offer now but promises and he had an inkling that promises would mean little to Fra Timoteo.

'Your eloquence and your piety, father, bear out the good report I have heard of you, and if my letter of recommendation to the Signory has the effect we both desire I am sure it will be to the spiritual benefit of the people of Florence.'

The monk bowed with a grave dignity, but Machiavelli saw that he was unmoved. He went on.

'A wise man does not put all his eggs in one basket. If a plan miscarries he tries another. Do not let us lose sight of the fact that if Bartolomeo is disappointed in his hopes he will adopt his nephews to the injury of his wife and his mother-in-law and to the loss of your church.'

'It would be a misfortune which it would be my Christian duty to persuade all concerned to bear with resignation.'

'We are told that God helps those who help themselves. You have not found me ungenerous in the past, you will not find me ungenerous in the future. It is to your interest as well as to that of the two ladies that Bartolomeo's hopes should not be disappointed.'

A faint smile for a moment lit Fra Timoteo's Roman features.

'You know that I would do much to oblige a person of your distinction, but supposing that the good Bartolomeo's hopes are disappointed, how do you propose that we should gain God's help by helping ourselves?'

Machiavelli suddenly got an idea. It amused him so much that he nearly burst out laughing.

'Father, like the rest of the world you have doubtless from time to time to take a purge, and suppose you take a dose of aloes at night, you have certainly discovered that its action is more satisfactory if you take a dose of salts in the morning. Does it not occur to you that the efficacy of Bartolomeo's pilgrimage to San Vitale would be increased if he made another to Rimini, for example, which would oblige him to absent himself from this city for another twenty-four hours?'

'You are a man of so many desires, Messere, that I cannot refuse you my admiration. But this one comes too late. Messer Bartolomeo may be a fool, but I should be more of a fool than he if I counted on his being more of a fool than he is.'

'Your influence over him is great.'

'That is all the more reason for my not losing it.'

'Then I can't count upon your aid?'

'I do not say that. Wait a month and then we will talk of it again.'

'To a lover a month is a hundred years.'

'Let us not forget that the patriarch Jacob waited seven years for Rachel.'

Machiavelli saw well enough that the monk was mocking him. He was going to do nothing until Machiavelli could make it worth his while. He was seething, but he knew it would be fatal to show his irritation. Controlling himself he parted from the monk with a pleasantry: he begged him to accept a florin for a candle to be burnt at the altar of the miraculous Virgin so that Bartolomeo's wishes might be fulfilled. There was no sting in a defeat accepted with spirit.

25

His only hope now of having his way with Aurelia was to enlist the aid of Monna Caterina. It was obvious that her concern at the misadventure which had frustrated their well-laid scheme must be great, greater than his indeed, for with him it was only a matter of satisfying his desire for a pretty woman; but her very security was at stake. He could no longer rely on the monk, but in her he had a self-interested ally, and that was an ally you could count on. He had a firm belief in the ingenuity of her sex; to deceive was food and drink to it, and it was to her manifest advantage to do everything she could to bring their plan to a successful issue. He decided to arrange a meeting with her. The secluded life the two women led made it none too easy, but fortunately Piero was there to act as a go-between. He congratulated himself on his foresight in urging the boy to make love to Nina.

Next day he bought a beautiful fish at the market and sent it by Piero to Bartolomeo's house at a time when he knew the fat man would be about his business in the city. It would be very unlucky if he could not get an opportunity to see her alone and make an appointment. Piero carried out his commission with his usual competence and returned to tell his master that Monna Caterina after some hesitation had agreed to meet him at such and such an hour, three days from then, at the church of St. Dominic. Her choice of place was adroit. It was evident that with her feminine intuition she had realized that Fra Timoteo could be trusted no longer and it was just as well that he should not see them together.

Machiavelli went to St. Dominic's without an idea in his head, but he was untroubled, for he was confident that Monna Caterina would be able to suggest something; his only fear was that it would cost too much money. Ah, well, if the worst came to the worst he would have to borrow once again from Bartolomeo; after all, it was only just that he should pay for the service Machiavelli was prepared to render him.

There was not a soul in the church. Machiavelli told

Monna Caterina how it had happened that he had not been able to keep the appointment and how he had stood knocking at the door in the rain and how he had caught a dreadful cold.

'I know, I know,' said Monna Caterina. 'Piero told us and we were greatly distressed. Aurelia kept on saying: "The poor gentleman, it would be on my conscience if he died."'

'I had no intention of dying,' said Machiavelli. 'And if I had been at the gates of Paradise the thought of Aurelia would have brought me back.'

'It was all very unfortunate.'

'Let us not think of the past. I have recovered my health. I am full of vigour. Let us think of the future. Our scheme has miscarried, we must devise another; you are a clever woman, and I find it hard to believe that you cannot arrange some way whereby all our wishes may be satisfied.'

'Messer Niccolo, I did not want to come here today; I only came because of your Piero's entreaties.'

'He said you had shown hesitation. I could not understand.'

'No one likes to be the bearer of ill tidings.'

'What do you mean?' cried Machiavelli. 'It is impossible that Bartolomeo should have conceived any suspicion.'

'No, no, it is not that. It is Aurelia. I have argued with her, I have gone down on my bended knees. I can do nothing with her. Ah, my poor friend, girls are not what they were when I was young; then it never occurred to them that they could disobey their parents.'

'Don't beat about the bush, woman. Tell me what you mean.'

'Aurelia refuses to go on. She will not do what you desire.'

'But have you put the consequences before her? Haven't you shown her what her position will be, and yours, if Bartolomeo adopts his sister's sons and Monna Costanza becomes mistress of your house?'

'I have said everything.'

'But the reason? Even a woman must have a reason for what she does.'

'She believes that by a special interposition of Providence she has been preserved from mortal sin.'

'Sin?' shouted Machiavelli, in his agitation forgetting the decorum due to the sacred building in which they were thus conversing.

'Do not be angry with me, Messer Niccolo. It is not for a mother to persuade her daughter to act contrary to the dictates of her conscience.'

'Saving your presence, Madonna, you are talking stuff and nonsense. You are an experienced woman and she is but an ignorant girl. It is your duty to point out to her that of two evils not only reason, but heaven itself commands us to choose the lesser. Who in his senses would refuse to commit a little sin, and one to which considerable pleasure is attached, in order to gain a great good?'

'It is no use, Messere, I know my daughter, she is as stubborn as a mule; she had made up her mind and I can do nothing with her. She wishes me to tell you that in memory of the interest you have taken in her she will always treasure the elegant gloves and the silk scarf you gave her, but she will accept no more presents from you and desires you to offer none. She desired you further to make no more attempt, either direct or indirect, to see her. For my part I shall always remember your kindness with gratitude and I only wish I could make up to you for the disappointment you have suffered.'

She paused for a moment, but Machiavelli made no reply.

'I need not tell a man of your wit and worldly wisdom that women are capricious and uncertain. If he chooses the right moment even the prude will accept the embraces of a lover, but if he misses it even the wanton will refuse them. I bid you a very good day.'

Monna Caterina gave him a curtsey in which according to his perspicacity an observer might have seen derision, resentment or civility, and was gone.

Machiavelli was confounded.

26

Notwithstanding all his attempts during the next month it was not till he was about to leave Imola that he saw Aurelia again. Fortunately his work kept him too busy to brood over his disappointment. The rebels were reported to be at loggerheads. At last, however, all signed the agreement which Agapito had shown Machiavelli except Baglioni of Perugia, who told them they were fools and dupes to put their hands to such a document, and when he found them determined to make peace at any cost strode in a passion out of the church in which they were meeting. The Duke appointed Pagolo Orsini governor of Urbino, which by the terms of the treaty he recovered, and to reward him for persuading the captains to sign it made him a present of five thousand ducats. Vitellozzo wrote humble letters in which he sought to excuse his actions.

'The traitor stuck a knife in our backs,' said Agapito, 'and now he thinks he can undo the harm with soft words.'

But Il Valentino appeared to be well pleased. It looked as though he were prepared to let bygones be bygones and restore the repentant rebels to his confidence. His amiability seemed suspicious to Machiavelli and he wrote to the Signory that it was hard to guess and impossible to know what the Duke had in mind. He had now large forces at his disposal and it was evident to all that he would make use of them. Rumours were current that he was making preparations for his departure from Imola, but whether he intended to march south and attack the Kingdom of Naples or north to wage war on the Venetians was more than anyone could tell. Machiavelli was disturbed to hear that influential persons from Pisa had come to offer him their city. Florence had spent time, money and lives in the attempt to recapture it, for its possession was necessary to their commerce, and if it was held by the Duke their position, both from the economic and the military standpoint, would be hazardous. Lucca was close, and the Duke, speaking of it, remarked in a way that Machiavelli thought ominous that it was a rich territory and a mouthful for gluttons. If after gaining possession of Pisa he seized Lucca, Florence would be at his mercy. In an interview with Machiavelli the Duke brought up again the matter of the *condotta*, and the wretched envoy was hard put to it to explain the Signory's hesitation to grant him the command he wanted in such a way as not to offend him. The plain fact was that they were determined not to place themselves in the power of an unscrupulous man whom they had every reason to distrust. But whatever sinister plans he turned round in that handsome head of his, the Duke was evidently not ready to resort to more than veiled threats to induce the Florentines to accede to his demands, for he listened to Machiavelli calmly enough. He ended by telling him that he was about to set out for Cesena with his army and once there would do what he decided was necessary.

He started for Forlì on the tenth of December and reached Cesena on the twelfth. Machiavelli made arrangements to follow him. He sent Piero with one of the servants ahead to make sure of a dwelling, and having taken leave of certain persons who had obliged him during his sojourn at Imola, empty now that the Duke, with his court and all the hangers-on, had left, finally went to say goodbye to Bartolomeo. He found him at home and was ushered into his study. The fat man received him with his usual boisterous cordiality. He had already heard of Machiavelli's approaching departure and expressed his regret in very handsome terms. He said how greatly he had enjoyed the acquaintance of such a distinguished visitor and how much he deplored that he would no longer have the opportunity to play with him those too infrequent games of chess and to entertain him at his house with music and such poor fare as he could provide. Machiavelli on his side paid him appropriate compliments and then with some embarrassment entered upon a matter which was on his mind.

'Listen, my dear friend, I am come not only to thank you for all your kindness to me, but to ask you to do me one more kindness still.'

'You have only to mention it.'

Machiavelli gave a slightly bitter laugh.

'I owe you twenty-five ducats. I haven't the money to pay you. I must ask you to wait a little longer.'

'It is a matter of no consequence.'

'Twenty-five ducats is a considerable sum.'

'Let it wait, let it wait, and if it's inconvenient for you to pay there's no reason why you should. Look upon it as a gift rather than a loan.'

'There is no reason why you should make me such a present. I couldn't possibly accept such a favour at your hands.'

Bartolomeo leaned back in his chair and burst into a great booming laugh.

'But didn't you guess? It is not my money. Our good Duke knew that with the rise of prices and the necessary expenses of your mission your circumstances were embarrassed. Everyone knows that the Signory is niggardly. I received instructions from His Excellency's treasurer to provide you with any sum you might need. If you had asked me for two hundred ducats instead of twenty-five I should have given them to you.'

Machiavelli went pale. He was dumbfounded.

'But if I had known the money came from the Duke nothing would have induced me to take it.'

'It was because the Duke knew your scruples and admired your integrity that he chose me to be the go-between. He respected your delicacy. I am betraying his confidence, but I do not think you should remain ignorant of so generous and disinterested a gesture.'

Machiavelli stifled the obscenity that rose to his lips. He had little belief in the Duke's generosity and none in his disinterestedness. Did he think to buy his good will for twenty-five ducats? Machiavelli's thin lips tightened so that his mouth showed as no more than a bitter line.

'You are surprised?' smiled Bartolomeo.

'Nothing the Duke may do can any longer surprise me.'

'He is a very great man. I have no doubt that we who have enjoyed the privilege of being useful to him shall on that account be remembered by posterity.'

'My good Bartolomeo,' said Machiavelli, 'it is not the great deeds men do that make them remembered by posterity, but the fine language with which men of letters describe their deeds. Pericles would be no more than a name if Thucydides had not put into his mouth the speech that has made him famous.'

While saying these words he got up.

'You mustn't go without seeing the ladies. It would grieve them not to bid you farewell.'

Machiavelli followed him into the parlour. There was a certain constriction in his throat and it seemed to him that his heart was beating at an unaccustomed rate. The women had not expected a visitor and they were in their everyday clothes. They were taken aback to see him and perhaps none too well pleased. They rose to their feet and curtseyed. Bartolomeo told them that Machiavelli was leaving for Cesena.

'What shall we do without you?' cried Monna Caterina.

Since Machiavelli had the conviction that they would do perfectly well without him, he merely smiled a rather sour smile.

'Messer Niccolo will doubtless be glad to leave a place which offers so little to divert a stranger,' said Aurelia.

Machiavelli could not but think there was a hint of malice in her tone. She resumed her work and he noticed that she was still busy with the elaborate embroidery of the shirts, the material for which he had brought from Florence.

'I hardly know which to admire most, Monna Aurelia,' he said, 'your patience or your industry.'

'They say the devil finds work for idle hands to do,' she replied.

'And pleasant work, too, on occasion.'

'But dangerous.'

'And hence more attractive.'

'Yet discretion is the better part of valour.'

Machiavelli didn't much like having his remarks capped, and though he smiled, his retort as acidulous.

'They say that proverbs are the wisdom of the multitude, but the multitude is always in the wrong.'

Aurelia was not looking her best. The weather had been bad for some time and she had waited too long to dye her hair. The roots showed black. One might have thought that she had made-up that morning in haste, for the natural olive of her skin was not quite disguised by the cosmetics she had applied.

'By the time she's forty she'll be no more desirable than her mother,' said Machiavelli to himself.

After a decent interval he took his leave. He was glad he had seen Aurelia again. He still desired her, but his desire was not so importunate as it had been. He was not a man who because he was disappointed of the fat quails he had promised himself for his dinner was disinclined to eat the pig's trotters that were set before him; and when he saw that to pursue Aurelia further was fruitless, he had on occasion assuaged his urgent passions in the arms of sundry not too expensive young women whose acquaintance he made through the good offices of La Barberina. Now when he looked into his heart he could not but see that, so far as Aurelia was concerned, he was suffering as much from wounded vanity as from the pangs of unrequited love. He came to the conclusion that she was rather stupid; otherwise she would not have gone to bed in a pet because he had kept her waiting a mere three hours; otherwise it would never have occurred to her that in going to bed with him she was committing a sin, at least till after she had committed it. If only she knew as much about life as he did, she would know that it is not the temptations you have succumbed to that you regret, but those you have resisted.

'Well, it'll serve her right if Bartolomeo adopts his nephews,' he said to himself. 'She'll be sorry then that she was such a fool.'

27

Two days later he arrived at Cesena. The Duke's artillery was approaching the city, his army was at full strength, and he was well provided with money. It was evident that something was afoot, but none knew what. Notwithstanding the activity that prevailed there was in the air a stillness like that which they say obtains before an earthquake: men are uneasy and restless, they know not why, and suddenly, without warning, the ground under their feet shakes and the houses come tumbling about their ears. Machiavelli twice requested the Duke to receive him, and the Duke, thanking him for his courtesy, returned the message that he would send for him when he had need of him. He could get no information from the secretaries. They repeated that the Duke told nothing till he was ready to act, and he acted as necessity dictated. It was obvious that they were as ignorant of his plans as anyone else. Machiavelli was sick and sore and he had no money. He wrote to the Signory asking for his recall and advised them to send in his place an ambassador with fuller powers than they had been willing to grant him.

But Machiavelli had not been in Cesena a week before an unexpected event occurred. Going one morning to the Palace which the Duke had requisitioned for his own use he found all the French captains there. They were angry and excited. It appeared that they had on a sudden received the order to take themselves off within two days, and they were deeply affronted by their abrupt dismissal. Machiavelli racked his brains to think of a plausible explanation for this step. His friends at court told him that the Duke could no longer stand the French, since they caused him more trouble than they were worth; but it seemed the height of folly to send away so important a part of his armed force when the troops left to him would not be superior to those under the command of the captains, Orsini, Vitellozzo, Oliverotto da Fermo and the rest, in whose loyalty, after their recent rebellion and unwilling submission, he could certainly place small trust. Was it possible that the Duke had so much confidence in himself that he wanted to show the King of France that he no longer needed his help?

The French went away and a few days later another occurrence took place which Machiavelli, a student of human nature as well as of politics, found of quite peculiar interest. Ramiro de Lorqua was summoned to Cesena. He had remained faithful to the Duke, he was a good soldier and an able administrator. He had been for some time governor of Romagna. But his cruelty and dishonesty had made him hated and feared by the people, and at last, driven beyond endurance, they sent representatives to lay their complaints before the Duke. When Ramiro arrived he was arrested and thrown into prison.

On Christmas Day Piero woke Machiavelli early.

'Come into the Piazza, Messere, and you will see a sight worth seeing,' he said, his young eyes sparkling with excitement.

'What is it?'

'I will not tell you. There is a great crowd assembled. Everyone is amazed.'

It did not take Machiavelli long to dress. It had been snowing and the morning was raw. In the Piazza, on a mat on the snow, lay the headless body of Ramiro de Lorqua, richly dressed, with all his decorations, and gloves on his hands. At a little distance was his head stuck on a pike. Machiavelli turned away from the shocking sight and slowly walked back to his lodging.

'What do you make of it, Messere?' asked Piero. 'He was the Duke's most valiant captain. They always said the Duke trusted him and relied on him as on nobody else.'

Machiavelli shrugged his shoulders.

'It has so pleased the Duke. It shows that he can make and unmake men at his pleasure according to their deserts. I suppose that the Duke had no further use for him and was not displeased to show by an act of justice that he had the interests of his people at heart.'

It was generally believed that Ramiro had been the lover of Lucrezia Borgia, and it was dangerous to be either the husband or the lover of Cæsar Borgia's sister. He loved her. Her first husband, Giovanni Sforza, escaped death only because she warned him that Cæsar had given orders for him to be killed. He threw himself

147

on a horse and rode for dear life till he reached the safety of Pesaro. When the Duke of Gandia was fished out of the Tiber with nine wounds in his body, common report ascribed his murder to Cæsar, and the reason given was that he also had loved Lucrezia. Pedro Calderon, a Spaniard and a chamberlain of the Pope, was killed at Cæsar's command 'because of something offending the honour of Madonna Lucrezia'. She was in point of fact, it was said, with child by him. Her second husband Alfonso, Duke of Bisceglie, was equally unfortunate. One day, a year after his marriage, when he was only nineteen, he was set upon by armed men as he was leaving the Vatican and desperately wounded; he was helped back to the papal apartments, where for a month he hovered between life and death; then, refusing to die of his wounds, Burchard relates, he was strangled in bed one hour after sunset. Alfonso of Bisceglie was the handsomest man in Rome and Lucrezia had made the mistake of loving him too fondly. No one in Italy doubted that he owed his death to Cæsar Borgia's jealousy.

Machiavelli had a good memory and he had not forgotten something that the Duke had said to him at Imola. Pagolo Orsini had complained of Ramiro's brutality and the Duke had promised to give him satisfaction. It was unlikely that he cared anything for the complaints of Pagolo whom he despised, but was it not possible that by his execution of Ramiro he would dissipate the last of the suspicions harboured by the rebellious captains? How could they fail to rely on his good faith when to gratify one of their number he had sacrificed the most competent and highly trusted of his lieutenants? Machiavelli laughed within himself. It was just the kind of thing that would appeal to Il Valentino, at one stroke to placate the outraged people of Romagna, assure his false friends of his confidence in them, and wreak his private vengeance on one who had enjoyed the favours of Lucrezia.

'At all events,' he said to Piero cheerfully, 'our good Duke has rid the earth of one more rascal. Let us find a tavern and drink a cup of hot wine to get the chill out of our bones.'

28

There was a very good reason why Machiavelli had not been able to discover Il Valentino's projects, and that was because they were still unsettled. Something had to be done, for there was no sense in having an army and not using it, but it was not so easy to decide what. The captains sent representatives to Cesena to discuss the matter with the Duke, but no agreement was reached, so after some days they dispatched Oliverotto da Fermo with a concrete proposition to put before him.

. This Oliverotto da Fermo was a young man who not long before had got himself much talked about. Having been left fatherless in early childhood he was brought up by his uncle, his mother's brother, called Giovanni Fogliati, and on reaching a suitable age was sent to learn the profession of arms under Paolo Vitelli. After Paolo's execution he joined his brother Vitellozzo, and in a short while, because he was intelligent and vigorous, became one of his best officers. But he was ambitious. He thought it base to serve when he might rule, and so concocted an ingenious plan to better himself. He wrote to his uncle and benefactor that since he had been away from home for some years, he would like to visit him and his native town and at the same time see to his paternal estate. And because his only concern had been to gain renown, so that his fellow-citizens should see that he had not spent his time in vain he desired to come in an imposing way with a hundred horsemen, his friends and servants, in his train; and he begged his uncle to see that he was received in an honourable manner, which would be not only a credit to him but to his uncle whose foster child he was. Giovanni Fogliati was gratified to see that his nephew was not forgetful of the care and affection with which he had treated him, and when Oliverotto arrived at Fermo very naturally took him to live with him. But after some days Oliverotto, not to be a burden on his uncle, moved into a house of his own and invited him and all the most important personages of Fermo to a solemn banquet.

When they had feasted and made merry, Oliverotto, broaching a topic that was of concern to all of them, spoke of the greatness of the Pope and his son Cæsar and of their undertakings; but getting up on a sudden with a remark that these were matters that must be discussed in private, he led his guests into another room. They had no sooner seated themselves than soldiers came out of their hiding-places and killed them one and all. Thus he gained possession of the city, and since all were dead who might have resisted him, and the regulations he made, both civil and military, were efficient, within a year he made himself not only safe in Fermo, but formidable to his neighbours. This was the man then whom the captains sent to Il Valentino. The proposition he brought was with their combined forces to invade Tuscany or if that did not suit him to seize Sinigaglia. Tuscany was a rich prize. The capture of Siena, Pisa, Lucca and Florence would provide great spoil to all who took part in the enterprise, and Vitellozzo and the Orsini had old scores with Florence which they would be glad to settle. But Siena and Florence were under the protection of the King of France and the Duke was not prepared to anger an ally of whom he might yet have need. He therefore told Oliverotto that he would not join in an attack on Tuscany, but would be well pleased to have Sinigaglia taken.

Sinigaglia was small, but not unimportant, for it was on the sea and had a good port. Its ruler, the widowed sister of the unfortunate Duke of Urbino, had signed the compact at La Magione along with the rebel captains; but after the reconciliation, in which she would have no share, she had fled with her young son to Venice, leaving Andrea Doria, a Genoese, to defend the citadel. Oliverotto marched on the city and occupied it without opposition. Vitellozzo and the Orsini advanced with their troops and quartered them in the vicinity. The operation had been conducted with only one hitch: Andrea Doria refused to surrender the citadel except to Il Valentino in person. It was strong, and to take it by storm would cost time, money and men. Common sense prevailed. Now that the Duke had sent away his French contingent the captains could no longer regard him as formidable, and so, informing him of Andrea Doria's demand, they invited him to come to Sinigaglia.

When he received this summons he had already left Cesena and was at Fano. He sent a trusted secretary to tell the captains that he would come to Sinigaglia at once and to request them to await him there. Since the signing of the treaty they had shown no inclination to encounter the Duke in person. Anxious to dispel the mistrust which their neglect indicated, he instructed the secretary to inform them in a friendly manner that the estrangement they persisted in maintaining could only prevent the pact they had agreed on from being effective; and that for his part his one and only desire was to avail himself of their forces and their counsels.

Machiavelli was astounded when he heard that the Duke had accepted the captains' invitation. He had closely studied the treaty and it was evident to him that neither side put the smallest trust in the other. On learning that the captains had asked Il Valentino to join them at Sinigaglia because the commander of the citadel refused to deliver it to one of his officers, he was convinced that they were setting a trap for him. The Duke had dismissed his French men-at-arms and so considerably diminished his strength. The captains had all their men at Sinigaglia or near at hand. It seemed obvious that the commander had made his condition with their connivance, and that when the Duke arrived with his mounted men they would attack him and cut him and them to pieces. It was incredible that he should hazard himself almost defenceless among his mortal enemies. The only explanation was that he trusted in his star and, blinded by arrogance, thought to cow those brutal men by the power of his will and the force of his personality. He knew they were afraid of him, but perhaps he had forgotten that fear may well make brave men out of cowards. True, fortune hitherto had favoured the Duke, but fortune was inconstant. Pride goeth before a fall. Machiavelli chuckled. If the Duke walked into the trap laid for him and were destroyed it would be to the great advantage of Florence. He was the enemy; the captains, held together only by their dread of him, could be separated by skilful manœuvres and disposed of one by one.

Machiavelli chuckled too soon. When the Orsini made the commander of the citadel an offer of money to refuse to deliver it except to the Duke in person he already had the gold the Duke had paid him to do exactly that. He had guessed his captains' design and foreseen what they would do to induce him to come among them. He was a secret man and it was not his habit to discuss his plans till the moment arrived to put them in execution. On the night before leaving Fano he called together eight of his most trusted followers. He told them that when the captains came to meet him one of them was to place himself on each side of each one of them and, as though to do him honour, accompany him till they reached the Palace which had been chosen as his residence. He bade them take care that none of them made his escape. Once in the Palace they would be at his mercy. None of them would leave it alive and free. He had scattered his troops about the country so that none should know how great a force he disposed of, and now he gave orders that they should assemble in the morning at a river about six miles on the way to Sinigaglia. As a sign of good faith he had sent his baggage wagons on ahead of him, and he smiled as he thought how the captains must lick their chops when they contemplated the great booty that awaited them.

All being settled he went to bed and slept soundly. He started betimes in the morning. It was the thirty-first of December, 1502. The distance between Fano and Sinigaglia was fifteen miles and the road ran between the mountains and the sea. The advance guard of fifteen hundred men was headed by Lodovico della Mirandola; then came a number of Gascons and Swiss, a thousand of them; after them the Duke in full armour on a richly-caparisoned charger; and then the rest of his cavalry. Machiavelli was not highly susceptible to æsthetic emotion, but he thought he had never seen a prettier sight than this army winding its slow way between the snow-capped mountains and the blue sea.

The captains were waiting at a point three miles from Sinigaglia.

Vitellozzo Vitelli, till his health was ruined by the French sickness, was a man of powerful physique, big and strong, but spare, even gaunt, with a sallow, clean-shaven face, an aggressive nose and a small, receding chin. His eyelids drooping heavily over his eyes gave them a strange, brooding expression. Ruthless, cruel, rapacious and brave, he was a fine soldier and had the reputation of being the best artilleryman in Europe. He was proud of his possession, Città di Castello, and of the fine palaces, adorned with frescoes, bronzes, marble figures and Flemish tapestries, with which he and his family had enriched it. He had loved his brother Paolo whom the Florentines had beheaded and he hated them for it with a hatred time could not lessen. But owing to the mercury with which the doctors dosed him he suffered from attacks of intolerable depression, and was but a shadow of his old self. When Pagolo Orsini at the time they were negotiating a reconciliation brought Il Valentino's terms to the assembled captains, Gian Paolo Baglioni, Lord of Perugia, would not accept them, and though for a time Vitellozzo, mistrusting the Duke's offers, sided with him, he had not the strength to withstand the nagging arguments of the others and in the end agreed to sign. But he signed against his better judgment. True, he had written humble letters of submission and apology, and Il Valentino in return had assured him that all was forgiven and forgotten; but he was uneasy. His instinct told him that the Duke had neither forgotten nor forgiven. One of the articles of the agreement had been that only one of the captains at a time should be on service in the Duke's camp, and there they were, all of them, gathered together. Pagolo Orsini reasoned with him. He had visited the Duke several times, they had talked together long and often, openly and frankly, as man to man, and it was impossible not to be convinced of his sincerity. What better proof of it could there be than that he had dismissed his French lancers and so could only conduct an enterprise with their assistance? And why had he executed Ramiro de Lorqua if not to show that he was prepared to listen to their demands?

'Believe me, the rebellion has taught the young man a lesson, and there's good reason to believe that in future we shall have no cause to be displeased with him.'

Pagolo Orsini did not, however, think it necessary to tell Vitellozzo of a certain conversation he had had with the Duke. The Pope was seventy, a man of a plethoric condition who lived the life of a man in his prime, and a stroke might kill him at any moment. If Il Valentino could control the votes of the Spanish cardinals and the cardinals his father had created; he was prepared in return for an assurance that his states would be secured to him to ensure the election to the papacy of Pagolo's brother Cardinal Orsini. The prospect was dazzling. Pagolo was the more inclined to trust the Duke, since it seemed certain that he needed the Orsini as much as they needed him. Vitellozzo was the first of the captains to come forward to greet the Duke. He was unarmed, dressed in a shabby black tunic, and over it he wore a black cloak lined with green. He was pale and troubled and you might have thought from the look on his face that he knew the fate in store for him. No one seeing him now would have supposed that this was the man who had once thought on his own resources to drive the King of France out of Italy. He was riding a mule and was about to dismount, but the Duke prevented him, and leaning over put a friendly arm round his shoulder and kissed him on both cheeks. Within a few minutes Pagolo Orsini and the Duke of Gravina rode up with their attendants and Cæsar Borgia received them with the courtesy due to their great birth and the happy cordiality of one who has been too long parted from dear friends. But he noticed the absence of Oliverotto da Fermo, and on asking for him was told that he was awaiting him in the city. He sent Don Michele to fetch the young man and while they waited engaged the captains in desultory conversation. No one could be more charming than he when it was worth his while, and to see him then you would have thought that nothing had ever happened to mar the harmony of his relations with the three commanders. He was gracious, as befitted his station, but without hauteur, so that there was no hint of condescension in his manner. He was composed, urbane and affable. He enquired after Vitellozzo's health and suggested sending his own surgeon to treat him. With an amused smile he gaily chaffed the Duke of Gravina about a love affair in which he was engaged. He listened with flattering interest to Pagolo Orsini's description of the Villa he was building in the Alban hills.

Don Michele found Oliverotto drilling his troops in a square beyond the river outside the city walls. He told him that it would be wise to let his men take possession of their quarters or they would be seized by the Duke's. The advice was good and Oliverotto, thanking him for the sensible suggestion, immediately acted on it. Having given the necessary orders he accompanied Don Michele to the spot where the others were waiting. The Duke welcomed him with the same warm friendliness as he had shown to the others. He would not let him do the homage he was prepared to do; he used him as comrade rather than as a subordinate.

The Duke gave the order to advance.

Vitellozzo was seized with terror. He had seen by now how great was the force that followed the Duke, and knew for a certainty that the plot the captains had made stood no chance of success. He made up his mind to rejoin his own troops, which were camped but a few miles away. His illness offered a convincing excuse. But Pagolo would not let him go. This was no time, he argued, to let the Duke think they were doubtful of his good faith. Vitellozzo was broken in spirit; he lacked the resolution to do what his instinct told him was his only chance to escape. He allowed himself to be persuaded.

'I have a conviction that if I go, I go to my death,' he said, 'but since you are determined to take the chance, whether it be to live or die, I am ready to face fate with you and with the others to whom destiny has linked me.'

The eight men whom the Duke had ordered to escort the captains took up their positions one on either side of each of the doomed men and, headed by their commander, splendid in his shining armour, the cavalcade rode into the city. On reaching the Palace that had been set aside for the Duke's residence the captains wished to take leave of him, but he urged them in his frank and open way to come in so that they might immediately discuss the plan he wished to put before them. He had much to say that could not fail to be of interest to them. Time was important. Whatever they decided to do must be done quickly. They agreed to what he asked. He ushered them through the doorway and up a fine flight of stairs that led to the great reception room. Once there he begged them to excuse him so that he might attend to a call of nature, and no sooner was he gone than armed men burst in and arrested them. Thus he played the same neat and simple trick on them that the graceless Oliverotto had played on his uncle and the chief citizens at Fermo, and it had not even cost him a banquet. Pagolo Orsini protested at the Duke's breach of faith and called for him, but he had already left the Palace. He gave orders that the troops of the four captains should be disarmed. Oliverotto's men, being near at hand, were taken by surprise and those who resisted were butchered, but the others who were encamped at some distance were more fortunate; they got wind of the disaster that had befallen their masters and combining their forces succeeded, though with serious losses, in fighting their way to safety. Cæsar Borgia had to content himself with putting to death the immediate followers of Vitellozzo and the Orsini.

The Duke's soldiers, however, were not satisfied with plundering Oliverotto's men. They set about sacking the city. They would have spared nothing but for the Duke's stern measures; he did not want a ruined city, but a prosperous one from which he could get revenue, and he had the looters hanged. The city was in a turmoil. The shopkeepers had put up their shutters and honest citizens cowered in their houses behind locked doors. Soldiers broke into the wine-shops and forced their owners at the sword's point to give them wine. Men were lying dead in the streets and mongrel dogs lapped their blood.

29

Machiavelli had followed the Duke to Sinigaglia. He spent an anxious day. It was dangerous to go out alone or unarmed and when obliged to leave the wretched inn where he had taken refuge he was careful to be accompanied by Piero and his servants. He had no wish to be killed by excitable Gascons the worse for liquor.

At eight o'clock that night the Duke sent for him. On all other occasions on which Machiavelli had had audience with him it had been in the presence of others, secretaries, churchmen or members of the suite; but on this occasion, to his surprise, the officer who ushered him into the room in which the Duke was seated immediately withdrew, and for the first time they were alone.

The Duke was in high spirits. With his auburn hair and neat beard, his cheeks flushed and his eyes shining, he looked handsomer than Machiavelli had ever seen him. There was assurance in his mien and majesty in his bearing. He might be the bastard of a wicked priest but he bore himself like a king. As usual he came straight to the point.

'Well, I have done your masters a great service in ridding them of their enemies,' he said. 'I desire you now to write to them to collect infantry and send it with their cavalry so that we can march together on Castello or Perugia.'

'Perugia?'

A cheerful smile lit up the Duke's face.

'The Baglioni refused to sign the treaty with the others and he left them saying: "If Cæsar Borgia wants me he

can come and fetch me at Perugia and come armed."
That is what I propose to do.'

Machiavelli thought that it had not done the others
much good to sign the treaty, but contented himself
with smiling.

'To crush Vitellozzo and destroy the Orsini would
have cost the Signory a lot of money and they they
wouldn't have done it half so neatly as I have. I don't
think they should be ungrateful.'

'I'm sure they are not, Excellency.'

The Duke, a smile still on his lips, but his eyes
shrewd, held Machiavelli with a steady gaze.

'Then let them show it. They haven't stirred a finger,
and what I've done is worth a hundred thousand ducats
to them. The obligation is not legal, but tacit, and it
would be well if they started to discharge it.'

Machiavelli very well knew that the Signory would
be outraged at such a demand and he had no wish to be
the transmitter of it. He was glad to have a way out.

'I should tell Your Excellency that I have asked my
government to recall me. I have pointed out to them
that they should have here an envoy of more consequence and with fuller powers than mine. Your Excellency could more profitably discuss this matter with my
successor.'

'You are right. I am tired of your government's temporizing. The time has come for them to make the decision
whether they will be with me or against me. I should
have left here today, but if I had the town would have
been sacked. Andrea Doria is to surrender the citadel
tomorrow morning and then I shall set out for Castello
and Perugia. When I have settled my business there I
shall turn my attention to Siena.'

'Would the King of France consent to your taking
cities that are under his protection?'

'He wouldn't and I'm not so foolish as to think so. I

propose to take them on behalf of the Church. All I want for myself is my own state of Romagna.'

Machiavelli sighed. He was filled with an unwilling admiration for this man whose spirit was so fiery and who was so confident in his power to get whatsoever he wanted.

'No one can doubt that you are favoured by fortune, Excellency,' he said.

'Fortune favours him who knows how to take advantage of his opportunity. Do you suppose it was a happy accident, by which I profited, that the governor of the citadel refused to surrender except to me personally?'

'I wouldn't do Your Excellency that injustice. After what has happened today I can guess that you made it worth his while.'

The Duke laughed.

'I like you, Secretary. You are a man with whom one can talk. I shall miss you.' He paused and for what seemed quite a long time looked searchingly at Machiavelli. 'I could almost wish that you were in my service.'

'Your Excellency is very kind. I am very well content to serve the Republic.'

'What does it profit you? The salary you receive is so miserable that to make both ends meet you have to borrow from your friends.'

This gave Machiavelli something of a turn, but then he remembered that the Duke must know of the twenty-five ducats Bartolomeo had lent him.

'I am careless of money and of an extravagant disposition,' he answered with a pleasant smile. 'It is my own fault if from time to time I live beyond my means.'

'You would find it hard to do that if you were employed by me. It is very pleasant to be able to give a pretty lady a ring, a bracelet or a brooch when one wishes to obtain her favours.'

'I have made it my rule to satisfy my desires with women of easy virtue and modest pretensions.'

'A good rule enough if one's desires were under one's control, but who can tell what strange tricks love can play on him? Have you never discovered, Secretary, to what expense one is put when one loves a virtuous woman?'

The Duke was looking at him with mocking eyes and for an instant Machiavelli asked himself uneasily whether it was possible that he knew of his unsatisfied passion for Aurelia, but the thought had no sooner come into his mind than he rejected it. The Duke had more important things to occupy him than the Florentine envoy's love affairs.

'I am willing to take it for granted and leave both the pleasure and the expense to others.'

The Duke gazed at him thoughtfully. You might have imagined that he was asking himself what kind of a man this was, but with no ulterior motive, from idle curiosity rather. So when you find yourself alone with a stranger in the waiting-room of an office, to pass the time you try from the look of him to guess his business, his calling, his habits and his character.

'I should have thought you were too intelligent a man to be content to remain for the rest of your life in a subordinate position,' said the Duke.

'I have learnt from Aristotle that it is the better part of wisdom to cultivate the golden mean.'

'Is it possible that you are devoid of ambition?'

'Far from it, Excellency,' smiled Machiavelli. 'My ambition is to serve my state to the best of my ability.'

'That is just what you will not be allowed to do. You know better than anyone that in a republic talent is suspect. A man attains high office because his mediocrity prevents him from being a menace to his associates. That is why a democracy is ruled, not by the men who are most competent to rule it, but by the men whose insignificance can excite nobody's apprehension. Do you know what are the cankers that eat the heart of a democracy?'

He looked at Machiavelli as though waiting for an answer, but Machiavelli said nothing.

'Envy and fear. The petty men in office are envious of their colleagues, and rather than that one of them should gain reputation will prevent him from taking a measure on which may depend the safety and prosperity of the state; and they are fearful because they know that all about them are others who will stop at neither lies nor trickery to step into their shoes. And what is the result? The result is that they are more afraid of doing wrong than zealous to do right. They say that dog doesn't bite dog: whoever invented that proverb never lived under a democratic government.'

Machiavelli remained silent. He knew only too well how much truth there was in what the Duke said. He remembered how hotly the election to his own subordinate post had been contested and with what bitterness his defeated rivals had taken it. He knew that he had colleagues who were watching his every step ready to pounce upon any slip he made that might induce the Signory to dismiss him. The Duke continued.

'A prince in my position is free to choose men to serve him for their ability. He need not give a post to a man who is incapable of filling it because he needs his influence or because he has a party behind him whose services must be recognized. He fears no rival because he is above rivalry, and so instead of favouring mediocrity, which is the curse and bane of democracy, seeks out talent, energy, initiative and intelligence. No wonder things go from bad to worse in your republic; the last reason for which anyone gets office is his fitness for it.'

Machiavelli smiled thinly.

'Your Excellency will permit me to remind him that the favour of princes is notoriously uncertain. They can exalt a man to great heights, but they can also cast him down to the depths.'

The Duke gave a chuckle of frank amusement.

'You are thinking of Ramiro de Lorqua. A prince must know both how to reward and how to punish. His generosity must be profuse and his justice severe. Ramiro committed abominable crimes; he deserved to die. What would have happened to him in Florence? There would have been people whom his death would have offended; there would have been people to intercede for him because they had profited by his misdeeds; the Signory would have hesitated and in the end have sent him on an embassy to the King of France or to me.'

Machiavelli laughed.

'Believe me, Your Excellency, the ambassador they propose to send to you now is of unimpeachable respectability.'

'He will probably bore me to death. There is no doubt about it, I shall miss you, Secretary.' Then, as if the idea had suddenly occurred to him, he gave Machiavelli a warm smile. 'Why don't you enter my service? I will find work for you to do that will give scope to your quick mind and wide experience, and you won't find me ungenerous.'

'What confidence could you place in a man who had betrayed his country for money?'

'I do not ask you to betray your country. By serving me you could serve it to better advantage than you will ever be able to do as secretary of the Second Chancery. Other Florentines have entered my service and I don't know that they have regretted it.'

'Adherents of the Medici who fled when their lords were driven out and were prepared to do anything that gave them a means of livelihood.'

'Not only. Leonardo and Michelangelo were not too proud to accept my offers.'

'Artists. They will go wherever there is a patron to

give them a commission; they are not responsible people.'

There was still a smile in the eyes that steadily held Machiavelli's when the Duke answered.

'I have an estate in the immediate neighbourhood of Imola. It has vineyards, arable land, pasture and woods. I should be happy to give it to you. It would bring you in ten times as much as the few beggarly acres you own at San Casciano.'

Imola? Why had Cæsar thought of that city rather than another? Once more the suspicion crossed Machiavelli's mind that he knew of his fruitless pursuit of Aurelia.

'Those beggarly acres at San Casciano have belonged to my family for three hundred years,' he said acidly. 'What should I do with an estate at Imola?'

'The villa is new, handsome and well built. It would be an agreeable retreat from the city in the heat of summer.'

'You speak in riddles, Excellency.'

'I am sending Agapito to Urbino as its governor. I know no one more competent than you take his place as my chief secretary, but I can see that it would make negotiations with the ambassador Florence is sending to replace you somewhat embarrassing. I am prepared to appoint you governor of Imola.'

It seemed to Machiavelli that his heart on a sudden stopped beating. It was a position of importance and one to which he had never dreamt of aspiring. There were cities that had come into the possession of Florence, either by capture or by treaty, but the men sent to govern them were of great family and with powerful connections. If he were governor of Imola Aurelia would be proud to be his mistress, and by the same token he could easily find pretexts to rid himself of Bartolomeo whenever it suited him. It was almost impossible that the Duke should make this offer without being aware of the circumstances. But how could he be aware of them? Machiavelli felt in himself a certain complacency as he noticed that the double prospect did not for a moment affect him.

'I love my native land more than my soul, Excellency.'

Il Valentino was unused to being crossed and Machiavelli thought it certain that on this he would dismiss him with an angry gesture. To his surprise, the Duke, playing idly with his order of St. Michael, continued to look at him reflectively. It seemed a long time before he spoke.

'I have always been frank with you, Secretary,' he said at last. 'I know you are a man not easy to deceive and I would not waste my time in trying. I will put my cards on the table. I do not ask you for secrecy if I divulge my plans to you; you will not betray my confidence because no one would believe that I gave it to you. The Signory would think you were trying to make yourself important by giving out your guesses as matters of fact.'

The Duke paused for a moment only.

'My hold on Romagna and Urbino is secure. In a little while I shall have control of Castello, Perugia and Siena. Pisa is mine for the asking. Lucca will surrender at my bidding. What will be the position of Florence when it is surrounded by states in my possession or under my authority?'

'Dangerous without doubt, except for our treaty with France.'

Machiavelli's reply seemed to amuse the Duke.

'A treaty is an arrangement two states make to their common advantage, and a prudent government will disavow it whenever its provisions are no longer advantageous. What do you think the French King would say if in return for his connivance while I seized Florence I offered to join my forces with his to attack Venice?'

Machiavelli shivered. He knew only too well that Louis XII would never hesitate to sacrifice his honour to his interest. He took some time to answer and when he did he spoke with deliberation.

'It would be a mistake on Your Excellency's part to suppose that Florence could be taken at small cost. We should fight to the death to preserve our liberty.'

'What with? Your citizens have been too busy making money to be willing to train themselves to defend their country. You have hired mercenaries to fight for you so that you shouldn't be disturbed in your avocations. Folly! Hireling soldiers do not go to war for any reason other than a little money. That is not enough to make them die for you. A country is doomed to destruction if it cannot defend itself and the only way it can do that is to create out of its own citizens a trained, well-disciplined and well-equipped army. But are you Florentines prepared to make the sacrifices this entails? I don't believe it. You are governed by business men, and a business man's only idea is to make a deal at any price. Short profits and quick returns, peace in our time even at the cost of humiliation and the risk of disaster. Your Livy has taught you that the safety of a republic depends on the integrity of the individuals that compose it. Your people are soft. Your state is corrupt and deserves to perish.'

Machiavelli's face grew sullen. He had no answer to make. The Duke drove his point home.

'Now that Spain is united and France, rid of the English, is strong, the time is past when small states could maintain their independence. Their independence is a sham, for it is not based on force, and they maintain it only so long as it suits the convenience of the great powers. The states of the Church are under my control; Bologna will fall into my hands; Florence is doomed. I shall then be master of all the country from the Kingdom of Naples in the south to the Milanese and Venetia in the north. I shall have my own artillery and the artillery of the Vitelli. I shall create an army as efficient as my army of Romagna. The King of France and I will divide among ourselves the possessions of Venice.'

'But should all this happen as you desire, Excellency,' said Machiavelli, grimly, 'all you will have achieved will be to increase the power of France and arouse the fear and envy both of France and Spain. Either of them could crush you.'

'True. But with my arms and my gold I should be so powerful an ally that the party I sided with would be certain of victory.'

'You would still remain the vassal of the victor.'

'Tell me, Secretary, you have been in France and have had dealings with the French. What is your opinion of them?'

Machiavelli shrugged a somewhat disdainful shoulder.

'They're frivolous and unreliable. When an enemy resists the ferocity of their first attack they waver and lose courage. They can stand neither hardship nor discomfort and after a little while grow so careless that it's easy to take advantage of their unpreparedness.'

'I know. When winter comes with cold and rain they slink of out of camp one by one and then they're at the mercy of a more sturdy foe.'

'On the other hand the country is rich and fertile. The King has broken the strength of the barons and is very powerful. He's somewhat foolish, but well advised by men as clever as any in Italy.'

The Duke nodded.

'And now tell me what you think of the Spaniards.'

'I have had little to do with them.'

'Then I will tell you. They're brave, hardy, resolute and poor. They have nothing to lose and everything to gain. It would be impossible to withstand them but for one circumstance: they have to bring their troops and armaments across the sea. If they were once driven out of Italy it shouldn't be difficult to prevent them from coming back.'

Silence fell upon them. Il Valentino, his chin resting on his hand, appeared to be sunk in thought, and Machiavelli watched him at his ease. His eyes were hard and brilliant. They looked into a future of tortuous diplomacy and of bloody battles. Excited as he was by the events of the day and the amazing success of his duplicity, no enterprise seemed too difficult or too dangerous for him to undertake, and who could tell what visions of greatness and glory dazzled his bold imagination? He smiled.

'With my help the French could drive the Spaniards out of Naples and Sicily: with my help the Spaniards could drive the French out of the Milanese.'

'Whichever you helped would remain the master of Italy and you, Excellency.'

'If I helped the Spaniards, yes; not if I helped the French. We drove them out of Italy before; we can drive them out again.'

'They will bide their time and return.'

'I shall be ready for them. The old fox, King Ferdinand, is not one to cry over spilt milk; if they attack me he will seize the opportunity of revenge and march his armies into France. He married his daughter to the son of the King of England. The English will not miss the chance to declare war on their hereditary enemies. The French will have more reasons to fear me than I to fear them.'

'But the Pope is old, Excellency; his death will deprive you of half your force and great part of your reputation.'

'Do you suppose I haven't taken that into consideration? I've provided for everything that may happen when my father dies. I am prepared for it and the next Pope will be of my choosing. He will be protected by my troops. No, I do not fear the Pope's death. It will not interfere with my plans.'

Suddenly the Duke sprang out of his chair and began to pace the room.

'It is the Church that has kept this country divided. She has never been strong enough to bring all Italy under her rule, but only to prevent anyone else from doing so. Italy cannot prosper till it is united.'

'It is true that if our poor country has become the prey of the barbarians it is because it has been ruled by this multitude of lords and princes.'

Il Valentino stopped walking and, his sensual lips curling with a sardonic smile, looked into Machiavelli's eyes.

'For the remedy we must turn to the Gospel, my good Secretary, which tells us to render unto Cæsar the things that are Cæsar's and unto God the things that are God's.'

The Duke's meaning was plain. Machiavelli gave a gasp of fearful amazement. He was strangely fascinated by this man who could calmly speak of taking a step which must arouse the horror of all Christendom.

'A prince should support the spiritual authority of the Church,' he went on coolly, 'for this will keep his people good and happy, and I cannot think of a better way to restore to the Church the spiritual authority she has so unfortunately lost than to deprive her of the burden of temporal power.'

Machiavelli was at a loss to know how to answer a remark in which there was so brutal a cynicism, but he was saved from the necessity of doing so by a scratching at the door.

'Who is it?' cried the Duke with sudden anger at the interruption.

There was no answer, but the door was flung open and a man entered whom Machiavelli recognized as Don Michele, the Spaniard known as Michelotto. It was he, they said, who had strangled with his own hands the handsome and unfortunate boy, Alfonso of Bisceglie, whom Lucrezia loved. Michelotto was a big, hairy man of powerful build, with bushy eyebrows, hard eyes, a short blunt nose, and an expression of cold ferocity.

'Ah, it's you,' cried the Duke, his look changing. '*Murieron*.'

Machiavelli knew little Spanish, but he could not fail to understand that one grim word. *They died*. The man had remained at the door and the Duke went over to him. They spoke in an undertone and in Spanish, and Machiavelli could not hear what they said. The Duke asked one or two abrupt questions and the other seemed to answer in detail.

Il Valentino gave that curious light, gay laugh of his which meant that he was pleased as well as amused. After a little Don Michele went and the Duke, a happy smile in his eyes, resumed his seat.

'Vitellozzo and Oliverotto are dead. They died less valiantly than they lived. Oliverotto cried for mercy. He put the blame for his treachery on Vitellozzo and said that he had been led astray.'

'And Pagolo Orsini and the Duke of Gravina?'

'I am taking them with me tomorrow under guard. I shall hold them until I hear from His Holiness the Pope.'

Machiavelli gave him a questioning glance and the Duke answered it.

'As soon as I had arrested the rascals I sent a messenger to the Pope to ask him to seize the person of the Cardinal Orsini. Pagolo and his nephew must await the punishment of their crimes till I am assured that this has been done.'

The Borgia's face grew sombre and it was as though a heavy cloud lurked between his eyebrows. There was a silence and Machiavelli, supposing the audience was at an end, rose to his feet. But the Duke with a sudden gesture of impatience motioned him to sit still. When he spoke it was in a low voice, but in accents that were hard, angry and resolute.

'It is not enough to destroy these petty tyrants whose subjects groan under their misrule. We are the prey of the barbarians; Lombardy is plundered, Tuscany and

Naples are laid under tribute. I alone can crush these horrible and inhuman beasts. I alone can free Italy.'

'God knows, Italy prays for the liberator who will deliver her from bondage.'

'The time is ripe and the enterprise will bring glory to those who take part in it and good to the mass of the people of the land.' He turned his bright-eyed, frowning gaze on Machiavelli as though by its force he thought to bend him to his will. 'How can you hold back? Surely there is not an Italian who will refuse to follow me.'

Machiavelli stared gravely at Cæsar Borgia. He sighed deeply.

'The greatest wish of my heart is to free Italy from these barbarians who overrun and despoil us, lay waste our territories, rape our women and rob our citizens. It may be that you are the man chosen by God to redeem our country. The price you ask me to pay is to join with you in destroying the liberty of the city that gave me birth.'

'With or without you Florence will lose her liberty.'

'Then I will go down to destruction with her.'

The Duke gave his shoulders a displeased, peevish shrug.

'Spoken like an ancient Roman, but not like a man of sense.'

With a haughty wave of the hand he indicated that the audience was terminated. Machiavelli got up, bowed and uttered the usual expressions of respect. He was at the door when the Duke's voice stopped him. And now, clever actor that he was, he changed his tone to one of affable friendliness.

'Before you go, Secretary, I should like you to give me the benefit of your advice. At Imola you became friendly with Bartolomeo Martelli. He's done one or two odd jobs for me not too badly. I need a man to go to Montpellier to conduct negotiations with the wool merchants, and it would be convenient if he went on to Paris to do various things for me there. From your knowledge of Bartolomeo, do you think I should be wise to send him?'

He spoke casually as though there were nothing more in the enquiry than the words signified, but Machiavelli understood what was at the back of them. The Duke was offering to dispatch Bartolomeo on a journey that would take him away from Imola for a considerable period, and now there could be no doubt that he knew of Machiavelli's desire for Aurelia. Machiavelli's lips tightened, but otherwise his face betrayed nothing.

'Since Your Excellency is good enough to ask my opinion I should say that Bartolomeo is so useful to you in keeping the people of Imola contented with your rule that it would be a grave mistake to send him away.'

'Perhaps you are right. He shall stay.'

Machiavelli bowed once more and left.

30

Piero and the servants were waiting for him. The streets were dark and empty. Dead men, most of them stripped to the bone, still lay about, and from a gallows in the main square looters hung as a warning to others. They walked to the inn. The heavy doors were locked and barred, but on their knocking they were examined through the judas and let in. The night was bitter cold and Machiavelli was glad to warm himself at the kitchen fire. Some men were drinking, some were playing dice or cards; others were asleep on benches or on the floor. The landlord put down a mattress for Machiavelli and Piero in his room at the foot of the great bed in which his wife and children were already asleep. They lay down side by side, wrapped in their cloaks, and Piero, tired after the morning's ride from Fano, the exciting events of the day and the long wait at the Palace, fell asleep instantly; but Machiavelli stayed wide awake. He had much to occupy his thoughts.

It was obvious that Il Valentino knew of his abortive intrigue with Aurelia, and Machiavelli smiled with bitter irony over the mistake that man of tortuous mind had made in thinking that he could use the passion he supposed him to feel to seduce him from the service of the Republic. Machiavelli would have credited him with more intelligence than to imagine that a man of sense could be so besotted with desire for a woman as to allow it to interfere with the serious business of life. Women were a-plenty. Why, when the Duke had kidnapped Dorotea Caracciolo, wife of the captain of the Venetian infantry, and Venice had sent envoys to demand her return, he had asked them whether they thought he found the women of Romagna so unapproachable that he was compelled to abduct transient females. Except to say goodbye to her Machiavelli had not seen Aurelia for several weeks, and if he wanted her now it was because he did not like to be thwarted rather than because his passion was still at fever heat. He knew that, and it would have seemed absurd to him to yield to such a petty emotion. But he was curious to know how the Duke had discovered his secret. Certainly not through Piero; he had tried him and found him true. Serafina? He had been very careful and there was no possibility that she had an inkling of what had gone on. Monna Caterina and Aurelia were too deeply implicated in the plot to have betrayed him. Nina? No, they had taken care of her. On a sudden Machiavelli slapped his forehead. Fool that he was! It was plain as the nose on his face and he could have kicked himself for not having guessed at once. Fra Timoteo! He must be in the Duke's pay; with his close association with Serafina and with Bartolomeo's household he was in a position to spy on the Florentine envoy's movements: and by him the Duke must have known all he did, who came to visit him, when he sent letters to Florence, and when the answers arrived. It gave Machiavelli a peculiar sense of discomfort to realize that he had been under surveillance. But this guess made everything clear. It was no coincidence that on the night when Bartolomeo was safely praying before the bones of San Vitale Il Valentino should have sent for him at the very hour appointed for him to knock at Aurelia's door. Fra Timoteo knew the arrangements and had passed the information on. Rage seized Machiavelli and he would gladly have wrung the sleek monk's neck. Cæsar Borgia, judging Machiavelli by himself, thought the disappointment would exacerbate his passion and so make him more malleable to his own designs. That was why Fra Timoteo had refused to help him further. It was certainly he who had persuaded Aurelia that Providence had prevented her from committing a sin and so she must refrain from it.

'I wonder how much he got besides my twenty-five ducats,' Machiavelli muttered, forgetting that he had borrowed them from Bartolomeo and Bartolomeo had got them from the Duke.

But for all that he could not but feel a certain complacency at the thought that the Duke was prepared to take so much trouble to inveigle him into his service. It was far from disagreeable to realize that he set so high a value on him. In Florence the Signory thought him an amusing fellow and his letters often made them laugh, but they had no great confidence in his judgment and never followed his advice.

'A prophet is not without honour save in his own country,' he sighed.

He knew that he had more brains in his little finger than all the rest of them put together. Piero Soderino, the head of the government, was a weak, shallow, amiable man, and it might have been of him that the Duke was thinking when he spoke of those who were more afraid of doing wrong than zealous to do right. The others, his immediate councillors, were timid, mediocre and irresolute. Their policy was to hesitate, to shilly-shally, to temporize. Machiavelli's immediate superior, the Secretary of the Republic, was Marcello Virgilio. He owed his position to his handsome presence and his gift for oratory. Machiavelli was attached to him, but had no great opinion of his ability. How it would surprise those silly fellows to hear that the agent whom they had sent to Il Valentino just because he was of small consequence had been appointed governor of Imola and was the most trusted of the Duke's advisers! Machiavelli hadn't the least intention of accepting the Duke's offers, but it amused him to play with the idea and imagine the consternation of the Signory and the wrath of his enemies.

And Imola would be merely a step. If Cæsar Borgia became King of Italy he might well become his first minister and occupy the same position as the Cardinal d'Amboise enjoyed with the King of France. Was it possible that in the Borgia Italy had found her redeemer? Even though it was personal ambition that spurred him on his purpose was lofty and worthy of his great spirit. He was wise and vigorous. He had made himself loved and feared by the people; he commanded the respect and confidence of the troops. Italy was enslaved and insulted, but surely her ancient valour was not dead. United under a strong ruler her people would enjoy the security they longed for to pursue their avocations and live in prosperity and happiness. What greater opportunity for glory could any man want than to give that suffering land the blessing of lasting peace?

But suddenly a notion struck Machiavelli with such force that he started violently, so that Piero, asleep by his side, was disturbed and made a restless movement. It had occurred to him that the whole thing might be nothing more than a practical joke that the Duke had played on him. He knew well enough that Il Valentino, notwithstanding his pretence of cordiality, was displeased with him because he felt that he had not exerted himself as much as he might have to persuade the Signory to grant the *condotta* which would enhance his prestige and augment his resources. This might be his revenge, and Machiavelli felt his whole body prickle as he thought that all that time at Imola the Duke and Agapito and the rest had watched his ingenious moves and guffawed as they devised ways to frustrate them. He tried to persuade himself that this was only an idle fancy which had better be quickly forgotten; but he couldn't be sure, and the uncertainty tortured him. He spent a very troubled night.

31

Next morning the Duke, leaving a small force to garrison the town, set out with his army on the first lap to Perugia.

It was New Year's Day.

The weather was bad, and the roads, poor at the best of times, were converted by the tramping horses, the baggage wagons and the marching soldiers into a slush of mud. The army halted at small towns in which there were no means of accommodation for so great a mass of men and those were lucky who found the shelter of a roof. Machiavelli liked his comfort. It affected his temper to sleep on the bare earth in a peasant's hut cheek by jowl with as many as could find room in which to stretch their weary limbs. One had to eat what food there was, and Machiavelli, with his poor digestion, suffered miserably. At Sasso Ferrato news came that the surviving Vitelli had fled to Perugia, and at Gualdo citizens of Castello were waiting to offer the Duke the town and its territories. Then a messenger arrived to announce that Gian Paolo Baglioni, with the Orsini, the Vitelli and their men-at-arms, abandoning hope of defending Perugia, had fled to Siena, whereupon the people had risen and next day ambassadors came to surrender it. Thus the Duke gained possession of two important towns without striking a blow. He went on to Assisi. There envoys from Siena came to ask what reason he had for attacking their city as according to common report was his intention. The Duke told them that he was filled with amicable sentiments towards it but that he was determined to expel Pandolfo Petrucci, their lord and his enemy, and that if they would do this themselves they had nothing to fear from him; but if not he would come with his army and do it himself. He set out for Siena, but by a circuitous route so that the citizens might have time to reflect, and on the way captured various castles and villages. The soldiery plundered the country. The inhabitants had fled before them, but when they found any that had stayed behind, old men or old women too infirm to leave, they hung them up by their arms and lit fires under their feet so that they might tell where valuables had been hidden. When they would not, or could not because they didn't know, they died under the torture.

Meanwhile good news arrived from Rome. On receipt of his son's letter telling him what had occurred at Sinigaglia, His Holiness sent a message to Cardinal Orsini not, naturally enough, to inform him of what had happened to his friends and kinsmen, but to impart the glad tidings that the citadel had surrendered; and next day, as in duty bound, the Cardinal went to the Vatican to offer the Pope his congratulations. He was accompanied by relations and retainers. He was conducted to an antechamber and there together with the other members of his family put under arrest. It was safe then for the Duke to dispose of his captives, and Michelotto strangled Pagolo Orsini, the fool who had been taken in by the Duke's smooth words, and his nephew the Duke of Gravina. The Cardinal was imprisoned in the Castle of San Angelo where after no long time he very obligingly died. The Pope and his son might congratulate themselves on having crippled the strength of the family that had been for so long a thorn in the flesh of the Vicars of Christ. It was indeed a cause for rejoicing that in disposing of their personal enemies they had done an important service to the Church. They proved thus that it was in point of fact possible to serve God and Mammon.

32

When the Duke arrived at a place called Città della Piave Machiavelli was relieved to learn that his successor was on the point of leaving Florence. Città della Piave was a town of some note, with a castle and a cathedral, and he had the luck to find a decent dwelling-place. The Duke proposed to stay there briefly to rest his troops, and by the time he set forth again Machiavelli hoped that Giacomo Salviati, the new ambassador, would have come. The long journeys on horseback had tired him, the bad food upset his stomach, and he had got little sleep in the wretched lodgings which at the day's end he had been obliged to put up with.

After two or three days it happened that one afternoon he lay on his bed to rest his way-worn limbs, but uneasily, for he was not a little troubled in mind. Though he had written almost daily to the Signory to tell them what it behoved them to know, he had hesitated to inform them of the more important parts of his conversation with the Duke at Sinigaglia. The Duke had offered him wealth and power; the opportunity was prodigious, and it might well occur to the Signory that since he occupied already as important a position as he could ever aspire to he might find the temptation irresistible. They were small men with the low suspiciousness of pettifogging attorneys. They would ask themselves what there was between them to make Il Valentino think him susceptible to such advances. It would be a black mark against him. He would be a man whom perhaps it was wise not to trust too much and it would not be difficult to find a plausible reason for his dismissal. Why, Machiavelli asked himself, should they suppose he would put the interests of Florence above his own when it was just because they did not do that that they were jeopardizing her safety? It seemed prudent to keep silence, and yet if somehow the Signory got wind of the Duke's proposals his very silence would condemn him. The situation was awkward. His reflections, however, were rudely interrupted by a booming voice asking the woman of the house whether Messer Niccolo Machiavelli lived there.

'Messer Bartolomeo,' cried Piero, who had been sitting at the window reading one of his master's books.

'What the devil does he want?' asked Machiavelli irritably, as he got up.

In a moment the burly fellow burst into the room. He flung his arms round Machiavelli and kissed him on both cheeks.

'It's been the very deuce to find you. I've been to house after house.'

Machiavelli disengaged himself.

'How is it you're here?'

Bartolomeo greeted his young cousin after the same exuberant fashion and answered:

'The Duke sent for me in connection with some business at Imola. I had to pass through Florence and I came with some of your ambassador's servants. He'll be here tomorrow. Niccolo, Niccolo, my dear friend, you have saved my life.'

He once more seized Machiavelli in his arms and again kissed him on both cheeks. Machiavelli once more extricated himself from this embrace.

'I am delighted to see you, Bartolomeo,' he began, somewhat frigidly.

But the merchant interrupted him.

'A miracle, a miracle, and I have you to thank for it. Aurelia is pregnant.'

'What!'

'In seven months, my dear Niccolo, I shall be the father of a bouncing boy, and I owe it to you.'

If things had gone differently Machiavelli might have been embarrassed by this remark, but as it was he was stupefied.

'Calm yourself, Bartolomeo, and tell me what you mean,' said he crossly. 'How do you owe it to me?'

'How can I be calm when the dearest wish of my heart has been gratified? Now I can go to my grave in peace. Now I can leave my honours and my possessions to the issue of my own loins. Costanza, my sister, is beside herself with rage.'

He burst into a great bellow of laughter. Machiavelli gave Piero a puzzled look; he could make neither head nor tail of it; and he saw that Piero was as surprised as he.

'Of course I owe it to you; I should never have gone to Ravenna and spent that cold night praying before the altar of San Vitale but for you. True, it was Fra Timoteo's idea, but I didn't trust him; he'd sent us on pilgrimages to the shrine of one saint after the other and nothing had come of it. Fra Timoteo is a good and saintly man, but with priests you have to be on your guard; you can never be quite sure that they haven't some ulterior motive in their advice. I don't blame them, they are faithful sons of our Holy Church; but I should have hesitated to go if you hadn't told me about Messer Giuliano degli Albertelli. I could trust you, you had only my welfare at heart, you are my friend. I said to myself that what had happened to one of the most notable citizens of Florence might just as well happen to one who is not the least notable citizen of Imola. Aurelia conceived on the night of my return from Ravenna.'

His excitement and his flow of speech had brought him out into a profuse sweat and he wiped his glistening forehead with his sleeve. Machiavelli stared at him with perplexity, distaste and vexation.

'Are you quite sure that Monna Aurelia is in this condition?' he said acidly. 'Women are inclined to make mistakes on these matters.'

'Sure, as sure as I am of the articles of our faith. We had our suspicions before you left Imola, I wanted to tell you then, but Monna Caterina and Aurelia begged me not to. "Let us say nothing," they said, "until we are certain." Did you not notice how poorly she looked when I took you to say good-bye to her? She was angry with me afterwards; she said she couldn't bear you to see her looking so hideous; she was afraid you'd suspect and she didn't want anyone to know until all doubt was removed. I reasoned with her, but you know what women's fancies are when they're with child.'

'I suspected nothing,' said Machiavelli. 'It's true that I have only been married a few months and my experience in these things is limited.'

'I wanted you to be the first person to know, since except for you I should never have been the happy father I now shall be.'

He gave every indication of being about to clasp Machiavelli in his arms again, but Machiavelli warded him off.

'I congratulate you with all my heart, but if my ambassador is arriving tomorrow I have no time to waste; the information should be conveyed to the Duke at once.'

'I will leave you, but you must sup with me tonight, you and Piero, to celebrate the occasion in style.'

'It would be hard to do that here,' said he ill-temperedly. 'There is scarcely anything to eat and the wine if there is any will be as bad as it has been all along the way.'

'I had thought of that,' said Bartolomeo, with a bellow of laughter, rubbing his fat hands together, 'and I brought wine with me from Florence, a hare and a sucking pig. We will feast and drink to the health of my first-born son.'

Though he was by now thoroughly out of humour, Machiavelli had fared too badly since leaving Imola to be able to resist the offer of a tolerable meal, and so with what amiability he could muster accepted.

'I will call for you here,' said Bartolomeo, 'but before I go I want you to give me some advice. Of course you remember that I promised Fra Timoteo that I would give a picture to be placed over the altar of our miraculous Virgin, and though I know I owe my good fortune to San Vitale I don't want to put an affront on her. She undoubtedly did her best. So I have decided to have a picture painted of Our Lady seated on a rich throne with her Blessed Son in her arms and with me and Aurelia kneeling on each side with our hands clasped like this.' He put his great paws together and raised his eyes to the ceiling with an appropriate expression of devotion. 'I shall have San Vitale standing on one side of the throne, and Fra Timoteo has suggested that on the other, since the church is dedicated to him, I should have St. Francis. Do you like the idea?'

'Very choice,' said Machiavelli.

'You're a Florentine and must know about such things: tell me to whom I should give the order.'

'I really don't know. They're a very unreliable, dissipated lot, these painters, and I've never had any truck with them.'

'I don't blame you. But surely you can suggest someone.'

Machiavelli shrugged his shoulders.

'When I was in Urbino last summer they talked to me

about a young fellow, a pupil of Perugino, who they say already paints better than his master and who they expect will go far.'

'What is his name?'

'I have no idea. They told me, but it meant nothing to me and it went in at one ear and out of the other. But I dare say I could find out and I don't suppose he'd be expensive.'

'Expense is no object,' said Bartolomeo with a grandiose wave of the arm. 'I'm a business man and I know that if you want the best you must pay for it. And only the best is good enough for me. I want a big name and if I have to pay for it I'll pay for it.'

'Oh, well, when I get back to Florence I'll make enquiries,' Machiavelli answered impatiently.

When he had gone Machiavelli sat down on the edge of the bed and stared at Piero with a look of complete bewilderment.

'Did you ever hear the like?' he said. 'The man is sterile.'

'It is evidently a miracle,' said Piero.

'Don't talk such nonsense. We are bound to believe that miracles were performed by our Blessed Lord and by His apostles, and our Holy Church has accepted the authenticity of miracles performed by its saints, but the time of miracles is past, and in any case why in the name of heaven should San Vitale go out of his way to do one for a fat stupid fool like Bartolomeo?'

But even as he spoke he remembered that Fra Timoteo had said something to him to the effect that even though San Vitale's singular power was an invention of Machiavelli's, Bartolomeo's absolute belief in it might effect the miracle he expected. Was it possible? At the time he had thought it only a hypocritical excuse on the man's part to avoid giving him more assistance till he received more money.

Piero opened his mouth to speak.

'Hold your tongue,' said Machiavelli. 'I'm thinking.'

He would never have described himself as a good Catholic. He had indeed often permitted himself to wish that the gods of Olympus still dwelt in their old abode. Christianity had shown men the truth and the way of salvation, but it asked men to suffer rather than to do. It had made the world feeble and given it over a helpless prey to the wicked, since the generality, in order to go to Heaven, thought more of enduring injuries than of defending themselves against them. It had taught that the highest good consisted in humility, lowliness, and contempt for the things of this world; the religion of the ancients taught that it consisted in greatness of spirit, courage, and strength.

But this was a strange thing that had happened. It shook him. Though his reason revolted he was aware within himself of an uneasy inclination to believe in the possibility of a supernatural intervention. His head refused to accept it, but in his bones, in his blood, in his nerves there was a doubt that he could not still. It was as though all those generations behind him that had believed took possession of his soul and forced their will upon him.

'My grandfather suffered from his stomach too,' he said suddenly.

Piero had no notion what he was talking about. Machiavelli sighed.

'It may be that if men have grown soft it is because in their worthlessness they have interpreted our religion according to their sloth. They have forgotten that it enjoins upon us to love and honour our native land, and to prepare ourselves to be such that we can defend her.'

He burst out laughing when he saw the blankness of Piero's face.

'Never mind, my boy, pay no attention to my nonsense. I will get myself ready to announce to the Duke the arrival tomorrow of the ambassador, and in any case we'll get a good supper out of that old fool.'

33

They got it. Under the influence of the first decent meal he had eaten since leaving Imola and the good Chianti Bartolomeo had brought from Florence, Machiavelli expanded. He made indecent jokes, he told obscene stories, he was lightly ribald, grossly coarse and gaily lewd. He made Bartolomeo laugh so much that his sides ached. All three of them got a little drunk.

The events at Sinigaglia had caused a stir in Italy and a multitude of imaginative Italians had related the story in their different ways. Bartolomeo was eager to hear the facts from an eye-witness, and Machiavelli, pleasantly mellow, was very willing to oblige him. He had written his account three or four times to the Signory, in part because of its importance and in part because at least one of his letters had not reached its destination. He had reflected upon the various incidents, he had had the opportunity to gather details from one or the other of those close to Il Valentino, and he had by now got to the bottom of much that at the time had puzzled him.

He made a thrilling story of it.

'When Vitellozzo left Città di Castello for Sinigaglia he bade farewell to his family and friends as though he knew it was for the last time. To his friends he left the charge of his house and its fortunes and he admonished his nephews to remember the virtues of their ancestors.'

'If he knew the danger he was running why did he leave the safety of his walled town?' asked Bartolomeo.

'How can man escape his destiny? We think to bend men to our will, we think to mould events to our purpose, we strive, we toil and sweat, but in the end we are nought but the playthings of fate. When the captains had been arrested and Pagolo Orsini was complaining of the Duke's perfidy, the only reproach that Vitellozzo made him was this: "You see how wrong you were and in what a plight my friends and I have been placed by your folly." '

'He was a scoundrel and he deserved to die,' said Bartolomeo. 'I sold him some horses once and he never paid me for them. When I demanded the money he told me to come to Città di Castello and get it. I preferred to pocket my loss.'

'You were wise.'

Machiavelli asked himself what had been the thoughts of that ruthless man, old, tired and sick, during the hours that passed between the time of his arrest and the time when tied to a chair, back to back with Oliverotto, Michelotto's cruel hands had wrung the life out of him. Michelotto was a pleasant fellow to meet, he would drink a bottle of wine with you and crack a lewd joke, play strange Spanish tunes on a guitar and by the hour sing wild, sad songs of his country. It was hard then to believe that he was the murderous brute you knew him to be. What fearful satisfaction did he get out of doing his foul work with his own hands? Machiavelli smiled as he thought that one of these days the Duke, having finished with him, would have him killed with no more compunction than when he had killed his trusted and loyal lieutenant Ramiro de Lorqua.

'A strange man,' he muttered, 'perhaps a great one.'

'Of whom are you speaking?' asked Bartolomeo.

'Of the Duke of course. Of whom else could I have been speaking? He has rid himself of his enemies by the exercise of a duplicity so perfect that the onlooker can only wonder and admire. These painters with their colours and their brushes prate about the works of art they produce, but what are they in comparison with a work of art that is produced when your paints are living men and your brushes wit and cunning? The Duke is a man of action and impetuous, you would never have credited him with the wary patience that was needed to bring his beautiful stratagem to a successful issue. For four months he kept them guessing at his intentions; he worked on their fears, he traded on their jealousies, he confused them by his wiles, he fooled them with false promises; with infinite skill he sowed dissension among them, so that the Bentivogli in Bologna and the Baglioni in Perugia deserted them. You know how ill it has served Baglioni: the Bentivogli's turn will come. As suited his purpose he was friendly and genial, stern and menacing; and at last they stepped into the trap he had set. It was a masterpiece of deceit which deserves to go down to posterity for the neatness of its planning and the perfection of its execution.'

Bartolomeo, a loquacious fellow, was about to speak, but Machiavelli had not yet said his say.

'He has rid Italy of the petty tyrants that were its scourge. What will he do now? Others before him have seemed to be chosen by God to effect the redemption of Italy, and then in the full current of action have been cast off by fortune.'

He rose to his feet abruptly. He was tired of the party and did not want to listen to Bartolomeo's platitudes. He thanked him for his entertainment and escorted by the faithful Piero went back to his lodging.

34

Next day Bartolomeo, his business transacted, set off for Perugia on his way home. Later on Machiavelli, with Piero and his two servants, and a number of the Duke's gentlemen, rode out to meet the Florentine ambassador. After Giacomo Salviati, for such was his name, had changed from his riding clothes to the dignified garb of a Florentine of rank, Machiavelli accompanied him to the castle to present his credentials. Machiavelli was eager to get back to Florence, but he could not leave till he had made known to the ambassador the various persons with whom it was necessary for him to be acquainted. Little was done at the Duke's court for love, and Machiavelli had to inform his successor what services such a one could render and what payment he expected. He had to give his opinion of the trustworthiness of one and the unreliability of another. Though Giacomo Salviati had read the letters that Machiavelli had written to the Signory, there was much that he had not ventured to say, since the danger was constant that letters would be intercepted, and so he had to spend long hours recounting by word of mouth a multitude of facts that it behoved the ambassador to know.

It was in consequence six days before he could set out on the homeward journey. The road was long and bad and none too safe, and so that he might get as far as he could before nightfall he had decided to start early. He was out of bed by dawn and it did not take him long to dress. The saddle-bags, packed the night before, were taken down by the servants, and the woman of the house in a few minutes came up to tell him that all was ready for him to start.

'Is Piero with the horses?'

'No, Messere.'

'Where is he?'

'He went out.'

'Out? Where? What for? Tiresome fellow, doesn't he know yet that I hate being kept waiting? Send one of my servants to find him and be quick about it.'

She hurried to do his bidding and had hardly closed the door behind her when it was opened again and Piero came in.

Machiavelli stared at him in amazement: he was dressed, not in his own shabby riding clothes, but in the scarlet and yellow of the Duke's soldiers. There was a mischievous smile on his lips, but it somewhat lacked assurance.

'I've come to say good-bye to you, Messer Niccolo. I have enlisted in the Duke's army.'

'I did not imagine you had put on that gaudy costume just for fun.'

'Don't be angry with me, Messere. During the three months and more that I've been with you I've seen something of the world. I've been witness to great events and I've talked with men who were concerned in them. I'm strong and young and healthy. I can't go back to Florence and spend the rest of my life driving a quill in the Second Chancery. I wasn't made for that. I want to live.'

Machiavelli looked at him reflectively. The suspicion of a smile hovered on that razor-blade which was his mouth.

'Why didn't you tell me what you had in mind?'

'I thought you would prevent me from doing it.'

'I should have looked upon it as my duty to point out to you that a soldier's life is hard, dangerous and ill-paid. He takes the risks and the commander gets the glory. He suffers from hunger and thirst and is exposed to the rigour of the elements. If he is captured by the enemy he is robbed of the very clothes on his back. If he is wounded he is left to die, and should he recover and be useless for combat little is left him but to beg his food in the streets. He spends his life among coarse, brutal and licentious men to the ruin of his morals and the peril of his soul. I should have felt it my duty to point out to you that in the Chancery of the Republic you would have a position at once respectable and secure in which by industry and subservience to the whims of your superiors you could earn a salary just enough to keep body and soul together, and after many years of faithful service, if you were adroit, slightly unscrupulous and very lucky, you could count on advancement if the brother-in-law or the nephew by marriage of an influential person did not at the moment happen to want a job. But having done my duty I should have taken no further steps to prevent you from doing what you wished.'

Piero laughed with relief, for though he was attached to Machiavelli and admired him, he was not a little afraid of him.

'Then you are not vexed with me?'

'No, my dear boy. You have served me well and I have found you honest, loyal and energetic. Fortune favours the Duke and I can't blame you for wanting to follow his star.'

'Then you will make it all right for me with my mother and Uncle Biagio?'

'Your mother will be broken-hearted. She will think I have led you astray and will blame me, but Biagio is a sensible man and will do his best to console her. And now, my dear boy, I must be off.'

He took the boy in his arms to kiss him on both cheeks, but as he did so noticed the shirt he was wearing. He pulled up the heavily-embroidered collar.

'Where did you get that shirt?'

Piero flushed to the roots of his hair.

'Nina gave it to me.'

'Nina?'

'Monna Aurelia's maid.'

Machiavelli recognized the fine linen he had brought Bartolomeo from Florence and he stared frowning at the elaborate needlework. Then he looked into Piero's eyes. Beads of sweat stood on the boy's forehead.

'Monna Aurelia had more material than she needed for Messer Bartolomeo and she gave Nina what she didn't want.'

'And did Nina do that beautiful embroidery herself?'

'Yes.'

It was a clumsy lie.

'How many shirts did she give you?'

'Only two. There wasn't material for more.'

'That will do very well. You will be able to wear one while the other is washed. You are a lucky young man. When I sleep with women they do not give me presents; they expect me to give them presents.'

'I only did it to oblige you, Messer Niccolo,' said Piero, with a disarming smile. 'You urged me to make advances to her.'

Machiavelli knew very well that Aurelia would never have dreamt of giving her maid several yards of costly linen, and he knew that the maid could never have drawn that intricate design; and Monna Caterina herself had told him that only Aurelia could do that delicate handiwork. It was Aurelia who had given the boy the shirts. And why? Because he was her husband's third cousin? Nonsense. The truth, the unpalatable truth stared him in the face. On the night of the assignation, when Machiavelli had been sent for by the Duke, it was not with the maid that Piero had slept, but with her mistress. It was by no miraculous intervention of San Vitale that Bartolomeo's wife was about to bear a son, but by the very natural instrumentality of the young man who stood before him. That explained why Monna Caterina had given him ridiculous excuses for not arranging another opportunity for him to meet Aurelia, and why Aurelia had avoided all further communication with him. Machiavelli was seized with cold fury. They had made a pretty fool of him, those two abandoned women and the boy whom he had befriended. He stepped back a little to have a good look at him.

Machiavelli had never set great store on masculine beauty; he considered it of small importance compared with the pleasant manner, the easy conversation and the audacious approach which had enabled him to get all the women he wanted; and though he had recognized that Piero was a personable fellow he had never troubled to look closely at him. He examined him now with angry eyes. He was tall and well-made, with broad shoulders, a slim waist and shapely legs. The uniform set off his figure to advantage. He had brown curly hair that covered his head like a tight-fitting cap, large round brown eyes under well-marked brows, an olive skin as smooth and clear as a girl's, a small straight nose, a red, sensual mouth, and ears that clung close to his skull. His expression was bold, frank, ingenuous and engaging.

'Yes,' reflected Machiavelli, 'he has the beauty that would appeal to a silly woman. I never noticed it or I'd have been on my guard.'

He cursed himself for having been so stupid. But how could he suspect that Aurelia, cousin though he was of her husband, would give a thought to a lad who after all was no more than an errand-boy just out of school? Machiavelli had used him to fetch and carry, to run hither and thither at his beck and call; and if he had treated him with an indulgence he now regretted, it was because Biagio was his uncle. Piero was not unintelligent, but he had none of the graces you learn by living in the great world, and having little to say for himself for the most part kept quiet in the presence of his betters. Machiavelli knew very well that, as for himself, he had a way with women; he had never failed to charm when to charm was his object, and he thought there was little anyone could teach him in the art and science of gallantry. Piero was no more than a callow youth. Who in his senses could have supposed that Aurelia would cast so much as a glance of her fine eyes on him when she had at her feet a man of distinction, wordly wisdom and urbane conversation? It was preposterous.

Piero suffered his master's long scrutiny with composure. He had recovered from his embarrassment and there was a wariness in his manner which suggested that he was alert.

'I've been very fortunate,' he remarked coolly, but as

though he were somewhat inclined to take good luck as his due. 'Count Lodovico Alvisi's page fell ill on the way from Sinigaglia and had to go back to Rome, and he's taken me in his place.'

This Count Lodovico, an intimate of Il Valentino's, was one of the Roman gentlemen who had taken service under him as a lancer.

'How did you manage that?'

'Messer Bartolomeo spoke to the Duke's treasurer about me and he arranged it.'

Machiavelli faintly raised his eyebrows. Not only had the boy seduced Bartolomeo's wife, but he had used him to get a sought-after position with one of the Duke's favourites. If he had not himself been so intimately concerned he would have found the situation humorous.

'Fortune favours audacity and youth,' he said. 'You will go far. But let me give you some advice. Take care that like me you do not get a reputation for wit, since if you do no one will think you sensible, but notice men's moods and adapt yourself to them; laugh with them when they are merry and pull a long face when they are solemn. It is absurd to be wise with fools and foolish with the wise: you must speak to each one in his own language. Be courteous; it costs little and helps much; to be of use and to know how to show yourself of use is to be doubly useful; it is idle to please yourself if you do not please others, and remember that you please them more by ministering to their vices than by encouraging their virtues. Never be so intimate with a friend that he may injure you should he become your enemy, and never use your enemy so ill that he can never become your friend. Be careful in your speech. There is always time to put in a word, never to withdraw one; truth is the most dangerous weapon a man can wield, and so he must wield it with caution. For years I have never said what I believed nor ever believed what I have said, and if it sometimes happens that I tell the truth I conceal it among so many lies that it is hard to find it.'

But while these old saws and homely commonplaces tripped off the end of his tongue Machiavelli's thoughts were intent on something much more important, and he scarcely listened to what he said. For he knew that a public man can be corrupt, incompetent, cruel, vindictive, vacillating, self-seeking, weak and stupid and yet attain to the highest honours in the state; but if he is ridiculous he is undone. Slander he can refute; abuse he can despise; but against ridicule he has no defence. Strange as it may seem the Absolute has no sense of humour, and ridicule is the instrument the devil uses to hinder aspiring man in his arduous quest of perfection. Machiavelli valued the esteem of his fellow-citizens and the attention that was paid to his opinions by the heads of the Republic. He had confidence in his own judgment and was ambitious to be employed in affairs of consequence. He was too clear-sighted not to see that in this abortive affair with Aurelia he cut a comic figure. If the story were told in Florence he would become a laughing-stock, the helpless victim of brutal jest and cruel innuendo. A cold shiver ran down his spine at the thought of the pasquinades, the epigrams that his misadventure would suggest to the malicious wit of the Florentines. Even his friend Biagio, the easy butt of his jokes, would welcome the opportunity to pay off many an old score. He must stop Piero's mouth or he was ruined. In a friendly way he put his hand on the lad's shoulder and smiled pleasantly; but the eyes he fixed on Piero's, the bright darting little eyes, were cold and hard.

'There is only one more thing I would say to you, dear boy. Fortune is inconstant and restless. She may grant you power, honour and riches, but also afflict you with servitude, infamy and poverty. The Duke also is her plaything and with a turn of her wheel she may plunge him to destruction. Then you will need friends in Florence. It would be imprudent of you to make enemies of those who can help you in distress. The Republic is suspicious of those who leave her service to enter that of those whom she mistrusts. A few words whispered in the right ear might easily lead to the confiscation of your property so that your mother, driven from her house, would have to live on the unwilling charity of her relations. The Republic has a long arm; if she thought fit, it would not be hard to find a needy Gascon who for a few ducats would drive a dagger into your back. A letter might be allowed to fall into the Duke's hands which would suggest that you were a Florentine spy, and the rack would force you to confess that it was true, and you would be hanged like a common thief. It would distress your mother. For your own sake then, and as you value your life, I recommend you to be secret. It is not wise to tell everything one knows.'

Machiavelli, his gaze fixed on Piero's brown, liquid eyes, saw that he understood.

'Have no fear, Messere. I will be as secret as the grave.'

Machiavelli laughed lightly.

'I did not think you were a fool.'

Though it would leave him with only just enough money to get back to Florence, he thought this was a moment to be generous even to excess, so taking out his purse he gave Piero five ducats as a parting gift.

'You have served me well and faithfully,' he said, 'and it will be a pleasure to me to give Biagio a good account of your zeal in my interests and in those of the Republic.'

He kissed him affectionately and they went downstairs hand in hand. Piero held the horse's head while Machiavelli mounted. He walked by his side till they came to the city's gate and there they parted.

36

Machiavelli gave his horse a touch of the spur and it
broke into an easy canter. The two servants followed
close behind. He was in a vile temper. There was no
denying it, they had made a perfect fool of him, Fra
Timoteo, Aurelia, her mother and Piero; he didn't know
with which he was most angry. And the worst of it was
that he didn't see how he could settle his account with
them; they had had a lot of fun at his expense and there
was no way by which he could make them pay for it.
Of course Aurelia was a fool, sly as all women were, but
a fool; otherwise she wouldn't have preferred a smooth-
faced pretty boy to a man in the flower of his age, a man
of affairs who was entrusted by his government with
important negotiations. No intelligent person could
deny that the comparison was all in his favour. No one
could call him repulsive; Marietta had always told him
she liked the way his hair grew on his head; it was like
black velvet, she said. Thank God for Marietta: there
was a woman you could trust; you could leave her for
half a year and be certain that she would look neither
to the right nor to the left. It was true that she had been
rather troublesome of late, complaining through Biagio
that he didn't come back and didn't write and had left
her without money. Well, in her condition one must
expect women to be peevish. He had been gone three
and a half months, she must be getting quite big, he
wondered when she would be delivered; they had
already made up their minds that the boy should be
called Bernardo after his own father now with God. And
if she grumbled at his long absence it was because she
loved him, poor slut; it would be well to get back to

her; that was the advantage of a wife, she was always there when you wanted her. Of course she wasn't the beauty that Aurelia was, but she was virtuous, and that was more than you could say for Monna Caterina's daughter. He wished he had thought of bringing her back a present, but it hadn't occurred to him till that moment and now he simply hadn't the money.

He wished he hadn't spent so much on Aurelia. There was the scarf, and the gloves and the attar of roses, and the gold chain, well, no, not gold, silver gilt, that he'd given to Monna Caterina; if she'd had a spark of decency she'd have returned that, it would have done very well to give to Marietta and would have pleased her. But when did women ever return the presents you made them?

An old procuress, that's what she was, and not even honest. She knew quite well that the chain was the price he was paying her to arrange things for him, and when she didn't deliver the goods surely the least she could do would have been to return the purchase price. But she was an abandoned old wanton, he'd guessed that from his first glance at her, and she got a filthy satisfaction out of helping others to the debaucheries which she could no longer herself indulge in. He was prepared to bet a ducat that she'd put Piero and Aurelia to bed herself. They must have had a fine laugh when they ate the capons and the pastries he'd sent in by Piero and drunk his wine while he was standing at the door in the pelting rain. If Bartolomeo hadn't been the fool he was he'd have known it was madness to entrust a woman like that with the charge of his wife's fidelity.

For a moment Machiavelli's thoughts turned on that gross and stupid man. It was his fault really that all this had happened.

'If he'd looked after her properly,' said Machiavelli to himself, 'it would never have occurred to me that there was anything doing and I shouldn't have tried.'

Bartolomeo was to blame for the whole thing. But what a fool he'd been, he, Machiavelli, to send her that expensive scarf to excuse himself for not having kept the appointment; and he'd sent it round in the morning, by Piero of all people, when he was feeling like nothing on earth and his voice was a croak, so that she could get it before Bartolomeo's return. How they must have sniggered! And did Piero take the opportunity to . . . they were a nice pair, he wouldn't put anything past them.

And the exasperating thing was that he'd not only lavished presents upon her, he'd told his best stories to amuse her, he'd sung his best songs to charm her, he'd flattered her, in short he'd done everything a man can do to ingratiate himself with a woman; and then, then that wretched boy came along and just because he was eighteen and good-looking got for nothing what he'd spent a month's time to get and much more money than he could afford. He would have liked to know how Piero had gone about it. Perhaps it was Monna Caterina, with her fear that Bartolomeo would adopt his nephews, who had suggested it. He invented her conversation.

'Well, what are we going to do about it? We can't wait all night for him. It seems a pity to waste the opportunity. In your place, Aurelia, I wouldn't hesitate. Look at him with his sweet face and his curly hair; he's like the Adonis in that picture in the Town Hall. I know if I had to choose between him and that Messer Niccolo with his sallow skin and his long nose and those little beady eyes – well, there's no comparison, my dear. And I dare say he can do what you want much better than that skinny Secretary.'

A bad woman. A wicked woman. And why she should prefer that boy to father her daughter's son rather than an intelligent man of the world was something he would never understand.

But perhaps there had been small need for Monna

Caterina to put her word in. It's true the boy looked so innocent and seemed even a trifle shy, but appearances were deceptive. He had a pretty power of dissimulation, for never had he given the smallest indication that there was anything between him and Aurelia; and he was a cool, brazen liar; the only embarrassment he had shown was when Machiavelli had noticed the shirt; but how quickly he had recovered himself and with what effrontery met his master's unspoken accusations! He was quite impudent enough just to have kissed Aurelia frankly on the mouth and when he found she did not object, slip his hand down her open bodice between her breasts. Anyone could guess what would happen then and Machiavelli's angry imagination followed them into Bartolomeo's bedchamber and into Bartolomeo's bed.

'The ingratitude of the boy!' he muttered.

He had taken him on this trip from sheer good nature, he had done everything for him, he had introduced him to persons worth knowing, he had done his best to form him, to show him how to behave, to civilize him in short; he had not spared his wit and wisdom to teach him the ways of the world, how to make friends and influence people. And this was his reward, to have his girl snatched away from him under his very nose.

'Anyhow I put the fear of God into him.'

Machiavelli knew that when you have played a dirty trick on your benefactor half the savour of it is lost if you cannot tell your friends about it. He found some small comfort in that.

But all the anger he felt for Aurelia, Piero, Monna Caterina and Bartolomeo amounted to nothing compared with that which he felt for Fra Timoteo. That was the treacherous villain who had upset all his well-laid plans.

'Much chance he has now of preaching the Lenten sermons in Florence,' he hissed.

He had never had any intention of recommending the

friar for that office, but it was a satisfaction to think that if he had had the intention he would now without hesitation discard it. The man was a rascal. No wonder Christianity was losing its hold on the people, and they were become wicked, licentious and corrupt, when there was no honesty, no sense of right and wrong in the religious by profession. Fooled, fooled, he'd been fooled by all of them, but by none so monstrously as by that rascally friar.

They stopped to eat at a wayside inn. The food was bad but the wine drinkable and Machiavelli drank a good deal of it, with the result that when he got into the saddle again to continue his journey the world looked a trifle less black to him. They passed peasants leading a cow or riding on the rump of a heavy-laden ass; they met travellers on foot or on horseback. For a while he pondered over the Duke's participation in his disappointment; if it was a joke he had kept it to himself as he kept his designs to himself, and if it was part of a scheme to get him in his power, he knew by now that it had failed. Then his thoughts reverted to Aurelia. It was no good crying over spilt milk. Four months ago he had never seen her; it was silly to make such a fuss over a woman whom he had only seen half a dozen times and with whom he had only exchanged as many sentences. He wasn't the first man whom a woman had led on only to let him down when it came to the point. That was the kind of thing a wise man took philosophically. Fortunately it was to the interest of the only people who knew the facts to say nothing about them. It was a humiliation certainly to have been made such a fool of, but anyone can put up with a humiliation that only he is aware of. The thing was to look at it from the outside as though it had happened to somebody else, and Machiavelli set himself deliberately to do this.

Suddenly with an exclamation he jerked his reins, and his horse, thinking he was meant to stop, pulled up so sharply that Machiavelli was thrown forward in his saddle. His servants rode up.

'Is anything the matter, Messere?'

'Nothing, nothing.'

He rode on. Machiavelli's exclamation and the instinctive movement had been caused by an idea that had flashed through his mind. At first he thought he was going to vomit and then he knew he'd had an inspiration: it had occurred to him that there was a play in the story. That was how he could revenge himself on those people who had mocked and robbed him; he would hold them up to contempt and ridicule. His ill-humour vanished and as he rode along, his imagination busy, his face beamed with malicious delight.

He would place the action in Florence, because he felt his invention would be more at home in those familiar streets. The characters were there and all he had to do was to emphasize their qualities a little in order to make them more effective on the stage. Bartolomeo, for instance, would have to be even sillier and more credulous than he was in fact, and Aurelia more ingenuous and more docile. He had already cast Piero for the pimp who was to engineer the deception by means of which the hero would achieve his ends, and a pretty scamp he proposed to make him. For the general outlines of the play were clear in his mind. He would himself be the hero and the name he would give himself came to him at once – Callimaco. He was a Florentine, handsome, young and rich, who had spent some years in Paris – this would give Machiavelli the chance to say some sharp things about the French whom he neither liked nor esteemed – and having come back to Florence had seen and fallen violently in love with Aurelia. What should he call her? Lucrezia. Machiavelli sniggered when he decided to give her the name of the Roman matron distinguished for her domestic virtues who had stabbed herself to death after having been outraged by

Tarquinius. Of course the play would end happily and Callimaco would spend a night of love with the object of his desire.

The sun was shining from a blue sky, there was still snow in the fields, but the road was crisp under the horses' hooves and Machiavelli, well wrapped up, was pleasantly exhilarated by the activity of his invention. He felt strangely exalted. There was in his mind as yet no more than a theme; the facts were too tame for his purpose, and he was aware that he needed to think of a comic stratagem that would give him a coherent plot on which he could string his scenes. What he was looking for was a fantastic idea that would make an audience laugh and not only lead naturally to the resolution of his intrigue, but allow him to show the simplicity of Aurelia, the foolishness of Bartolomeo, the rascality of Piero, the wantonness of Monna Caterina, and the knavery of Fra Timoteo. For the monk was to be an important character. In imagination Machiavelli rubbed his hands as he thought how he would show him in his true colours, with his avarice, his lack of scruple, his cunning and his hypocrisy. He would give false names to all of them, but he would leave Fra Timoteo his own so that all should know what a false and wicked man he was.

But he remained at a loss for the idea that should set his puppets in motion. It must be unexpected, outrageous even, for it was a comedy that he proposed to write, and so funny that people would gasp with astonishment and then burst into a roar of laughter. He knew his Plautus and his Terence well, and he surveyed them in his memory to see whether there was not in their plays some ingenious fancy that would serve his purpose. He could think of nothing. And what made it more difficult to apply his mind to the problem was that his thoughts willy-nilly presented odd scenes to him here and there, amusing bits of dialogue and ridiculous situations. The time passed so quickly that he was surprised when they arrived at the place where they had decided to spend the night.

'To hell with love,' he muttered as he got off his horse. 'What is love beside art!'

37

The place was called Castiglione Aretino, and there was an inn which at all events looked no worse than any of those he had slept at since leaving home. What with the exercise in the open air and his fancy running wild, he had developed a healthy appetite and the first thing he did on entering was to order his supper. Then he washed his feet, which, being a cleanly man, he liked to do every four or five days, and having dried them he wrote a short letter to the Signory which he sent off at once by a courier. The inn was full, but the innkeeper told him there would be room for him in the large bed he and his wife slept in. Machiavelli gave her a glance and said that if they could put a couple of sheepskins on the kitchen floor he would rest comfortably enough. Then he sat down to a great dish of macaroni.

'What is love in comparison with art?' he repeated. 'Love is transitory, but art is eternal. Love is merely Nature's device to induce us to bring into this vile world creatures who from the day of their birth to the day of their death will be exposed to hunger and thirst, sickness and sorrow, envy, hatred and malice. This macaroni is better cooked than I could have expected and the sauce is rich and succulent. Chicken livers and giblets. The creation of man was not even a tragic mistake, it was a grotesque mischance. What is its justification? Art, I suppose. Lucretius, Horace, Catullus, Dante and Petrarch. And perhaps they would never have been driven to write their divine works if their lives had not been full of tribulation, for there is no question that if

I had gone to bed with Aurelia I should never have had the idea of writing a play. So when you come to look at it, it's all turned out for the best. I lost a trinket and picked up a jewel fit for a king's crown.'

The good meal and these reflections restored Machiavelli to his usual amiability. He played a game of cards with a travelling friar who was on his way from one monastery to another and lost a trifle to him with good grace. Then settling himself down on his sheepskins he quickly fell asleep and slept without a break till dawn.

The sun had only just risen when he set out again, and it looked as though it were going to be a fine day. He was in high spirits. It was good to think that in a few hours he would be once more in his own house, he hoped Marietta would be too glad to have him back to reproach him for his neglect of her, Biagio would come round to visit him after supper, dear kind Biagio, and tomorrow he would see Piero Soderini and the gentlemen of the Signory. Then he would go and call on his friends. Oh, what a joy it would be to be back in Florence, to have the Chancery to go to every day and to walk those streets he had known since childhood, knowing by name, if not to speak to, almost everyone he passed!

'Welcome back, Messere,' from one, and 'Well, well, Niccolo, where have you sprung from?' from another. 'I suppose you've come back with your pockets bulging with money,' from a third, and 'When is the happy event to be?' from a friend of his mother's.

Home. Florence. Home.

And there was La Carolina, at a loose end now because the Cardinal who'd kept her had been too rich to die a natural death. She was a grand woman, with a clever tongue, whom it was a treat to talk to, and sometimes you could cajole her into giving you for nothing what others were prepared to pay good money for.

How pretty the Tuscan landscape was! In another month the almond-trees would be in flower.

He began once more to think of the play that was simmering in his head. It made him feel happy and young and as light-headed as though he had drunk wine on an empty stomach. He repeated to himself the cynical speeches he would put in the mouth of Fra Timoteo. Suddenly he pulled his horse up. The servants came up with him to see if there were anything he wanted and to their surprise saw that he was shaking with silent laughter. He saw the look on their faces and laughed all the more, then without a word clapped his spurs to the horse's flanks and galloped hell for leather down the road till the poor brute, unaccustomed to such exuberance, slackened down to its usual steady amble. The Idea had come to him, the idea he had racked his brains to invent, and it had come on a sudden, he could not tell how or why or whence, and it was the very idea he wanted, ribald, extravagant and comic. It was almost a miracle. Everyone knew that credulous women bought the mandrake root to promote conception, it was a common superstition and many were the indecent stories told about its use. Now he would persuade Bartolomeo – to whom by then he had given the name of Messer Nicia – that his wife would conceive if she drank a potion made from it, but that the first man who had connection with her after she had done so would die. How to persuade him of that? It was easy. He, Callimaco, would disguise himself as a doctor who had studied in Paris, and prescribe the treatment. It was obvious that Messer Nicia would hesitate to give his life to become a father, and so a stranger must be found to take his place for one night. This stranger, under another disguise, would of course be Callimaco, that is to say Machiavelli.

Now that he had a plot the scenes succeeded one another with inevitability. They fell into place like the pieces of a puzzle. It was as though the play were writing itself and he, Machiavelli, were no more than an amanuensis. If he had been excited before, when the notion of making a play out of his misadventure had first come to him, he was doubly excited now that it all lay clear before his mind's eye like a garden laid out with terraces and fountains, shady walks and pleasant arbours. When they stopped to dine, absorbed in his characters he paid no attention to what he ate; and when they started off again he was unconscious of the miles they travelled; they came nearer to Florence, and the countryside was as familiar to him, and as dear, as the street he was born in, but he had no eyes for it; the sun, long past its meridian, was making its westering way to where it met earth and sky, but he gave no heed to it. He was in a world of makebelieve that rendered the real world illusory. He felt more than himself. He *was* Callimaco, young, handsome, rich, audacious, gay; and the passion with which he burnt for Lucrezia was of a tempestuous violence that made the desire Machiavelli had had for Aurelia a pale slight thing. That was but a shadow, this was the substance. Machiavelli, had he only known it, was enjoying the supreme happiness that man is capable of experiencing, the activity of creation.

'Look, Messere,' cried his servant Antonio, riding up to come abreast of him. 'Florence.'

Machiavelli looked. In the distance against the winter sky, paling now with the decline of day, he saw the dome, the proud dome that Bramante had built. He pulled up. There it was, the city he loved more than his soul; they were not idle words that he had spoken when he had said that to Il Valentino. Florence, the city of flowers, with her campanile and her baptistery, her churches and palaces, her gardens, her tortuous streets, the old bridge he crossed every day to go to the Palazzo, and his home, his brother Toto, Marietta, his friends, the city of which he knew every stone, the city with its great history, his birthplace and the birthplace of his ancestors, Florence, the city of Dante and Boccaccio, the city which had fought for its freedom through the centuries, Florence the well-beloved, the city of flowers.

Tears formed in his eyes and rolled down his cheeks. He clenched his teeth to restrain the sobs that shook him. She was powerless now, governed by men who had lost their courage; corrupt; and the citizens who once had been quick to rise up against those who threatened their liberties, were concerned only to buy and sell. Free now only by the grace of the King of France, to whom she paid unworthy tribute, her only defence faithless mercenaries, how could she resist the onslaught of that desperate, audacious man who thought her of so little danger that he did not trouble to conceal his evil intentions? Florence was doomed. She might not fall to the arms of Cæsar Borgia, but if not to his, then to another's, not that year perhaps, nor next, but before men now in their middle age were old.

'To hell with art,' he said. 'What is art beside freedom! Men who lose their freedom lose everything.'

'If we want to get in before dark we must push on, Messere,' said Antonio.

With a shrug of the shoulders Machiavelli tightened his reins, and the tired horse ambled on.

EPILOGUE

Four years passed and in that period much happened. Alexander VI died. Il Valentino had provided for everything that might occur on his father's death, but he had not foreseen that when it took place he would himself be at death's door. Though ill, so desperately ill that only the strength of his constitution saved him, he managed to secure the election to the papacy of a cardinal, Pius III, whom he had no reason to fear; but the lords whom he had attacked and driven to flight seized the opportunity to regain their dominions, and he could do nothing to prevent them. Guidobaldo di Montefeltro returned to Urbino, the Vitellis recovered Città di Castello and Gian Paolo Baglioni captured Perugia. Only Romagna remained faithful to him. Then Pius III, an old man and a sick one, died, and Giuliano della Rovere, a bitter enemy of the Borgias, ascended the papal throne as Julius II. In order to obtain the votes of those cardinals whom Il Valentino controlled he had promised to reappoint him Captain General of the Church and confirm him in possession of his states. Cæsar thought that the promises of others were more likely to be kept than his own. He made a fatal error. Julius II was vindictive, crafty, unscrupulous and ruthless. It was not long before he found an excuse to put the Duke under arrest; he then forced him to surrender the cities of Romagna which his captains still held for him, and that accomplished, allowed him to escape to Naples. Here after a short while by order of King Ferdinand he was again thrown into prison and presently conveyed to Spain. He was taken first to a fortress in Murcia and then for greater safety to one at Medina del Campo in the heart of Old Castile. It looked as though Italy were rid at last and for good of the adventurer whose boundless ambition had for so long disturbed her peace.

But some months later the whole country was startled to hear that he had escaped, and after a hazardous journey, disguised as a merchant, had reached Pamplona, the capital of his brother-in-law, the King of Navarre. The news raised the spirits of his partisans and in the cities of Romagna there were wild scenes of rejoicing. The petty princelings of Italy trembled in their cities. The King of Navarre was at the time at war with his barons and he put Cæsar Borgia in command of his army.

During these four years Machiavelli was kept hard at

work. He went on various missions. He was given the difficult task of constituting a militia so that Florence should not be altogether dependent on mercenaries, and when not otherwise occupied had handled the affairs of the Second Chancery. His digestion had always been poor and the journeys on horseback through the heat of summer, in the cold, wind, rain and snow of winter, the extreme discomfort of the inns, the poor food at irregular hours had exhausted him, and in February – February of the year of Our Lord fifteen hundred and seven – he fell seriously ill. He was bled and purged and took his favourite remedy, a pill of his own concoction, which to his mind was a specific for every human ailment. He was convinced that it was to this, rather than to the doctors, that he owed his recovery, but his illness and its treatment had left him so weak that the Signory granted him a month's leave of absence. He went down to his farm at San Casciano, which was some three miles from Florence, and there quickly regained his health.

Spring had come early that year, and the countryside, with the trees bursting into leaf, the wild flowers, the fresh green of the grass, the rich growth of wheat, was a joy to the eye. To Machiavelli the Tuscan scene had a friendly, intimate delight that appealed to the mind rather than to the senses. It had none of the sublimity of the Alps, nor the grandeur of the sea; it was a plot of earth, graceful, lightly gay and elegant, for men to live on who loved wit and intelligent argument, pretty women and good cheer. It reminded you not of the splendid solemn music of Dante, but rather of the light-hearted strains of Lorenzo de' Medici.

One March morning Machiavelli, up with the sun, went to a grove on his small estate that he was having cut. He lingered there, looking over the previous day's work, and talked with the woodmen; then he went to a spring and sat himself down on a bank with a book he had brought in his pocket. It was an Ovid, and with a smile on his thin lips he read the amiable and lively verses in which the poet described his amours and, remembering his own, thought of them for a while with pleasure.

'How much better it is to sin and repent,' he murmured, 'than to repent for not having sinned!'

Then he strolled down the road to the inn and chatted with the passers-by. For he was a sociable creature and if he could not have good company was willing to put up with poor. When his hunger told him that it must be getting on towards dinner-time he sauntered home and sat down with his wife and the children to the modest fare his farm provided. After dinner he went back to the inn. The innkeeper was there, the butcher, the miller and the blacksmith. He sat down to play a game of cards with them, a noisy, quarrelsome game, and they flew into a passion over a penny, shouted at one another, flung insults across the table and shook their fists in one another's face. Machiavelli shouted and shook his fist with the best of them. Evening drew near and he returned to his house. Marietta, pregnant for the third time, was about to give the two little boys their supper.

'I thought you were never coming,' said she.

'We were playing cards.'

'Who with?'

'The usual lot, the miller, the butcher and Batista.'

'Riff-raff.'

'They keep my wits from growing mouldy, and when all's said and done they're no stupider than ministers of state, and on the whole not more rascally.'

He took his eldest son, Bernardo, now getting on for four, on his knees and began to feed him.

'Don't let your soup get cold,' said Marietta.

They were eating in the kitchen, with the maid and the hired man, and when he had finished his soup the maid brought him half a dozen larks roasted on a skewer. He was surprised and pleased, for as a rule supper consisted of nothing but a bowl of soup and a salad.

'What is this?'

'Giovanni snared them and I thought you'd like them for your supper.'

'Are they all for me?'

'All.'

'You're a good woman, Marietta.'

'I haven't been married to you for five years without finding out that the way to your heart is through your stomach,' she said dryly.

'For that sound piece of observation you shall have a lark, dear,' he answered, taking one of the tiny birds in his fingers and popping it, notwithstanding her remonstrance, into her mouth.

'They fly towards heaven in their ecstasy, their hearts bursting with song, and then, caught by an idle boy, they're cooked and eaten. So man, for all his soaring ideals, his vision of intellectual beauty and his yearning for the infinite, in the end is caught by the perversity of fate and serves no other purpose than to feed the worms.'

'Eat your food while it's hot, dear, you can talk afterwards.'

Machiavelli laughed. He slipped another lark off the skewer and while crunching it with strong teeth looked at Marietta with affection. It was true she was a good woman; she was thrifty and good-tempered. She was always sorry to see him go on one of his journeys and glad to see him come back. He wondered if she knew how unfaithful he was to her. If she did, she had never given a sign of it, which showed that she was sensible and good-natured; he might have gone farther and fared worse; he was very well pleased with his wife.

When they had finished and the maid was washing up, Marietta put the children to bed. Machiavelli went upstairs to take off the clothes, muddy and dirty, that he had worn all day, and put on what he liked to describe as courtly and regal garments; for it was his habit to spend the evening in his study reading the authors he loved. He was not yet dressed when he heard a horseman ride up and in a moment a voice he recognized asking the maid for him. It was Biagio, and he wondered what had brought him out from the city at that hour.

'Niccolo,' he shouted from below. 'I have news for you.'

'Wait a minute. I'll come down as soon as I'm ready.'

Since it was still a trifle chilly as the day drew in he slipped his black damask robe over his tunic and opened the door. Biagio was waiting for him at the foot of the stairs.

'Il Valentino is dead.'

'How do you know?'

'A courier arrived from Pamplona today. I thought you'd want to know so I rode out.'

'Come into my study.'

They sat down, Machiavelli at his writing-table and Biagio in a carved chair which was part of Marietta's dowry. Biagio told him the facts as he had learnt them. Cæsar Borgia had established his headquarters at a village on the Ebro and planned to attack the castle of the Count of Lerin, the most powerful of the insurgent barons. Early in the morning, on the 12th of March, there was a skirmish between his men and the Count's. Cæsar Borgia was still in his rooms when the alarm sounded; he donned his armour, mounted his horse and flung himself into the fray. The rebels fled, and he, without looking round to see if he was followed, pursued them down into a deep ravine, and there, surrounded and alone, unhorsed, he fought fiercely till he was killed. Next day the King and his men found the body, naked, for they had stripped him of his armour and his clothes, and the King with his own cloak covered his nakedness.

Machiavelli listened to Biagio attentively, but when he had finished remained silent.

'It is good that he is dead,' said Biagio after a while.

'He had lost his states, his money and his army, and yet all Italy feared him still.'

'He was a terrible man.'

'Secret and impenetrable. He was cruel, treacherous and unscrupulous, but he was able and energetic. He was temperate and self-controlled. He let nothing interfere with his chosen course. He liked women, but he used them only for his pleasure and never allowed himself to be swayed by them. He created an army that was loyal to him and trusted him. He never spared himself. On the march he was indifferent to cold and hunger, and the strength of his body made him immune to fatigue. He was brave and mettlesome in battle. He shared danger with the meanest of his soldiers. He was as competent in the arts of peace as in the arts of war. He chose his ministers with discrimination, but took care that they should remain dependent upon his good will. He did everything that a prudent and clever man should do to consolidate his power, and if his methods did not bring him success it was through no fault of his, but through the extraordinary and extreme malice of fortune. With his great spirit and lofty intentions he could not have conducted himself otherwise than he did. His designs were thwarted only by Alexander's death and his own illness; if he had been in health he could have surmounted all his difficulties.'

'He suffered the just punishment of his crimes,' said Biagio.

Machiavelli shrugged his shoulders.

'Had he lived, had fortune continued to favour him, he might have driven the barbarians out of this unhappy country and given it peace and plenty. Then men would have forgotten by what crimes he had achieved power and he would have gone down to posterity as a great and good man. Who cares now that Alexander of Macedon was cruel and ungrateful, who remembers that Julius Cæsar was perfidious? In this world it is only necessary to seize power and hold it, and the means you have used will be judged honourable and will be admired by all. If Cæsar Borgia is regarded as a scoundrel it is only because he didn't succeed. One of these days I shall write a book about him and what I learnt from my observation of his actions.'

'My dear Niccolo, you're so impractical. Who d'you think would read it? You're not going to achieve immortality by writing a book like that.'

'I don't aspire to it,' laughed Machiavelli.

Biagio looked suspiciously at a pile of manuscript on his friend's writing-table.

'What have you there?'

Machiavelli gave him a disarming smile.

'I had nothing much to do here and I thought I'd pass the time by writing a comedy. Would you like me to read it to you?'

'A comedy?' said Biagio doubtfully. 'I presume it has political implications.'

'Not at all. Its only purpose is to amuse.'

'Oh, Niccolo, when will you take yourself seriously? You'll have the critics down on you like a thousand of bricks.'

'I don't know why; no one can suppose that Apuleius wrote his Golden Ass or Petronius the Satyricon with any other object than to entertain.'

'But they're classics. That makes all the difference.'

'You mean that works of entertainment, like loose women, become respectable with age. I've often wondered why it is that the critics can only see a joke when the fun has long since seeped out of it. They've never discovered that humour depends upon actuality.'

'You used to say that not brevity, but pornography was the soul of wit. You've changed your mind?'

'Not at all. For what can be more actual than pornography? Believe me, my good Biagio, when men cease to find it so they will have lost all interest in reproducing their kind, and that will be the end of the Creator's most unfortunate experiment.'

'Read your play, Niccolo. You know I don't like to hear you say things like that.'

With a smile Machiavelli took his manuscript and began to read.

'*A Street in Florence*.'

But then he was seized with the slight misgiving of an author who reads something for the first time to a friend and is not sure that it will please. He interrupted himself.

'This is only a first draft and I dare say I shall make a good many changes when I go over it again.'

He flipped the pages uncertainly. The play had amused him to write, but one or two things had happened that he had not counted on. The characters had taken on a life of their own and had diverged a good deal from their models. Lucrezia had remained as shadowy as Aurelia had been, and he had not seen how to make her more substantial. The exigencies of the plot had obliged him to make her a virtuous woman induced by her mother and her confessor to submit to something her conscience disapproved of. Piero, whom he had called Ligurio, on the contrary played a much greater part than he had intended. It was he who suggested the scheme by which the foolish husband was taken in, he who got round Lucrezia's mother and the monk, he in short who staged the intrigue and conducted it to a happy conclusion. He was astute, ingenious, quick-witted and pleasantly unprincipled. Machiavelli found it very easy to put himself into the rascal's shoes, but by the time he had finished discovered that there was as much of himself in the artful schemer as in the love-sick gallant who was his hero.

Thinking how odd it was that he should play two parts in one play, he looked up and asked Biagio:

'By the way, have your heard anything lately of your nephew Piero?'

'In point of fact I have. I meant to tell you, but with all the excitement of Il Valentino's death I quite forgot. He's going to be married.'

'Is he? Is it a good match?'

'Yes, he's marrying money. You remember Bartolomeo Martelli at Imola? He was some sort of relation of mine.'

Machiavelli nodded.

'When Imola revolted he thought it safer to get away till he saw how things were going. You see, he'd been one of the Duke's chief partisans and he was afraid he'd have to pay for it. He went to Turkey, where he had a business. The papal troops got to the city before there were any real disturbances, and as luck would have it Piero was with them. It seems he was well liked by some influential men who had the ear of the Pope and he managed to protect Bartolomeo's property. But Bartolomeo was banished, and lately the news has arrived that he died in Smyrna, and so Piero is going to marry the widow.'

'Very right and proper,' said Machiavelli.

'They tell me she's young and good-looking; evidently she needed a man to protect her, and Piero has a head on his shoulders.'

'That was the impression he gave me.'

'There's only one fly in the ointment. Bartolomeo had a little boy, between three and four years old, I think he is, and that won't improve the prospects of any children Piero might have.'

'I think you may be sure that he will cherish the little boy as if he were his own,' said Machiavelli dryly.

He returned to his manuscript. He smiled with some complacency. he could not help thinking that he had succeeded with Fra Timoteo. His pen had been dipped in gall and as he wrote he chuckled with malice. Into that character he had put all the hatred and contempt he felt for the monks who fattened on the credulity of the ignorant. By that character his play would stand or fall. He began again.

'*A Street in Florence.*'

He stopped and looked up.

'What is the matter?' asked Biagio.

'You say that Cæsar Borgia suffered the just punishment of his crimes. He was destroyed, not by his misdeeds, but by circumstances over which he had no control. His wickedness was an irrelevant accident. In this world of sin and sorrow if virtue triumphs over vice it is not because it is virtuous, but because it has better and bigger guns; if honesty prevails over double-dealing, it is not because it is honest, but because it has a stronger army more ably led; and if good overcomes evil it is not because it is good, but because it has a well-lined purse. It is well to have right on our side, but it is madness to forget that unless we have might as well it will avail us nothing. We must believe that God loves men of good will, but there is no evidence to show that He will save fools from the result of their folly.'

He sighed, and for the third time started reading.

'*A Street in Florence.*'

THE END

A Selected List of Mandarin Classics

While every effort is made to keep prices low, it is sometimes necessary to increase prices at short notice. Mandarin Paperbacks reserves the right to show new retail prices on covers which may differ from those previously advertised in the text or elsewhere.

The prices shown below were correct at the time of going to press.